11-5-12

These Muddy Waters

Molly's Story

Libby Draper

Inspiring Voices®
A Service of Guideposts

Copyright © 2012 Libby Draper

All rights reserved. No part of this book may be used or reproduced by any means, graphic, electronic, or mechanical, including photocopying, recording, taping or by any information storage retrieval system without the written permission of the publisher except in the case of brief quotations embodied in critical articles and reviews.

Taken from the Holy Bible New Living Translation copyright 1996 used by permission of Tyndale House Publishers, Inc. Wheaton, IL 60189. All rights reserved

Inspiring Voices books may be ordered through booksellers or by contacting:

Inspiring Voices
1663 Liberty Drive
Bloomington, IN 47403
www.inspiringvoices.com
1-(866) 697-5313

Because of the dynamic nature of the Internet, any web addresses or links contained in this book may have changed since publication and may no longer be valid. The views expressed in this work are solely those of the author and do not necessarily reflect the views of the publisher, and the publisher hereby disclaims any responsibility for them.

Any people depicted in stock imagery provided by Thinkstock are models, and such images are being used for illustrative purposes only.

Certain stock imagery © Thinkstock.

ISBN: 978-1-4624-0092-8 (sc)
ISBN: 978-1-4624-0091-1 (e)

Library of Congress Control Number: 2012935062

Printed in the United States of America

Inspiring Voices rev. date: 3/30/2012

For my husband Danny who always believed in me.

For my friend Rebekah without whose encouragement and help I could have never finished this work

And to my Children, Jason and Corie, Jeff and Brenda and Grand Children, Loran, Abbey, and Madeline

For he shall be like a tree planted by the waters, Which spreads out its roots by the river, And will not fear when heat comes...
(Jeremiah 17:8 NKJV)

There was a time in America, when the rivers and streams were a major part of transportation for goods and people. Even with the railroad becoming more and more important, the river still flowed with cargo and people. For the young people in this story, set in the tumultuous times after the Civil War, the river is always there, deep and muddy and full of trouble. Only God's Grace and The Faith in their hearts can good come from heartache.

Chapter 1

A brisk March wind tugged at Molly's cloak as she pushed against the stubborn door at Jake's Mercantile. March was without doubt coming in like a lion. A few flurries of snow stung at her face suggesting that the weather could take a turn for the worse. The door opened with a creak that went unnoticed by the two men at the front counter. Molly silently made her way to the pot bellied stove in the corner and extended her cold hands toward its warmth. Her slim frame shivered a little as she leaned over the stove to soak up the welcome heat after her trek through the cold to get tobacco for her father. The men carried on their conversation unaware of Molly's presence and her close scrutiny of them. She knew Jake, the proprietor of course, but the other man was a stranger. He was tall and fair with long hair and a beard. He wore buckskin clothing and boots and he was discussing with Jake the trade of supplies for the winters' furs.

"These are some of the best furs I've seen in a while, Nathan," Jake told the man. "Looks like you've had a good winter."

"I've had a great winter. The furs are fine and my place is shaping up real good. This is my first spring to try putting in a garden. A man can't live on wild meat, beans and coffee forever."

Jake glanced at Nathan with a smirk on his face,

"Sounds like you're itching to settle down a bit."

"Yeah, too bad you can't sell me a woman along with the seeds and the flour. She could take care of the garden for me and keep me warm on a cold night."

From the corner of the store near the stove, a soft feminine voice whispered,

"I'd go."

Startled, both men turned to see where the sound came from. As their eyes met hers, it felt as though they were staring right through her as she attempted to hide behind the stove. The blood rushed up her throat to spread an embarrassing stain on her face as she realized that she had spoken out loud. Her thin face was framed by thick chestnut colored hair; her eyes large and sparkling. She grasped her cloak around her neck awkwardly and ran to the usually stubborn door, opening it with ease as she hurried out into the cold and began running toward home. The men stood there in silence for a moment staring at the door that Molly hadn't bothered to close, and then Nathan spoke.

"Who was that?"

Jake stepped from behind the counter and went to close the door, watching Molly briefly as she ran down the trail away from the store. "Molly Meyers," he said.

"I didn't even hear that little gal come in."

"Well," Nathan answered. "I'm glad I didn't add anymore to my remark about being warmed on a cold night. Wouldn't want to say that kind of thing in front of a child."

"Oh, I don't think Molly's that much of a child. She's turned sixteen. I know she's just a little bitty thing, but I reckon she's old enough to want to be with a man. She'd probably be more than willing for a chance to leave home.."

Nathan scowled as he questioned Jake.

"Well, her old man drinks and from what I've seen, he's rough on those kids. Molly's the oldest and because of that, he makes her work like a dog."

" Does she have a Ma?", Nathan's mind was taking it all in, already feeling a little sad for the small wisp of a woman child he'd just seen flittering out the store"

"Yeah, she's got a Ma. She can't stand up to Meyers none, though. He was quite a bit older than her when she married him. He don't do much toward making a living for them. Just works for the Wood Hawks on the river every once in a while, supplying fuel for the boats. Spends a good part of what he earns on liquor. When he's sober, he ain't so bad, but when he's drinking, he gets mean."

Jake shook his head as the men stood silent for a moment, then they were back to the business at hand, talking trade and making a list of the supplies that Nathan needed.

"Let's see, I'll need flour and meal; plenty more beans. It'll have to be beans 'til my garden comes up. Oh yeah, molasses, salt, salt meat, sugar. You got any more of those tinned biscuits?"

As Molly ran back out into the cold, she was mortified. She could hardly catch her breath! There she'd been warming herself and eaves dropping on somebody else's doings. Hadn't her Ma told her over and over how such a thing was not polite? And above all that, Molly had gone and done the one thing her Ma fussed at her about over and over; you don't speak until you're spoken to. Her Ma's voice echoing in her mind just made it all the worse.

"Molly, when are you ever gonna learn?"

She hurried toward home with her face down partly so that the stinging bits of snow didn't hit her directly in the face, partly because of the continued humiliation. It wasn't until Molly reached for the door knob at the farm that she realized she didn't have Pa's tobacco. Even though she was out of breath from running she intended to go back, when their hound, Old Mo announced her presence. Almost immediately her Pa threw open the door. One look at her anxious face told him that she hadn't gotten his tobacco.

With a scowl on his leathered face he leaned toward her, "Where's my 'baccy, girl?"

"Pa, I..." Molly stuttered a little. "There was a stranger at the store. Somebody I hadn't seen before, I..."

"What's a stranger got to do with you forgetting my 'baccy, Missy?" With a quick hand he grabbed at the razor strap hanging by the door on the porch. In two quick strides he was at Molly's side. She cringed and stepped back as he grabbed her arm. Her cloak fell from her shoulders and the quick wind bit into her flesh like the strap her father swung. Her lip quivered, and tears rolled down her cheeks but she took the licks without crying. She had known there'd be consequences if she didn't do what she was sent to do. She promised heaven right then, that if she ever had a little girl, and she forgot her chores, Molly'd help her own child remember without making it hurt so bad. Meyers shoved her toward the cabin, dragging her shoulder by the porch post as Molly gathered her cloak as though it were a security blanket. By this time, anxious eyes were peering at her from behind the door.

"I can't depend on you to do nothing right. I'll get the tobacco myself. You get in there and help your Ma get supper on the table." With that, Meyers strode down the trail back towards the Mercantile while Molly's Ma grabbed her hand and pulled her toward her.

"You saw a stranger at the store?" queried her brother Earl. The Meyers kids were always quick to change the subject after one of them got a whipping. It was their way of dealing with what was a common occurrence around the farm.

Molly brushed the tears away from her cheek and sighing, she hung her cloak on a nail near the door. Glancing at her Ma but turning her attention to her brother, she found it helped to talk about what little excitement she found at the store. "Yeah, I hadn't seen him before. I guess he's a trapper from across the river. Jake was buying furs from him."

"When I'm big enough, I'm going to live across the river to get furs." the youngest boy, Seth exclaimed. He pointed an imaginary gun at prey and popped off a few "POW POW POW's"

"You girls get over here and help me get supper on the table before your Pa gets back." The kids may have accepted the harsh discipline they received, at least to a certain extent, but Winifred Meyers knew her kids didn't deserve all that her husband doled out. Her half smile belied her heart aching to defend them. But she was a timid woman and had felt the sting of his temper herself. She constantly strived not to cross him. Her children obeyed her immediately. Not from fear of her, but because they knew to have supper ready when their Pa came back.

Back at the Mercantile, Nathan and Jake were still at the counter when Samuel Meyers swaggered in. Unlike his daughter, his entrance did not go unnoticed.

"Hello, Meyers," Jake nodded a greeting to the man.

Nathan looked at the unkempt older man with a critical eye after having been told a little about him by Jake. Meyers wasn't a big man. He was hardly the type to stand against someone bigger and stronger than himself. But of course, many men who would feel intimated by other men were capable of dishing out intimidation to those weaker and under their authority.

"I sent my girl down here to get my 'baccy," Meyers said as he strode over to the front where the two stood. "You men ain't privy as to why she got so addled in here that she'd forget do you?"

Jake reached over to get the man's tobacco and answered him cautiously. "She was in and out so quick; I didn't realize she was in to buy something. Sometimes when it's cold, kids will stop in and warm a bit when they're out this way. Could be she was afraid that it was going to come up a blizzard before she could get on back home."

Meyers pulled a coin out of his pocket and laid it on the counter.

"Could be you fellows said something to her that was out of line for a gentleman to say to a young lady. My Molly's been taught to steer clear of men folk, especially if she don't know 'em. Could be the stranger there scared my girl."

Nathan bristled at the man's insult, but held his tongue. He knew that with men like this, there wasn't any point wasting time trying to reason with them.

"Now, Meyers," Jake responded. "You know I have always been respectful toward your wife and kids. Whatever reason Molly didn't get what she was sent for, it wasn't anything we done."

"Just you remember. Any man who gets out of line with one of my girls will have to answer to me!" With that Samuel Meyers turned abruptly and left the store before either man could speak.

"Kind of over-protective isn't he?" Nathan asked, raising his eyebrows slightly.

Jake scratched his head, wondering if he should say all that was on his mind,

"It's more than that. Sometimes he's downright mean. I have seen him show some kindness towards those kids, but more often than not, he just bullies them. There's been more times than once that I thought I was going to have to interfere when he was in here with his family but he usually seems to check himself before it gets nasty. He's careful not to do much in front of others but it's just something you know. Those kids don't dare open their mouths in front of him unless they have permission, his wife too. There's just this look about them. They never let their guard down and have fun like kids should."

"Well, I've seen his kind before. They can't hold their own, man to man, so they got to be tough to the women and children. He'd better not let me catch him getting out of line."

Just then a ping of sleet began to hit the window. Glancing toward the sound, Jake noticed the large swirling snowflakes that were coming down much faster now.

"Nathan, you weren't planning to head out toward home today, were you? Maybe you ought to go ahead and stay over a couple of more nights."

"You don't have to ask twice. A warm bed in back of the store seems a sight more interesting than trying to make it to the halfway house when a storm's brewing."

Chapter 2

At the Meyers cabin, Molly continued helping her mother prepare the table. Hearing the weather sound a little different on the tin roof, she looked out to see sleet tapping at the panes of the window mixed with little tiny flakes of late snow. Suddenly she remembered Pa. He was going to be in a foul mood all evening at having to go back to the store and getting caught in the snow coming back. Shaking off the dread, her mind wandered back to that trapper. Did he really want a wife? What would it be like to be married to him? She sighed, as she poured out milk for the others. She wasn't so sure life would be any easier to be married. It sure hadn't been for her Ma. She glanced up at Winifred ladling the steaming hot beans onto the plates. Ma's face was showing tired little lines and her hands were worn and calloused. Molly couldn't remember the last time she had heard her mother laugh. If she did, it was only when Pa wasn't home. The rest of the time, Ma stayed busy doing the chores or waiting on Pa for one thing or another. Molly's daydreaming about a handsome stranger carrying her away was one thing, but there was just a little fear when who could know what reality would bring.

Pa came in just then, stomping his feet and cursing under his breath, which called Molly out of her reverie, and Ma quickly shushed them all to the table. Customarily they ate their meal in silence careful not to make eye contact with Pa while he ranted on about the storm. As soon as the meal was consumed, Molly stoically helped her Ma get the little ones ready for bed. As soon as they were tucked in and cozy under the heavy quilts, she and Sissy poured hot water from the kettle into the dish pan and washed the dishes. Sissy was a frail child, with a bluish cast to her skin. She wasn't ever going to be a strong girl. Nevertheless her sweet spirit made up for it. Being the oldest girl made Molly want to mother the others, especially Sissy, even though nobody could tell by looking, who was barely younger than herself. Sometimes they laughed and talked when they cleaned up after supper, but tonight no one was talking much. Finally it was time for the older ones to go to bed. Molly shared a bed in the loft with Sissy. At least they had a little privacy there. Earl had a bed on the other side of the loft separated by a wooden partition. Long after Sissy was asleep Molly lay there letting her thoughts drift towards the handsome trapper. She imagined he'd call on her, bringing flowers. A picnic basket would be ready and she'd be wearing a lovely new dress ordered from the catalog at the Mercantile. They'd walk, hand in hand down to the creek and spread their lunch in the shade of that big old oak tree. She blushed to herself as she dreamed he'd touch her cheek softly and gradually her fantasies floated away as she drifted off to sleep.

Chapter 3

When at last Nathan had settled in the bunk in the back room of the Mercantile, he found he couldn't get right off to sleep. Folding his arms beneath his head, he closed his eyes and saw a wisp of a girl with a solemn face and big brown eyes staring at him in embarrassment. He realized it was a right pretty face to tell the truth. Brown hair peeped out from under her cloak with a few little unruly waves framing her face. He found himself wondering how long it was. Did it hang all the way down her back? He soothed himself with thoughts of her hair trailing onto the soft skin of her back. With a start he realized he was letting his thoughts have too full a reign. He tossed on the bed and thumped his knapsack of a pillow. He gave himself a talking to, "She was after all, only sixteen, just a girl. What could he be thinking?" As he drifted off to the wind howling and a window banging somewhere nearby, his dreams were filled with a young brown haired girl, running with him near his meadow, laughing and teasing. They shared kisses and laughed and talked and played. When morning brought an end to the delight, Nathan realized that Jake was right. He was itching to settle down. Feeling pretty good about the idea, he jumped up and went to the stove to stoke the coals and add some wood to the fire whose embers were barely glowing. By the time Jake got up, the store was warm and the coffee pot was on.

"Looks like we'll see some sunshine today," Jake said peering out the window hopefully. "Maybe it'll get warm enough to melt some of last night's snow. That weather sure rip snorted through here in the night."

"Yeah, I guess it is going to be a nice day," Nathan answered. "I ought to try and head on home. Maybe this will be the last snow for the winter."

"Don't count on it. We nearly always get one more good snow just before April sets in. Boy, I'm ready for spring though. Winter can't be over soon enough if you ask me" Jake poured himself a cup of scalding coffee and sat down.

"I don't mind it so much. When I'm out running my traps, it always seems like a wonderland, all white and so pure and clean. When the sun is shining and the wind ain't blowing, it don't even feel so cold."

"Yeah and you still got youth on your side." Jake responded with a shiver. "Now when you get to be as old as I am, then you ain't going to want to be out there in that cold day after day trapping."

"Trapping is the way to make a good living though. It really don't take as much out of a man as say, trying to farm, you know? In between running my traps and curing my pelts, I've had plenty of time to work on my place. My cabin is finished, I've got a smoke house built, and just about done with the spring house. I've put two good years into that place and I'm right proud of how it's turned out."

"You really are ready to settle down and find a wife, ain't you? I thought you was just kidding yesterday."

Nathan paused and looked pensive.

"I thought about that girl, Molly, a lot last night, but she don't seem hardly old enough. Are there any more women around these parts that ain't taken already?"

"Lots of girls get married by the time they're sixteen, Nathan." Jake answered. "Ain't no good reason to wait. If a girl is strong enough to work hard and old enough to have babies, then that's all a man needs, right?"

"Yeah, but is that one strong enough? Sure wasn't big as nothing and looked like a little scared rabbit at that. Wouldn't I have my hands full trying to take on a girl that's probably scared to death of me?"

"Listen, Nate." Jake stood up and faced Nathan as he talked. "I know that girl. She ain't done nothing but work hard her whole life. Oh, she'd be scared of you at first I know, but a man like you, well, if you was patient with her, I'm thinkin' she'd turn out to be a right decent wife."

"Jake, are you trying to talk me into taking that girl?" Nathan laughed and poured himself another hot cup of coffee. He spilled a little as he poured, might have been because his hand was shaking just a little thinking about that girl.

"Tarnation Nathan! No, you wouldn't want to mess with her Pa anyway. You saw what he's like yesterday. There are more burrs in that man's saddle than you'd want to deal with. You're the one that brought this up anyhow. How'd you think you'd go about it? Just ride out there and get her?"

At that, both men burst out laughing at the absurdity of it.

"I can just see you riding out there and rescuing her like a knight or something." Jake was really howling now, but suddenly Nathan was not laughing so hard. Jake paused a second, "Oh, man you're thinking serious about this, ain't you?"

Nathan hesitated to admit that was exactly what he was thinking about. Maybe Jake was right. Maybe she was old enough and strong enough to go with him. And hadn't she said it, right there in front of them both. "I'd go." Well he was going to see if she'd go. In a split second he'd made up his mind.

"I'm going!" he told Jake. "You convinced me that she would be good for me. I'm going to go out there and see if she'll come with me." Nathan strode over to get his coat and his hat setting his jaw with determination. Every step made the idea seem better. "Where do they live, Jake? How far is it?"

"Man you're crazy. You can't just ride out there and get that girl. Her old man'll meet you at the door with his shotgun. Molly don't even know you. She might have said it. She might have said she'd go, but she won't. Besides, he'd never let her."

"I'm going to try. I'm riding out there before I change my mind."" Nathan headed out the door to saddle his horse, with Jake on his heels.

"Nathan, I know you're crazy." Jake's voice rose as he tried to stop the determined man. "But this'd be the craziest thing you ever did."

Nathan eyes his friend with a smile, "Help me load my supplies in the wagon, Jake."

The two strong friends made quick work of the loading and Nathan was off.

Chapter 4

It was late morning when Nathan finally rode up to the Meyers place. Sweat dripped from his brow even though it was still cold. He wondered about himself and hoped that his carefully laid plans would not be in vain.

The cabin showed neglect and sorely was in need of repair. The outbuildings that were still standing had cracks so wide you could see through them. Some of the shingles were crooked and some were totally gone. It made them look as though they were a face with teeth missing. Still, the yard was clean and smoke curled out of the chimney. Someone worked around here.

Molly was cleaning up in the cabin when Old Mo commenced to baying. "Someone's coming!" Seth cried, dropping the wood he was carrying into the wood box. He ran to the door and pulled it open as though something magical were appearing before them. After all they didn't get visitors much.

"Who is it?" Samuel Meyers barked harshly from his chair by the fire. He wasn't leaving his comfortable spot for just anybody.

"Don't know, Pa," Seth called back. "I ain't never seen him before."

Meyers grudgingly rose and went to the door, peering guardedly around his son.

Molly too, walked over and looked out. One glance told her it was the trapper she'd seen at the Jake's store yesterday. Suddenly her heart fluttered in her chest. What on earth could that stranger be wanting here?

"Morning," the man called, tipping his hat to Meyers.

"Whatta you be wantin'?" Meyers asked him not even returning the courtesy of looking Nathan in the eye.

"I came to see Molly," He answered. His horse moved restlessly in an effort to move from the dog's annoyance.

Molly's breath caught and she put her fingers to her mouth. He was here to see her? She could scarcely believe what she was hearing.

"You got no business with Molly," Meyers snapped. "I thought I made that clear to you yesterday. My Molly's off limits to the likes of you."

"Maybe so, maybe not. In any case, I've come to see." With that Nathan called out, " Molly". He could see her just behind her Pa in the doorway.

"And I'm telling you she ain't coming out!"" Samuel stepped back from the door and reached for his shotgun, leaving Molly in full view of Nathan.

"Molly," Nathan called again. "Yesterday, you said you'd go with me. Did you mean it? If you did, I'll take you."

Samuel Meyers rushed out the door with his shotgun in hand. "Get off my place," He roared. "You ain't touching my girl!" He grabbed at Molly but she was just out of reach.

In a flash, Nathan had pulled a pistol and pointed it directly in Meyers' face. "Molly, I'll marry you. Make it legal. I'm offering you a chance to go if you want to. It's up to you."

By this time Molly's whole family was standing in the doorway. You could hear a pin drop with how quiet it had gotten. Molly looked to her Ma for encouragement. She couldn't believe this was happening. Yesterday she was daydreaming about just such a thing. He was here and he was asking her to go. "Ma?" she questioned. Her lips quivered and her heart raced.

"Molly, you don't even know this man," her mother bent close and whispered, "You can't even think such a thing."

"But…" Molly bit her lip partly to keep herself from bursting out crying and partly to make herself remember where she was."Girl, get yourself back inside if you know what's good for you," her Pa bellowed. With that, she darted back inside like a gopher in a hole. Nobody ever disobeyed Pa. It wouldn't pay to do it now. Tears began to roll down her cheeks as she disappeared, wiping at her face with the back of her hand.

"Molly!" Again Nathan called out to her, leaning forward on his horse hoping to make himself heard better. "Molly! I'll give you five minutes. If you don't come out, then I'll leave and we'll forget about it forever. It's up to you."

It felt like an eternity as Molly stood in the middle of the cabin trembling and crying. Her thoughts were a jumble of agony. As she wiped more tears, she looked at her hands. They were already showing signs of wear for such a young thing. She pictured her own mother's hands – worn, calloused, red and aching from all the hard work. Why her Ma was hardly 30 years old! Suddenly she sprang into action. She ran to the curtained off corner where her clothes were. Her shaking hands began to grab everything she could and she ran for her cloak and a flour sack to stuff the items in. Surprisingly she found an inner determination she'd never had before. Her mother ran to her side and pulled on her arm.

"Molly!" she whispered a cry. "Don't do this. You don't know what you're doing!'

Touching her Ma's arm she spoke with assurance, "I trust him, Ma. I just feel inside that it will be alright." She gave one more anxious look around, mentally taking it all in. At the last moment she ran over to a box just behind the stove. Reaching down she tenderly grabbed a fuzzy kitten, barely old enough to leave its mother, and hid it in her cloak. With that she rushed out the door past her mother's clutching hands. Molly pushed her mother away, while trying to shut out the woman's protests. She knew she couldn't look her Ma in the face or she might lose her determination.

Nathan was watching the door when she rushed out toward him. She stopped abruptly as she looked at her Pa between her and Nathan. Her Pa turned toward her threateningly and suddenly Nathan cocked the pistol in his hand. He pointed it straight at Meyers with the hammer pulled back.

"Let her come," he told the man.

Time seemed to stand still for Molly as she forced her rubbery legs to run to Nathan. With one strong arm he swiftly pulled her up into the saddle behind him. Nathan turned his horse to leave but kept his eyes and his gun on the girl's pa as they rode out of the yard. Behind him, Molly's family looked on in amazement as she rode away with the handsome stranger.

As soon as Nathan was out of site of the Meyers cabin, he urged his horse into a run. The rough motion of the horse frightened the kitten inside Molly's cloak. She could feel its little claws digging and hear the faint noises it made. As if she wasn't scared enough, now she worried that the man would hear her stowaway. Thankfully the noise of the horse's hooves and the sound of its labored breathing drowned out the muffled cries of the kitten.

When he reached the creek, Nathan slowed his horse and directed him into the water. Molly grabbed at him with her free hand to hold on as they went down the embankment. She was not at all surprised that his back was muscular and as she held close she smelled him for the first time. It was a comforting aroma and an entirely new sensation for her.

The snow had melted some here and Nathan knew the horse would leave no tracks. Before long the thickness of the brush and the noise of the gurgling creek hid them from anyone who might try to follow down the trail. When she thought she heard something behind them, Molly gave a terrified glance back wondering if Pa was right there. Nathan, focused on handling his mount in the rocky creek bed was silent and Molly wondered if she was dreaming all of this.

Would Ma be scolding her to wake up and be about her chores soon? The kitten scratched once more and Molly knew for certain this was no dream. She let go of Nathan to reach in and secure the kitten a little better. Her little stowaway seemed to be settling in.

Before long Nathan was guiding the horse up out of the creek and was circling back toward the way they had come. For one fleeting second Molly thought he must have changed his mind and was taking her back, but he was headed in a more southerly direction. "Where on earth could they be going?" she wondered. Finally as their ride became less hurried and on more level ground, Nathan looked back at her and spoke tenderly.

"Are you okay, girl?"

"Yes," Molly managed a soft reply although she certainly wasn't sure that she was. "Where are we going?" She finally managed to ask.

"To Preacher Brown's place." He answered. "I said I'd marry you. Besides, if we can be married before your Pa finds us, he can't take you back."

Back, she thought. Suddenly it was everything she could do to keep from crying out to him to take her back. She'd get a whipping for sure, but that was better than not knowing what would happen with this stranger. How on earth could she upset her Ma like this? She bit into her lip, to keep from crying out and could taste the blood from the cut it made. It was one thing to have fantasies of running off with a handsome stranger to live happily ever after, but reality was a totally different thing. Besides, Ma hadn't had much good to say from the little bit she'd shared about marriage. Ma was very modest and shy. She was training her girls to be ladies and ladies didn't talk about such things. The girls at school would whisper and giggle but Miss Prue would usually settle them back down with a stern "Girls!" Just as quickly as the fear had tried to return, Molly felt peace wash over her soul. She knew one thing for sure and that was that God was with her. As He had protected her so many times from her father's wrath, she knew in her heart that she was safe. She remembered the story of Isaac and Rebekah her mother read a few times. Rebekah went with Abraham's servant to marry a stranger and she was not afraid. Molly would not be afraid either. She would trust in God. As the peace washed over again she realized she was growing up.

Back at the store Jake was wiping the counter, trying not to fret about his friend and his outrageous plan when Samuel Meyers and his oldest boy, Earl, burst into the room. Meyers was brandishing his shotgun and had the look of a wild man.

"Where are they?" He demanded, striding up to the counter.

Jake kept wiping the counter and hoped he appeared composed and unconcerned. "Who you looking for?" he replied.

Meyers's spat as he defiantly replied, "That trapper that was here yesterday. He's got Molly. He just came out to my place and took her. Now I'm thinking you might know all about this business. You'd best tell me where he took her."

Earl said nothing, just stood behind his father, his face chalky white. He was scared on the outside, but inside he was relieved that Molly had gotten away. He also longed for the day when he'd have a place to go to escape the misery at home.

"If you're talking about Nathan Smith, he left here early this morning and I ain't seen him since." At least Jake could answer him truthfully.

"Are you telling me you don't know nothing about his doings?" The older man trembled with anger as he shook his shotgun menacingly towards Jake.

The storekeeper raised his hands up from behind the counter and shook his head, staying calm, which made Meyers glare all the more.

"If your girl's run away, well, I'm just real sorry to hear about it, but I honestly can't tell you where she's gone."

"She ain't run away, I'm telling you he came and took her!" Meyers was near boiling now like a kettle about to pop its lid off on the stove.

"Pa," Earl offered timidly, "She did go with him of her own accord. Maybe she knew him already. Maybe they been meeting somewhere." He was thinking about his own hide as well as Molly's happiness. Not only did he want his sister to have a better life, he didn't want to be the brunt of his father's wrath when they returned home. Somebody surely would be. "She ain't already knowed him, boy." He twirled to stare harshly at Earl, "When could she have ever sneaked out of that house without my knowing it. I've half a mind to…" and noticing that Jake was walking around the counter towards him, he quickly changed his look and lowered the arm aimed at the brow of the now terrified boy.

No longer satisfied with the answers Jake gave him, Meyers strode out of the store with Earl at his heels. Jake breathed a sigh of relief that the man had not taken his anger out on him and hoped fervently that Nathan knew what he was doing and had gotten safely away. He thought of the look on Earl's face, too. That boy's probably gonna get it.

Molly's mother stood in her little house anxiously waiting for someone to come back to the house and tell her what was happening. Seth and Sissy hovered around her. It could be a long wait. Somewhere from deep within Winifred began to pray.

Chapter 5

Dogs began barking in the yard of Preacher Brown's house, at the presence of someone coming down the trail. Prudence Brown went to the window and peered out. "Pa," she called. "Here comes the young man who was here this morning early. I guess he's bringing his bride. Are you ready?" she smiled.

"I'm coming." Grabbing his jacket and shrugging it on, he continued, "Let 'em in so's they can warm up a bit. Now where did you put my marrying book? And where's my 'spectacles'?"

"I didn't put it anywhere. Just look where you had it last. And, your spectacles are on the top of your head, sir." Turning her thoughts to the couple on the horse she clucked,

"You young folk come on in now, where it's warm."

Nathan slid off the horse and reached up for Molly. For some reason she only extended one hand, keeping the other tucked in her cloak. As she landed in his arms and he placed her onto the ground, he heard the mewing noises of the kitten. Molly looked to the ground not wanting to face him. For a moment he was surprised and then he reared back his head and began to laugh. "How'd you manage to keep *that* a secret for five miles?"

Molly raised her head and grinned faintly. If he could laugh about the kitten then he couldn't be too angry with her for bringing it. He stroked a wayward tendril of hair off her forehead and together they walked into the house where Prudence closed the door behind them.

"Why, you didn't tell me it was Molly Meyers you were bringing! Land's sakes child, I didn't even know you had a beau, and here you are coming to be married." Prudence's joyful banter changed as she furrowed her brow in concern, "Why didn't your Ma come with you?"

Molly clutched her kitten tightly trying to think of an answer. Nathan put his hands on her shoulders.

"Molly's folks didn't take too kindly to me taking Molly so far away from them. That won't change things with you and the Preacher will it?'

"No, I guess not. Come to think of it, my folks didn't care too much for George taking me either, and I was about the same age as Molly here when we decided to get married." Dusting her skirt as though dismissing her own worry, she spoke to the girl soothingly. "Now, Molly just put your kitten down for a spell. He can have some breakfast if old Tom will let him. Say, have you young folks had breakfast yet? I'd be glad to warm up something for you. It'd be no problem at all."

"Thanks, but we've already eaten," Nathan lied. "We've a long way to travel today, so I hope you don't mind if we hurry this up a bit."

"No, not at all. I forgot all about the journey you two have ahead of you. Pa, did you find your marrying book yet?" She glanced towards her sweet husband with open affection and it caught Molly's heart. Marriage must be good for some folks after all, she decided right there and then.

"I've got it, Prue. Now if you young folks want to take off your coats, we'll get started with this" George Brown had his worn leather Bible and another leather bound book which he placed reverently on the table. From the Bible he began to read about Adam and how the Lord saw that it wasn't good for man to be alone and so he created a woman from the rib of man while he slept. Hurry Preacher, hurry, Nathan's mind was racing. He could hardly concentrate on what the man was saying. He was ready to get on with this new life.

"Do you Nathan Smith, take this woman Molly Meyers to be your wife?"

"Yes, sir, yes I do."

Nathan, Molly wondered. She remembered now that she'd heard Jake call him that. Nathan Smith. How nice it sounded. Molly Smith, that sounded good as well. Mrs. Nathan Smith sounded even better.

"And Molly, do you take Nathan to be your Husband?"

Molly's answer was barely above a whisper. "I do."

"I now pronounce you man and wife."

"Congratulations!" Prue gushed. "I just love a wedding!" Molly found herself enveloped in rosewater and glycerin, being hugged by a very affectionate and joyful woman.

"Now Prue, wait just a minute," the Preacher said. "They need to sign the wedding book."

He searched around looking for something to write with and again Nathan felt impatience surge through him. Sweat began to bead on his upper lip under his mustache and it certainly wasn't from the heat of the room. Finally a writing instrument was found and first Nathan and then Molly signed the book. Then Preacher Brown signed the date and pronounced that it was finished and now they were Mr. and Mrs. Nathan Smith.

Prudence took Molly's hand and led her to the back room. " N o w Molly, I'd like to give you some things. They're not much, just some things I don't need anymore and you'll likely be needing them. That'll be my wedding present to you."

When they were in the other room away from the men, Molly looked up into Prue's kind face. "Miss Brown, could you please be sure and let my Ma know that I'm okay and that everything's going to be all right?" Tears glistened in the corner of Molly's eyes.

"Why sure hon, I can remember how I worried about my Ma when George and I married. Oh, that was so many years ago and I'd not thought about that in years. But it's been good, as I'm sure yours will be with Nathan. My, such a handsome young man you've got Molly."

She's right, Molly thought, suddenly welling with pride. He is handsome.

Prudence bent over her cedar chest and took out some cloth.

"I've had this for some time now and I'm never going to get around to sewing it up. I want you to have it. And I've got some other stuff here too."

Molly looked on in amazement as the older woman took out soft white muslin and some floral print cloth offering it to Molly.

"You might need some extra sewing things too. I've got some extra needles around here somewhere. I'll just let you take a few for yourself."

She didn't really have that many extra, but she could get some more. She knew the girl didn't have any decent clothes. "Oh and here's a thimble and some scissors you can have too. Just let me get something to wrap these things in." Just then her eye caught a box that had come to them recently from back east; a box of Bibles that the Mission ladies in New York had sent. "Let me give you one of these hon. You can keep your family records in it." She opened the box and took one out for Molly presenting it to her as though it were made of gold.

This felt like Christmas, but she wondered how she would ever carry all of this on the horse.

Just then Nathan and the Preacher came into the room.

"Molly we'd best be going," Nathan said. "I've got my wagon out back. Let me take those things and I'll load them in the back."

It hadn't occurred to Molly that Nathan had a wagon. She felt relieved. It would have been hard to ride for two days doubled up on one horse. Prudence took the rest of the Bibles out of the box.

"Why don't we see if we can put some old rags in here and fix a warm place for kitty to ride?" She suggested. "You go on to the outhouse before you leave, Molly. I'll get the little thing and fix him right up for you."

Molly went as bidden. She found herself wishing that Prudence Brown could have been her Ma, and then felt guilty for thinking such a thing. She loved her Ma with all of her heart. Once again, the tears threatened to spill down her cheeks, but her new found inner strength prevailed and she recovered.

Before she knew it, Preacher Brown was putting the box enclosing the kitten ever so snugly into the wagon under the canvas and then Nathan was offering his hand to help her up. A lap robe was waiting to wrap around her to keep her warm as they traveled. The horse was already hitched so Nathan was up beside her on the buggy seat swiftly and they were off down the trail. Behind them the Preacher and Mrs. Brown waved and Molly thought Mrs. Brown wiped away a tear.

Nathan gave a sigh of relief as he snapped the reins. If Samuel Meyers was looking for them, at least now, he could prove Molly was his wife. He reached into his pocket to feel again the crinkle of the paper that the Preacher had given him. Molly was now safely his and he'd see to it that her father never mistreated her again. He glanced at her with a wink and she shyly looked away as they headed for home - their home.

Samuel and Earl searched in vain for any tracks that might be Nathan's. The more Earl thought about the situation, the less afraid he was. He reasoned that if Jake was friends with the trapper then he had to be a decent sort. Any time that Earl had the chance, he'd spend time with Jake and knew him to be a man of good judgment. Jake had treated Earl like a kid brother. Always ready with advice and adult conversation. The girls weren't allowed to hang around the store, but Ma didn't mind Earl going down there as long as his chores were done. Jake had taught him to play chess. They had spun stories and tall tales and the like. Things between friends. Earl trusted Jake and Jake seemed to trust this man. Maybe the preacher's sermon was right; God does take care of folks if they just wait and watch. Earl decided that even though he had to side with Pa while searching for his sister, when he had a chance, he would comfort their Ma that Molly was not in any jeopardy. Although he didn't know Molly felt the same way, it was just this inner sense that somehow it was meant to be and that God was directing this whole event. Maybe God was a mite kinder and more generous than his Pa.

Chapter 6

The warm sun beat down on the traveling couple, turning the snow into a messy, mucky slush. At last Nathan felt they were far enough ahead of Samuel Meyers that they could stop and eat something. He pulled over to a rocky knoll where the snow was long gone and the sun had created a dry place.

"Are you hungry Molly?" It was the first words that had been spoken between them since they'd left the preacher's house.

"Yes," she answered. Her fear had subsided to some extent. She'd spent most of the morning wondering if her Pa knew which course they'd taken. She fretted a little just thinking how, any minute he could ride up and demand that she go back with him.

Just as though he could read her thoughts, Nathan touched her shoulder in reassurance,

"Don't worry none about your Pa, Molly. I don't think he will try to face me one on one. He'll get word from the Preacher soon enough that we're married and he'll back off. Preacher thinks we've known each other for a while and I asked him to go and talk to your Pa."

Relief flooded through her, both at his reassuring touch and his response.

"I asked Miss Prudence to talk to Ma too." She leaned towards Nathan, feeling more relaxed in his presence. "I never meant to hurt them."

"Of course you didn't. Why Molly girl, if you want, I'll take you back to see them – when the time's right."

For the first time since she could remember, Molly felt a surge of joy. This strong kind man would surely take care of her. She jumped down from the wagon and began searching under the canvas on the wagon for her tiny companion. He was curled up in a warm ball under the rags Miss Prue had fixed for him and when he was pulled out he stretched his little body and gave a big yawn. Molly set him down on the ground and his little tail stood straight up when he felt the cold on his paws. Nathan pulled out a small box and went over and sat on a large rock.

"Come and sit down. I've got some biscuits and ham left over from mine and Jake's breakfast."

Molly took a biscuit and sat down beside him. She averted her gaze from his face and watched the stowaway instead. The kitten found a spot to his liking and began to dig to squat.

"Hey now, little fellow," Nathan chuckled. "You don't need to be doing that in our dining room." It was at that moment that the horse chose to relieve himself too.

Molly let out a little laugh. "Our dining room? I think we must be dining in a stable."

"Thankfully, we won't have to muck this stable out." Nathan looked at her and realized when she smiled her whole face lit up. You've done a good thing, old boy, he smiled to himself as he munched another biscuit half. With the warmth of the day and a full tummy, Molly began to relax and find her hesitation subsiding. She was pleasantly surprised that she could look "her husband" in the eye. When she did, Nathan smiled back and they laughed together and continued to enjoy their lunch. It reminded her of her little fantasy from last night. She had to pinch herself to be sure that this was for real. Thinking of stables would forever keep this moment special. It was also a precious reminder that the Lord was born in a stable. All these years she had wondered how something so special could happen in a dirty old barn, but now she understood. It must have been a comforting place, there with the animals, as Mary and Joseph looked at their child and Savior.

Nathan stepped away to the bushes and Molly cleaned up the scraps, setting aside a scrap of ham for the kitty, and put the rest of the leavings back in the box. She picked up the box along with the kitten and deposited them in the wagon again. When they were finally on their way, they were no longer riding in silence. They were beginning to make each other's acquaintance. Molly found him easy to warm up to and began telling him about her Ma and her brothers and sisters. She wasn't even thinking about her Pa as she began recounting good times and family stories. She talked about Miss Prudence and Preacher Brown. There were the Sunday School lessons she'd learned and the affection she felt for the Preacher and his wife. In turn Nathan told her a little about his family. They lived back East. Molly was surprised to discover that she had married an educated man. He had moved out here two years ago to be on his own. His Grandfather had taught him hunting and trapping and he'd had no problems adapting to the wilderness life he had chosen. He was proud of the home he'd carved out for himself. His face was animated as he recounted clearing his land and cutting the tall trees for the walls of the cabin. He talked of a friend and fellow trapper who lived nearby who helped him.

Molly told him she had managed to finish eighth grade. That was more than most girls. She enjoyed reading and writing, but hardly ever got the chance. Miss Prudence had taught school in the same building they used for a church. At home, she'd learned sewing and cooking from her Ma.

Watching out for the younger children had been part of her responsibility also and she recounted playing games with them, helping them learn or just entertaining them. The picture she painted of her life for Nathan was colored with good things, but he noticed that she didn't mention much of her Pa.

Night was creeping upon them and the cold was beginning to penetrate through Molly's inadequate clothing as they came upon the halfway house. It was merely an abandoned homestead in run down condition but it was out of the weather and it had a fireplace, which made it a good place for travelers to spend the night. There was an outhouse and Molly thankfully made use of it, while Nathan carried in a few things from the wagon. From the stack of wood left on the porch, he started a fire. When she was through, it was his turn to go out and with the dim light of the fire, Molly looked through the box he had brought in and found bread and cheese to fix for them to eat. They ate hurriedly as the fire had not yet warmed the cabin and Molly offered the crumbs that were left to the kitten. She amusingly watched her little friend bat a crumb and then pounce on it as though finding a prized mouse. Staring briefly at what was a pleasant scene to his heart and seeing the light of the fire licking at the gold in Molly's long brown hair, Nathan turned and went back out to the wagon to bring in some blankets for spreading on the old bed in the corner. As he worked to make them a fitting spot for the night, it suddenly dawned on Molly that they would be sleeping there alone together and that she was his wife. Her face paled as the pleasantness of the afternoon vanished and she wished for morning desperately. She didn't think she was ready for all this. Romantic daydreams were one thing, but this was for real. What should she do? She looked around the room for an imaginary answer and stole a glance to the corner where Nathan worked on their sleeping spot. Suddenly she was warmer than she wanted to be.

Nathan too was thinking on this. He remembered what Jake had said. Maybe he should be patient about this. He caught a glimpse of her face in the firelight. When he saw the sheer terror reflected there he knew that he couldn't force this on her. Not yet, not now. She might submit and feel obliged to him, but he wanted more for her. Remembering Meyers and his reputation, Nathan's heart melted even more for Molly. He would need to win her affections slowly and carefully. There should be a courtship. And with not a little pride, he also knew in his heart that Molly was worth the time. Besides, he remembered the look in her Ma's face at the door of that old ramshackle cabin and he never wanted to see Molly like that. Not if he had anything to do with it.

"Molly,"

When he spoke her name, she started visibly.

"Molly," he said again speaking clearly but carefully. "I know this isn't the time to ask anything of you."

Oh, she reflected. What do I say to him? I don't have the right to keep anything from him. This is his wedding night and I am his bride.

"Don't be afraid," he assured her. "We need each others warmth tonight, but I don't intend to ask anything of you that you aren't ready to give. We've got nothing but time ahead of us. I can wait."

Feeling relieved, but trying not to show it on her face, she timidly approached the makeshift bed and without removing any of her clothing, she quickly crawled in and positioned herself in the far corner with her back to him and waited. As he slid into place beside her, he placed the kitten near her face and she tucked it safely under the covers. Being careful not to startle her, he carefully covered up as well. Almost immediately fatigue overtook her and she slept. Nathan lay there quietly thinking about Molly and the events of the day. Who would have dreamed that he'd be taking a wife back with him to the home he was so proud of. In the dim glow of the firelight he studied her sleeping face as flickers danced across it. Her long lashes lay against her smooth cheek and her breath softly whispered in the night. Sleep had caused her face to relax and she looked more like a woman than a scared fawn. Unexpectedly, she turned towards him in her sleep and before Nathan knew what was happening she had cuddled up against him. Her breath was sweet and he began to rest feeling the covers warming him up. Gently he placed his arm around her and before long he too had drifted off to sleep.

Molly moved in the bed as the smell of salt meat frying and coffee bubbling filled her senses. She sat up. Ma had let her oversleep. She had best get up and help with breakfast before Pa was awake. She threw back the covers and jumped out of bed. The sleepy kitten tumbled to the floor and let out a surprised meow at his rude awaking. Just then she remembered! No Ma, no Pa, no brothers and sisters, just a strange man standing at the fire in a strange cabin. He turned to look at her.

"Good morning, Molly. Did you sleep well?"

Her husband. She was married now. Pa wasn't here to scold her for over sleeping.

"Why didn't you wake me?" She ventured. "I should be fixing your breakfast, not the other way around."

"I figured you needed the rest" Nathan smiled, "Besides, I'm not used to having someone do for me. You'll get your chance to do chores soon enough. Maybe you need to put the kitten out for a bit. Does he have a name?"

She scooped the little package up and headed toward the door.

"I think Seth had named all of them, but I forget which one was which. Maybe he needs a new name to go with his new life."

"Sure thing! Lets call him Boots. Those white feet sure look like boots. Okay, Boots, you go out now and take care of business. Molly you come on and have some breakfast."

"I will, but first I need to take care of a little business myself." And with that Molly threw Nathan a little smile and went out with her kitten.

When she came back in, she was overwhelmed once more with shyness. They had talked together so well yesterday afternoon, but this morning it was as if they needed to get acquainted all over again. Would it be like this every morning?

After breakfast Nathan packed their things back in the wagon and Molly straightened the cabin. Her wedding night had come and gone.

"You'll have to do better than this, girl" she scolded herself, feeling more grown up than she ever had. Her fear was turning into resolve and she liked the feel of it.

Chapter 7

The day promised to be nicer and soon Molly and Nathan were on their way once more. Inside her heart Molly was thankful that Nathan had been so considerate the night before. How much time he'd give her to adjust she didn't know but at least she had today to think about it.

Molly no longer feared that her Pa would come riding up. She and Nathan laughed and talked about many things. Oh, he was so full of fun and life. She had missed that growing up. He pointed out the geese and ducks that were flying back from the south. She noticed that certain trees were showing signs of budding. Near one place however, the woods were bare. A lot of the large trees had been cut. The place looked unsightly where wagons had left deep ruts and dead limbs lay everywhere having been stripped from the downed trees.

"What happened here?" Molly questioned.

"Oh," Nathan replied. "Looks like the Wood Hawks have been working here. They're no longer content to cut only the trees by the river bank. They're up here ripping out the forest as well."

"Wood Hawks." Molly knew about them. Occasionally her Pa would go work with them. They felled trees, cut them up and stacked them near the river bank. When the Riverboats came through, they'd stop and buy fuel for their ever hungry boilers.

"But they need to cut the trees don't they? The boats need fuel."

'You're right," Nathan replied. "The boats do need fuel. But they could be more selective about the way they cut timber. When they just go in and cut everything in one place like this, the land tends to wash out and make gullies. Then all that sand washes into the river and creates navigation problems. I've helped more than one boat get off a sand bar."

"Are we near the river?"" Molly was curious. "I've always lived this close to the river, but I've never seen it."

"We're not too far," Nathan responded. "But we're headed in the opposite direction. Sometime in the summer, we'll come back and see it."

Thinking about the river, Molly remembered the times when her Pa came back after spending a few weeks with the Wood Hawks. He'd always have a little money then and would bring them candy from the Mercantile. He used to talk about a man who worked up on the Missouri River. He called him Liver Eatin' Jonson. They'd all laugh about that name. They'd just picture this big bearded man lapping slices of calf liver dangled by huge hands. None of the Meyers kid's liked liver. Pa would always make them eat it though. Funny how sometimes Pa could be so nice and tell them stories and make them laugh and then before you knew it, he'd be shouting at them, until they were all hushed and afraid. Just as they felt like songbirds, they'd get flushed like a covey of quail, not knowing which way to fly. Finally she turned her thoughts back to the present. They had been riding for a long time and her seat was feeling harder and harder.

It was late evening when they rode upon a beautiful little meadow. Early spring flowers and blades of green were poking through scattered patches of snow. The horse whinnied his delight at being home and picked up his step. A babbling creek flowed to one side of the meadow and on a hill to the far side stood a beautiful cabin, large with real windows and a solid door. A front porch ran the full length of it with an open dog trot right through the middle. Behind it, higher on the hillside, Molly could see a smokehouse and a stable. Another tiny little house in need of a few finishing touches stood close to the creek with a small stream of water trickling out from under it spilling its way down to the creek. Molly stood to her feet in absolute awe of such a beautiful place, feeling she'd just arrived at heaven on earth.

"Do you like it?" Nathan asked, watching her reaction.

"Is all this *yours*?" She breathed, barely able to contain her excitement.

"*Ours*, Molly" He answered, his chest swelling with pride at what he had done with his own hands and at the obvious satisfaction showing on Molly's face. "This place is ours. Home Sweet Home."

He pulled the wagon up to the porch and stopped. The horse neighed again and shook his head anxious to be turned loose, his harness metal making a sing song sound as he snorted in obvious pleasure. Molly flew from the wagon and ran up on the porch, forgetting all about Boots meowing protest in the box. She ran her hands across the wood that was stacked neatly at one end, lots of it already split and ready to use. On the outside walls of the cabin, pelts were secured. She savored the softness of them as though she were touching the finest down. She turned to look at Nathan who was unhitching the restless horse. "Can I go in?" She asked.

"Sure, the latch string is out. Go on in."

Molly stepped joyfully inside leaving the door open wide, with the sunshine streaming in behind her. On this side of the cabin was one big room. A cook stove stood against the center wall. A cook stove! Molly ran to it and touched it. "Oh" she reflected, "I must have married a rich man." It was a beautiful modern stove with an oven and a tank built right in for heating water. There was a long wooden table and a large cupboard. Inside the cupboard were tin dishes and pans. Large sealed tin cans were there to store the beans and flour that Nathan had purchased at the Mercantile. That would protect the food from bugs and other varmints and allow the supplies to last. Molly ran from place to place in the big room. When Nathan walked in she was darting about like a butterfly touching everything she looked at.

"There's more on the other side of the dog trot," He told her.

She smiled warmly at him as she ran across the hall and pulled open the door there. Two rooms were on this side. A big fireplace was placed against the far wall with a wide opening between the rooms so that the heat could warm them both. Here also was a ladder built right onto the wall leading to the loft where the vegetables could be stored for the winter.

Suddenly Molly realized that Nathan was doing all the work, bringing in the supplies from the wagon. Embarrassed at herself for being so inattentive, she hurried back out the door to help him.

"Don't try to carry those heavy bags of seed and things. You get your things and bring in the blankets."

Happy to be useful and feeling like she'd burst out singing any minute, she carried everything that she could and soon the wagon was empty. Nathan left it where it stood. There would be time tomorrow to put it in the stable where it belonged. Before long, Nathan had a fire going in both the stove and in the fireplace and Molly began poking around in the goods for something to make a meal with. Nathan grinned. For the first time in more than two years, he didn't have to fix his own supper. He went outside to put up his horse for the night and brought in Molly's kitten from the porch. After supper Molly washed up using nice warm water from the tank on the stove and Nathan went to the spring house to bring in water for the morning. Then he discreetly left her in the big room alone and she drew a basin of the warm water and bathed herself and prepared for bed. Once more they slept together chastely. But this night Molly dreamt of a golden haired lover touching her softly and whispering sweet words of comfort in her ear.

A week passed. The days grew warmer and Molly and Nathan settled into a routine. During the day, they worked in the meadow making a garden. Digging in the rich earth was hard work but rewarding. Molly pulled weeds until her back ached. Then she would just sit down in the dirt working it with a little garden fork until it was loose and ready to accept the seeds. Boots often played at their feet getting in the way and making them laugh at his kitten antics. They laughed a lot and friendship blossomed between them. In the evenings by the lamp light, Molly sewed while Nathan observed her from his rocking chair near the fire. She was making a new dress from the pretty cotton fabric that Miss Prue had given her. Her small hands busily stitched tiny tight stitches and gradually the material became a delicate work of art. Molly loved sewing. It was peaceful and relaxing work, done by the firelight. Any tiny scrap was carefully hoarded to start a scrap box for quilt making.

At night while he lay near her warm body, it was all Nathan could do to keep from touching her, but he knew that it wasn't the time just yet. Patiently he allowed her trust in him to build.

One day as Nathan looked up from his work, he saw Molly chasing after Boots in the garden, and remembered the dream he'd had in the store. He found himself chasing after her. He grabbed her from behind and they fell laughing to the ground. He brushed her face softly with his beard.

Her heart began to pound and she stopped laughing. Her breath became uneven. He nuzzled her nose with his, rubbing gently. Ever so slowly he sought out her mouth and kissed her . She tasted the salt of his lips and when he raised his head, she raised her face to him for more. They kissed and nuzzled and unexpectedly Boots' tail rubbed against their faces as he meowed his disapproval at being left out. With that the moment was broken and Nathan scrambled to his feet, still unable to believe the inner joy and longing he felt. He reached for Molly's hand pensively and she too stood up weak in the legs from their encounter. Secretly she wished he'd take her to this place she could only see dimly. It was awkward and yet exciting. Neither one said a word and the seconds ticked and her heart beat began to settle when Nathan turned and went back to his work. Molly just stood there. The utter warmth of that moment again flooded her body; she trembled slightly. She ignored Boots as he insistently rubbed against her legs and meowed. Finally she caught her breath and barely whispered,

"I guess I need to go in and start supper."

"Sure," Nathan told her, not looking as he didn't want to embarrass her more.

"I'll just finish up here." He was dropping potato pieces into the prepared ground, all the while trying not to dwell on the wonderful awe he felt with Molly. "Law that girl's mine!" He pounded the dirt with his fist, shook his head as though to dislodge a cobweb and concentrated on the job at hand.

In the kitchen, Molly's hands trembled as she peeled potatoes and sliced salt meat. Still weak at the knees, she nicked a finger and immediately it was in her mouth, soothing the pain. Time seemed to have slowed tremendously. When she got her composure enough to finish the meal she called Nathan in to eat. He stopped on the porch and washed his face and hands.

Supper was quiet. It was as if they were totally unfamiliar with one another again. Both were caught up in the privacy of their own thoughts. Nathan stared noncommittally at the plate before him, trying to keep his mind off his own delight. He was almost fearful, this strong and viral young man, that he would not be able to take it, his love for her was so great! Such a strange sensation for Nathan, that he suddenly stabbed the salt meat as though it were an enemy. Molly jumped a little in her chair at Nathan's sudden movement. Molly was wondering if Nathan would make love to her tonight. She was no longer afraid of what it would be like. She realized that her wonderings were turning to hopes. Her face flushed slightly and she choked a little as she tried yet again to gain her composure.

Bedtime came and Molly took longer than usual to wash up for the night. Their night, she thought to herself, as she pulled out the new muslin gown that she'd been sewing on for three days. She slipped it on and once again the desire she'd never felt before rose up in her. Although she still felt a little awkward, she knew in her heart that he was waiting for her. She stepped quietly and quickly across the chilly wooden floor, through the hall and into the room where Nathan waited. He did not smile at her as she entered the room, but by his eyes, she could tell what he saw when he looked at her. She slipped towards his bed and he rose up to meet her, pulling her closer to him. Once more he kissed her lips and at first she shyly responded to his touch. There was much softness from those calloused hands, such tenderness in each caress. She eagerly welcomed his gentle loving and afterward felt a contentment and joy like she'd never felt before. She was no longer a child, but a woman for sure. And from this experience, she felt stronger, a seed of maturity and confidence beginning to grow. As she drifted to sleep in her man's arms, Nathan looked at her, this beautiful woman of his. The coal oil lamp flickered and gave a glow to her satin shoulder and throat. He caressed her neck and she sleepily responded. He wrapped her up close to him and sighed with pure pleasure. There'd be plenty of time for their love. He smiled to himself, gave her one more glance and fell into a deep sleep.

Chapter 8

The next morning when Nathan awakened he heard her across the hall singing as she prepared breakfast. Although he was unfamiliar with the grogginess he was experiencing, he grinned at the happy sound. He found himself recounting the night's love and wished that she'd stayed in bed just a little longer. Oh well, he'd talk her into this again when breakfast was over. Right now he was hungry as a bear. He jumped out of bed and bounded into to the kitchen.

"Woman, who said you could leave my bed without permission?" Nathan grabbed Molly and spun her round. He planted eager kisses all over her face and she giggled and squirmed to get loose.

"Please Nathan, if I don't stir this mush it will be full of lumps." She pounded his chest with her fists in mock displeasure.

"Let the mush be lumpy woman! There are things that are far more important than mush without lumps." He grabbed the pan from the stove and placed it on the table and grabbed at Molly again.

She laughed and protested, but her protests were false and he knew it. Again she tasted his sweet lips and he carried her back to the bed. Breakfast was forgotten as their marriage bed became more intimate. Molly's knowledge of womanhood grew with each touch from this man and she realized she was beginning to love him as she'd never loved anyone before.

Days grew into weeks, the summer bloomed and the two lovers settled into life as one. Molly cooked and cleaned and sewed while Nathan gardened, cleared some more of the land and replenished firewood. Each of them would catch the other whistling or humming and stealing glances at one another. Although Molly still blushed, it was no longer with embarrassment. It was that inner knowledge that all was well with their home and their nights.

Little radish tops and green onions poked out of the dark, soil. Tender young lettuce leaves burst forth in the warming sun. The two of them ate fresh vegetables until they were sick of them. As the days grew longer and hotter, tender vegetables were spread on a clean sheet in the sun to be dried and stored in the attic for the winter. Never had Molly felt such joy working the way she did when she was storing away food in her own little attic and cellar. This was truly a dream come true – a dream she'd not even known she could dream. She hoped she'd never wake up. In the cool of the mornings Nathan would clear brush near the edge of the yard and Molly would bring him water. He accepted the drink as though she were offering him nectar. Sweet tender kisses would often interrupt the work. Once when Molly was helping to drag brush to a pile for burning, she startled a little green snake. Her frightened squeal brought Nathan running to her side only to laugh and pick up the offending reptile throwing him safely away from his beautiful young wife.

"Mercy me," Molly said, her hand rushing to her flushed cheek. "If I'd only took a good look, I'd have known it was just a little green snake. What you must think of me screaming like that over a little old snake."

"What I think," Nathan grinned, pulling her into his arms, "is that you'll try any trick to get my attention."

"Well," Molly responded coyly. "Sometimes a girl needs a Knight in Shining Armor to rescue her."

Nathan was quiet for a moment as he recalled the morning when he had ridden up to her family home. Molly was remembering too. He truly was her Knight and he did rescue her.

"Molly," He uttered soberly. "I love you more than life itself and rescuing you is a privilege that I take very seriously. Small green snakes or vicious dragons, Nathan Smith to the rescue."

Chapter 9

With winter long gone, Samuel Meyers headed to the river to work for the Wood Hawks. As he rode up to the camp, he was greeted by Charlie Johnson. Charlie was the nephew of old Liver Eatin' Johnson, the most famous, or infamous, wood hawk on the upper Missouri River.

"Hey, Samuel, ain't seen you in a spell. You needing work?'

Samuel dismounted and reached for Charlie's extended hand to give it a good shake.

"Yeah, I could use some work." He scratched his beard as though thinking better of it. " Maybe I could work up enough for a fare to New Orleans on one of the boats."

"Yeah, I guess you could," Charlie answered. "You plan on going to New Orleans?"

"Could be," Samuel responded.

"Sit a spell and have some stew."" Charlie told him as he turned to stir the black caldron full of potatoes and squirrels. "I can tell you for sure, there's plenty of wood to cut. Did you bring your own tools with you?"

"I got tools," Samuel replied nodding towards his horse. "Just let me know which crew you want me working with." In the simple log corral nearby, two mules rested from their day's work. They shifted their feet and stomped to rid themselves of the pesky biting horse flies. Suddenly one raised his head and brayed, the awful racket echoing through the woods. It didn't matter how accustomed a person was to the sound, it was always startling.

In the dusk of the evening, the lumberjacks gathered around the campfire, eating and talking, sharing jokes and the day's events. Charlie pointed toward the crew he wanted Samuel to work with. Before long, the men began stretching out their bedrolls to settle in for the night. A chorus of tree frogs began their evening calls and just beyond the light of the campfire, other night creatures began to stir. From the bedrolls, snores commenced from first one tired logger and then another. Grunts and groans could be heard throughout the darkness as the men turned in their sleep to find a more comfortable spot. With the morning light the men of the camp came to life, readying themselves to work another day in the heat and humidity. Even the mules were at attention, patiently waiting to be harnessed. A friendly slap on the neck and they trotted toward their human partner to begin the day. Samuel worked with the men for some time. The work was plentiful but he wasn't too fond of the hardness of it. Still and all, the cash was good and for a few week's work he could do what he determined to accomplish later. Yep, he said to himself, I got me an idea and I'm gonna get it done. He rubbed at his back as though working through the soreness and headed out with the rest of his crew.

Throughout the woods, the metallic ring of axe heads sang out against the tall trees like claps of thunder. As each tree began to heave and give up it's standing in the forest, one man would holler out "TIMBER!" and the others would scramble to get out of the way. The tree would crack and fall with a mighty crashing groan. The earth moved underneath the weight as one mighty tree after another hit the ground. Quick work was made of cutting away branches and the racks of wood would start accumulating. Day after day the work droned on. Sweat would pour down a man's brow as the saltiness sting their eyes, and muscles would ache under the tremendous strain.

Each night the campfire would again host the men for a time of relaxing. Some men would sit and spit, others would laugh and joke with each other. Some of the men would slump under the effects of hard drink and tiredness. Almost as regular as clockwork, one boat after another tied off near the bank to purchase the wood needed to feed their ever hungry boilers. Watching those big river ships chug down the river, blowing smoke and churning the water, you knew the great logs of wood were no match for the mammoth fire belching with each turn of the waterwheel.

Once the Wood Hawks had depleted the supply of timber, they'd simply move their camp to another part of the river with a virgin stand and begin the demolition again. They left each place looking as though a hurricane had come through, not caring that they were leaving behind barren banks that would wash into the river with the next heavy rain. In the reasoning of the timber cutters there was a never ending supply of the natural resources of the forest.

One evening as the men sat around camp, Samuel leaned over to question Charlie about the folks that lived to the north of the river.

"You know many of the folks around here?" he asked trying to appear nonchalant.

"Yeah, some I do, some I don't" Charlie answered.

"Well, I'm wondering about one fellow in particular." Samuel said hunching towards the campfire. "Trapper fellow. Talks like an Eastener."

"Only two trappers that I know of in this general area.'" Charlie responded noncommittally. "One of them is a Frenchman."

"No, that ain't the fellow I'm thinking of. Ain't no Frenchie." Samuel answered.

"Well, that just leaves that Smith fellow. Nathan Smith I believe is his name."

"You wouldn't know how to get to his place by any chance?" Samuel didn't want to sound too eager, lest somebody get the idea he was up to no good.   "Sure," Charlie answered. He proceeded to give Samuel the information he craved.

Chapter 10

As the afternoon sun dappled the porch, shining through the leaves of nearby trees, Molly sat in her rocker, mending a shirt and watching her beloved working the garden. She was surprised when she heard a horse whinny as both the steed and rider appeared on the trail. Molly cupped her hand over her brow to make out who it was from the porch. As Molly leaned forward, the thread slipped from her lap and the kitten squealed as the rocker caught the tip of its tail. Looking at her little friend she looked back as she watched Nathan approach the rider. Nathan gave him a friendly slap on the back and a handshake that let Molly know Nathan must be familiar with him. She picked up her thread and looked again as the two talked for a minute as first one and then the other looked toward the cabin and back to each other. As the horse stomped, the man dismounted and they turned and walked toward the cabin together leading the man's horse. They were smiling as Molly stood up and waited for her husband to introduce her.

"Molly, this is Frenchie. He's a trapper too. He's our nearest neighbor and has been my friend for a long time."

"Hello little lady," With his thick accent, the man reached out his hand toward Molly, taking his hat off in the process. "I had no idea that Nate brought home such a beautiful Petite Femme! My woman Clara she be glad to hear about you." Frenchie's voice was musical and friendly. Instantly she liked him. "Molly, looks like we're gonna have company for supper!", Nathan invited with confidence in his woman, "Frenchie, eat with us and visit for a spell."

The men sat down at the table talking while Molly ladled up beans, some fried salt pork and poured black cups brimming with strong coffee.

"Bon ami", Frenchie addressed Nathan as friend. "I came over here to see if you had a little time to help me fix my roof tomorrow. That last heavy snow we had did quite a bit of damage. I just haven't had the time to get around to fixing it. I took Clara to see her Ma for a spell. She just didn't want to be out here away from her folks with it being about time for the baby to come."

He looked both delighted and a little embarrassed at speaking so in mixed company.

"No problem, I'll be more than glad to help you. I sure couldn't have done all the things around this place without the help you gave me. If Clara's not home, you might as well stay over tonight."

"Sure thing. I'll enjoy the company. It's too quiet without my Clara. I'll be glad when my cherie can come home." He shook his head wistfully.

After supper Nathan found a deck of playing cards. He and Frenchie were really enjoying themselves. Molly took up her sewing and sat down in the corner. She found herself feeling left out. For the first time since they'd left for home, Nathan's attention wasn't wholly hers. Finally, not being able to stand it any longer, she got up and went to bed by herself. Nathan barely noticed the door closing a little too loudly as he and Frenchie were deep in conversation. The men's loud talk and laughter lasted long into the night and finally the singsong of their voices helped her drift off to sleep. When morning came, she found that her mood was still a bit sour as she fixed breakfast for the two men. Nathan sensed her mood, but couldn't put his finger on the problem. Since he couldn't figure it out, he decided it was nothing and dismissed it. When it was time to head out for Frenchie's place he was surprised when she didn't want to go.

"Molly, I'd rather you didn't stay here by yourself.' He felt a swell of concern for this child bride of his. A nagging feeling he wasn't sure about.

"No, you go on with your friend. If his wife was there, I wouldn't mind going. It would be nice to have some company and visit with a woman.

Don't worry about me. I'll be fine. I just want to finish up the dress I'm making."

Still not sure, but shrugging it off, he accepted her decision to stay behind. His excitement to help a friend overtook him and he gave his wife a perfunctory peck on the cheek before they mounted their horses. After he and Frenchie got down the trail a bit, Nathan commented on it. He was feeling just a little frustrated.

"I apologize for my wife's rude behavior. I can't imagine what got into her"."

"Don't let it worry you none, Nate. Women get that way from time to time. Especially when it's that time of the month."

"Yeah, sure." Nathan agreed, but inwardly he thought about that. He didn't remember Molly mentioning anything about it being her time. He was surprised. Why hadn't she said something? Could she simply have forgotten about it? A glimmer of hope crossed his mind as he pondered her mood. Could it be something else? The thought that there could be a baby was incredible. Maybe she didn't even know it herself. He'd have to sweeten her up a little when he returned. They had things to talk about. He slapped the reigns and laughing aloud challenged his friend to a race down the way.

At home Molly was close to tears. Frustrated with herself for acting so childish a tear spilled over her cheek. To be jealous of Nathan's friend when it was apparent how happy he was to see Frenchie made her all the more mad at herself. It would probably have gone better if she'd had someone to visit with. The thought of getting to know Clara cheered her up a bit. And Clara would have a new baby to show off. That would be a delight. Mentally preparing a blanket for the neighbor, Molly wondered if she'd ever have a baby of her own. How would she know if she was expecting? For a moment, she saw her Ma's face and wished she could talk to her. She hadn't had her flow since she'd been with Nathan. Was that how she'd know? She remembered hearing the women talking about that at the quilting bee at Miss Prudence's house. But everytime they saw the younger girls listening, of whom Molly was one, they'd look at each other and smile and hush their talk.

The young wife could hold back the tears no longer. With the dishes untouched, she just sat in the rocker and gave way to the pent up emotions.

The tears had a cleansing effect and she began to rock, daydreaming and praying about a someday baby. She must have fallen asleep because she jumped awake with excitement as she heard a horse outside. Nathan was home! She flew to the door planning to throw herself into Nathan's arms. Only the man who dismounted from the horse wasn't Nathan. It was Samuel Meyers! Molly's hand flew to her forehead as she held her breath; just then she felt a terrible panic well up inside of her. She tried to scream but felt so sick in the pit of her stomach when out of the blue everything began to swirl and turn black. For the first time in Molly's life, she fainted.

What luck, Meyers thought, as he realized things could not have gone better for him. Having Molly unconscious was a great advantage. He hastily scooped her up and threw her over the back of his horse like a sack of meal and took off. He didn't dare waste a moment. He figured Nathan had to be somewhere close by. He had no way of knowing that he had arrived at the only possible time to make away with Molly, since Nathan was at his friend's homestead and had no idea that Molly needed him.

When Molly came to, she felt like her insides were being jarred out. Pa was holding her tight, her head was down and she felt so sick she thought she'd die.

"Pa, let me go. I have to go back. Please Pa don't do this."

"It's okay Molly. I've got you away from that terrible man. You're safe with your Pa now. I'm taking you where he can't find you. You're safe now." Meyers believed his own tales as he thought of himself as some sort of savior of a damsel in distress. Besides, he couldn't stand women pleading for anything.

"No, Pa, no! Take me back. I'm safe with Nathan. Pa, he's my husband." She grabbed at his shoulder, but he thrust her away like a rag doll with no emotion whatsoever.

Slowly it dawned on her that her cries were truly in vain. She let the faintness overtake her for a blessed rest from the terrible fix she was in. At last Meyers stopped; more for the horse's sake than for Molly's. If only she could stop being so sick and dizzy! Then she could run as soon as she had the chance. Where were they? Could she find her way back? They were near the creek and Pa wet his handkerchief and began to wash her face. Maybe he did think he was rescuing her, Molly thought. Who could ever know with him. When she had calmed down a bit, she attempted to reason with him on a more rational level.

"Pa, I'm sorry. I know it was wrong for me to run away with Nathan, but I love him. We got married all legal. Didn't Preacher Brown tell you? I asked him to let y'all know I was okay and we were happy. Listen, Pa, you can't take a man's wife away from him. For sure not when I think I'm…" She bent her head low, embarrassed at her realization and as though she were in mourning. She would not have wanted to tell this man, her Pa, about a baby before she told Nathan. It was all so wrong. How could it be that only this morning she was planning to make up with her man and now she didn't know how she'd ever get back to him? With head still bent, she pleaded,

" Oh Pa, take me back. We have a baby coming. I won't even tell Nathan about this. He's not home right now, he'll never even have to know."

Molly's revelation soothed Meyers a bit. If Nathan wasn't near the homestead then he'd been given the edge. That gave him a window of opportunity to work with. Meyers breathed in as he now felt time was on his side. His plan was to put Molly on a boat, pay her fair and ship her down to New Orleans where his brother lived. Nathan would never find her there. The news about the baby would make things easier. He'd just explain to his brother's wife that Molly'd gone bad. She'd understand and wouldn't believe Molly if she tried to explain. Yep, that'd be his reason for sending her down there. Maybe they could find a home somewhere for the baby. His sister-in-law would like that. She was such a pompous fool. She'd take in Molly thinking she could straighten her right out. With a woman like that keeping a tight rein on his girl there was no way she'd get a chance to run away from there. It'd be so easy to hoodwink them into helping him out.

"Now, Molly, you gotta get a hold of yourself. Don't you know how you broke your Ma's heart, running away like you did? You didn't even know that man. She cries 'bout near every night for you. The kids, well, they have it all the more harder because of what you done. Specially Sissy."

Now it was his turn to make his play for he knew Molly had a soft spot for her siblings.

Molly felt so awful thinking what her family had gone through because of her leaving with Nathan. She had to clear her head to remember she was fighting for her life – their life – their baby's life.

"But, I do now Pa. I'm sorry I didn't mean to hurt anybody. Nathan is good to me. He loves me. Pa, please. I need to go back."

Samuel had that look about him that always made his children fear.

"We'll have no more talk of it! You hear me girl?" He raised his fist and Molly cringed. He looked around as though worried someone would see him treating her badly. It wouldn't do to be found like this with her all whimpering and sick.

" Someday you'll thank me for this. Now hush!" Once again he wielded his fist through the air with severity.

Molly knew when to back off. Maybe if she just kept quiet and did what he said, everything would smooth over. As soon as they got home, Nathan would come. She knew that she could count on it.

Chapter 11

If they were headed to her old home, they sure were going in a round about way. Molly figured this see saw trip was designed to throw Nathan off track. Although she hated to admit it, she was really getting tired. She tried as hard as she could to keep her wits about her so that if the opportunity arrived, she'd take it. Didn't matter where they were, she'd just run. Pa was bigger than her and she might have a chance if she darted under the brush and through the briars. She also knew he was lazy, something she'd never let herself admit. She had been raised to be so afraid of the man that she couldn't even think her own thoughts, even if they were true. She shook her head, incredulous that she had been kept so dull for so long. Her poor Ma. Probably was a smart woman, but beneath the hatefulness and ill will of her husband all her good feelings had worn away, like the flower on the coffee cup Ma used so often. Oh Ma… Oh Nathan… Oh Lord, help me! Her Pa saw her head drop slightly and took it for fatigue. Little did he know that wherever Molly was, she wasn't lost; God was with her and heaven help the one who worked against His plan.

As they topped a hill and came to a clearing, she could make out the river below meandering like a serpent looking for a victim. Although Molly remembered how much she had wanted to see the river with her husband, it now looked awful. The cliff was menacing and the water just looked dirty. Dirty as the plan her Pa had. Once again she wiped away tears. No point in showing Pa any weakness.

The horse made its way gingerly carrying the load down to the sandbar. A steamboat was there just off shore with people milling around a small dock. Anxious though she was, Molly was in awe. It was the Ohio River, which began it's life at the confluence of the Allegheny and Monongahela Rivers in Pennsylvania hundreds of miles away. It was a majestic river only to be outdone by the Mighty Mississippi in Illinois as the Ohio emptied itself into Old Muddy. She made note of the flatboats seen along the shore and up and down the way. These were the cheapest of the many types of boats used and were the standard conveyance for families moving west. There were strong men at the poles and some were using oars for steering in the swift current.

She remembered Mr. Jake at the Mercantile talking one time how these mighty machines with huge paddlewheels moved everything that could possibly be moved, people, lumber, food, gold, silver, cattle and livestock, cotton, mail, machinery, bricks, tar, railroad ties and their rails for railroads, and...Well you name it a steamboat probably delivered it somewhere, at least once.

She saw shifting sand bars, snags and rocks and remembered him describing the seasonal floods that made river travel dangerous. He had said that river pilots were required to memorize every foot of the river in order to steer safely through the many hazards. She had sat enthralled listening to his stories about the boats that were wrecked and how the increasing amount of trade on the rivers made navigating safely so important. Mr. Jake had said it would take an act of Congress to do something about it. That or somebody important drowning.

She returned to reality wondering why she and Pa were going to the river. She turned to ask him when she saw he was busy pouring something from a little bottle onto an old handkerchief. She tried to see what it was, that small amber bottle he held gingerly in his hands, but before she could say anything he held the cloth up to her face. Oh, the smell. The sick feeling came back and then the blessed blackness.

Chapter 12

Nathan dusted his hands on his jeans and realized he was more than glad to be headed back home. Maybe Molly would be in a better humor this evening. He figured with just a little teasing and loving, she'd be right back to her old self. They had already learned a lot about each other and he remembered with a chuckle that she was easy to figure out.

Dang that girl, she's got me wrapped around her heart tighter than a hug! As he dismounted, he rehearsed just how he had planned to greet her. It was some things Frenchie said that made him realize that maybe, just maybe, something more was going on than just an ill temper or melancholy. Wouldn't that be something? Resolved to be his old generous self, he reached the porch. The door was hanging just ajar. Must be too hot in the house for cooking he thought. "I'll have to fix a little place outside for her to cook on really hot days," He muttered to himself and let out a little whistle. Grabbing the reigns that lay at the porch steps, he decided to go ahead and put the horse up. After all, there might not be time or wherewithal to rub the horse down and put the tack up later. As he returned to the house, he was a bit surprised that Molly still hadn't come out to meet him. Was she still peeved? Boots met him at the door wrapping his furry body around Nathan's boots but still no Molly.

"Molly?" He called out.

That's strange he thought. It was much too quiet around here. As he entered the room, he surveyed it closely. She hadn't even cleaned up from breakfast. The fire had gone out and the dishes were all strewn around.

Hmmm, her apron lay on the floor near the table. He called again. He went across the dog trot to the bedroom. Where in the world was she? One by one he checked all of the outbuildings calling loudly.

A flood of panic welled up inside him. He could of whipped himself! He shouldn't have taken no for an answer when she declined to come along to Frenchie's. He went back out front and bent to examine the earth by the porch steps, sifting dirt through his fingers and looking intently. Sure enough he spied another set of hoof prints besides his and Frenchie's. Suddenly it hit him. He felt a stream of cold air run across the back of his neck. By all creation, it couldn't have been anyone but Meyers! Cursing under his breath and making an oath to God Himself, he grabbed a bed roll and his gun. Carrying Boots out with him,

"You'll just have to get along on your own for a bit", he latched the door and bounded to the stable.

His horse was saddled in seconds and as the creeping twilight settled in, Nathan headed down the trail. He was going after his wife and no one not even the devil himself could stop him.

Chapter 13

Captain Jack Brennen was none too happy about taking on an unconscious passenger.

"I ain't got no one to look after a sick one." He said as he eyed the young slip of a fare. "Besides, whatever she's got might be catching. My crew needs their health so's they can do their work." He spat and wiped his chin. Nope he didn't like this at all. But money's money."Ain't none of your crew going to catch what's ailing this girl. She got herself in the family way. I gotta be sending her away. I'm sorry she's feeling poorly, but I don't want her missing the boat. She ain't married you know. I'm sending her to my brother's family in New Orleans till her time comes. That good for nothing boy ain't gonna stand by her. And, the Mrs., her Ma, well her heart's plumb broke. When that boy run off, Molly here just kinda went crazy. Staying at the farm, I'm sure she'd harm herself. She's bout lost her senses over it all. She may talk a little crazy to you, but don't pay no mind to what she says. You just get her to my brother safe and sound."

Samuel Meyers had to do some fast talking to persuade the Captain to take Molly. He'd had to work for the Wood Hawks most of the summer to get fare. He didn't want his plans to go afoul at the last minute. He had to get her on that boat before Nathan showed up or there'd be hell to pay.

"Well, I can sympathize with you. Ain't nothing worse than a girl what's gone bad. I still can't take no sick passenger." Eyeing the gold coins jingling in Meyers' fist, he knew himself well enough.

"She'll be better in the morning, I swear. Look, I'll take her to the cabin and tuck her in. Come morning when she's had something to eat and gets her strength up a bit, she'll be able to take care of herself alright. She may be a little upset but just give her a little time and let it go at that. She just needs to adjust some, that's all"

An older woman who was on the boat inched closer to the two men. She was curious about the young unconscious girl the man had carried on board. Very unusual state of affairs. The boat seldom picked up passengers at a wood camp. She eavesdropped on the conversation.

Jumping in, partly for curiosity and partly because she loved a mystery, "I'll help look out for your girl Mister. One of my girls went bad like that. I didn't have no place to send her though. She had to live with her shame always, and her babe too."

"Well now," the Captain relented, shaking his head and wiping the bead of nervous sweat from his brow.

"This changes things a might. Now that I don't have to try and be responsible for her and all, I guess she can stay aboard."

"Thank you sir, now if you'll just show me where she'll need to bunk, I'll get her settled in before I leave."

Meyers was trying to hide the sweat beading on his neck. This was not easy, but it would work.

"Why don't you just put her in my cabin," said the woman. " It'll be a whole lot easier to look after her that way."

"That'd probably be best," said the Captain. He let the woman lead Meyers away.

Meyers settled Molly on the bunk and turned to leave.

"Where's her luggage, Mr. uh?"

"It's Meyers, ma'am. Samuel Meyers and my girl here is Molly. I left her luggage out on the deck."

The woman turned her attention to the young woman and didn't remember until much later that Samuel Meyers never returned. Afterwards, when she questioned the Purser on the whereabouts of the girl's things, she was told they were probably up front with the freight. She would look for them in the morning. The girl was sleeping right now.

"More's the pity. But I'll try to find out more what this is all about in the morning."

With that the woman went to see what else she could find for interest on the boat.

Chapter 14

Nathan wasn't bothering to stay overnight at the half way point. In fact he would not have stopped at all had his horse not needed to rest. The sun was just beginning to climb over the horizon when he passed the Mercantile on his way to the Meyers cabin. He was feeling pretty good that he had gotten this far so quickly. Maybe Molly wouldn't be too upset yet. Nathan was sure her Ma would want to keep her, but if what he suspected was right, Mrs. Meyers would have no choice but to give her up. And, Meyers himself wouldn't want to take a chance someone might kill him over this.

Chapter 15

When Molly woke up, it was to a the heaving motion of the mighty Mississippi. They'd already left the Ohio while she was sleeping. The sound of the paddles slapping the water in rhythm should have been soothing but Molly's head was throbbing severely. She tried to raise up to see where she was and as she did a strange woman bent over her bed.

"Oh my dear, you awake at last? You're going to feel much better once you have a little breakfast. Now, would you like for me to go and find your things for you so you can clean up a bit?"

"Where am I?" Molly asked groggily.

"Why you're on the City of Louisville. Girl, don't you remember? You're on your way to your Aunt and Uncle's in New Orleans."

Satisfied that she was part of a great plan, with the wave of her kerchief, the woman sat down and folded her hands like church goers.

The boat. She recalled the boat as she waked up a little more. Pa had put her on the boat. Molly jumped to her feet. She had to get off before they left the dock. There was that sick feeling again. Molly was forced to sit down as quickly as she had gotten up.

"There dear, you just lie back down for a minute. I'll go and get you some tea and some toast. You need to try and get your strength up."

The woman patted the pillow beneath Molly's head, but it didn't help. She had to do something!

"I can't," she moaned. "I have to get off this boat."

"Oh you can't get off the boat now, Molly. We're way out in the middle of the river."

Panic flooded Molly's very soul. How could Pa do such a thing? Nathan would never find her here. There had to be a way to get off this boat.

"Nathan. I have to go to Nathan."

"Oh, hon. I'm so sorry about that. Your Pa has told me all about how that young man just left like that. And you in the condition you're in. You should be thankful to have folks who can take you in at a time like this."

Tears flowed down Molly's cheeks. "It wasn't like that. It wasn't like that at all."

"It never is, child. Now you just need to try and calm yourself. You're never going to get to feeling better if you don't. Now you stay right here. I'm going to get you some breakfast."

When the woman had left the tiny cabin, Molly had time to think. Yes, she must calm herself. There had to be a way to get back to Nathan. She would never get back to him if she didn't stay calm and think rationally. When the woman finally returned, she found her young charge sitting up. Molly's color had improved a lot.

"You're feeling better already, aren't you dear? You were so sick last night that the Captain almost wouldn't let you board. If I hadn't intervened, you would have missed the boat."

She was so proud of herself to have 'helped' this young thing.

Molly just sat there. She sensed that she needed this woman for a friend and not an enemy. One wrong word and she wouldn't be in control of this situation.

"Here is some tea and toast. It should help you get your strength up."

"Thank you, ma'am, I really appreciate this."

Molly took the tray. She really was hungry. "

What did you say your name was?"

"Oh, I'm so sorry. I'm Carrie Merriweather. Is this your first trip on a River boat?"

"Yes ma'am."

"Oh, I've traveled lots before. My husband and I had a plantation in Mississippi. After the war was over and then he was took by the fever, I just couldn't bear to be there. My son runs the place now. That's where I'm going, to see my son and his family. I'm really thinking that this time I just might stay."

The woman chattered incessantly, mostly it seemed to entertain herself. Molly was thankful in a way. It gave her time to think.

"Mrs. Merriweather?"

"Yes, dear?""

"Where are we?"

Molly realized she should play this hand very carefully.

"We're somewhere near Paducah, I think. We will probably dock there sometime later today."

Paducah. She'd get off there. Somehow she would find her way back to Nathan.

"My, but it's getting quite warm in here,"

Carrie fanned herself with her handkerchief.

"Do you feel up to going on deck? It'll be much cooler out there."

"Yes ma'am. I would like to cool off."

"We also need to ask the Purser about your things, Molly. You will feel much fresher when you've changed."

"My things?"

More confusion entered Molly's mind as she knew she didn't bring anything with her. Pa had just grabbed her. Nathan would be so worried. She held back more tears as she pictured her beloved ransacking the world for her.

"Yes. Your Pa must have left them up on the deck. I asked about them last night but didn't find them."

Molly knew there were no things. She'd just go on and let Mrs. Merriweather think they were simply misplaced.

Once they were out on deck Molly drank deeply of the fresh air. They found a couple of deck chairs and sat down. There were a few more passengers, but not many. It appeared that on this trip anyway, the boat was mostly transporting goods. Molly knew that in the winter, this was how Nathan's furs made it to market. Other things were transported as well such as molasses, corn, bolts of cloth and other goods for the Mercantile and sometimes furnishings that people shipped out to their homesteads.

"Young man,"

Carrie waved down one of the mates.

"Did you ever find Miss Meyers' satchel?"

"Yes, ma'am, I did." He answered, "I'll fetch it."

Molly gave a start. She knew there was no satchel. What on earth could the young man mean?

Actually, Jeremy Barnes, the young mate, knew Molly had no satchel. He'd watched her father bring her aboard and like Carrie Merriweather had listened in on the conversation between Samuel and his Captain. Unlike Carrie, however, he didn't think things were on the up and up. Just now he'd seen where a previous passenger with lots of luggage had failed to retrieve all of her things. It was possible whatever was in that left behind satchel could be useful to the young woman. He'd already inspected the contents and knew them to be garments for a young lady. When he brought the satchel to Molly, she took it hesitantly.

"It's yours alright ma'am. Your Pa gave it to me personally. Told me to be sure and see that you got it."

He was so convincing that Molly took the case and thanked him.

"If you'd like you can go on back to the cabin and change," Mrs. Merriweather persuaded her. "I'll save your seat for you."

Molly took the bag and went back to the cabin. What she found when she opened the satchel was a surprise. Inside were soft delicate under things and pretty print dresses. There was also sweet smelling soap, a silver handled brush and even a hand mirror. When Molly held up one dress to shake it out, a small handbag fell to the floor. It was empty save for a small amount of money. When she at last joined Mrs. Merriweather on deck she looked like a different girl. She sincerely hoped that the true owner of the satchel didn't show up just now.

"My, you look lovely dear." Mrs. Merriweather nodded approvingly. "Who could know looking at you now that you were so ill last night?"

From a distance Jeremy saw her and smiled. The young lady who had left the satchel behind had so many things she more than likely had never missed this one. Molly certainly looked delightful in the fancy garment. Jeremy was glad that he'd remembered the satchel.

In no time at all, the boat was docking in Paducah. Molly's heart began to race as she tried to think of how she might make her escape. The big boat put the engine in reverse. Slowly the twin paddles changed their direction and the boat shuddered to a standstill. Then the Captain expertly brought her round and maneuvered into the slip. Soon there was activity all around as the crew began their tasks. Molly watched in fascination as the men handled the ropes, tying off the boat and securing it. Soon goods were being transferred from dock to boat. Some passengers disembarked as others came on board. Some of the deck hands were singing their orders. Others called out to one another, throwing small crates and mail sacks across as if they weighed nothing. Flour, furs and kegs of maple syrup were loaded for the trip down south. Cotton would be brought up on the return trip delivered to Memphis for the many textile and garment factories.

"Why don't we go ashore, Molly? There are some nice places to eat within walking distance."

Nothing could have suited Molly more. She would have liked to have brought the satchel but there was no way to get that by Mrs. Merriweather's attention. The little purse in hand, she followed the older woman off the boat and up the dock to the levee. This was Molly's first visit to a real city. There were so many buildings. A throng of people and horses on the streets bustled around seeming to go everywhere and yet nowhere. Folks strolled on sidewalks made of boards so their feet wouldn't get all dirty.

As Molly surveyed her surroundings, she saw the huge building with the banging sounds from deep inside and it was covered with great heaps of dust. There were huge stacks of bricks, the likes of which Molly hadn't seen. There weren't brick buildings back home. Thick black smoke furled from another building down the street. She could see the smoke over the tops of the other buildings. There were men walking from that area and they were talking about the foundry. Molly saw their huge stacks of train rails. This was nothing like the blacksmith's shop back home.

Mrs. Merriweather touched her elbow and Molly realized the older lady was trying to get her attention. They headed over to a multi story building that took Molly's breath as she looked up. Mrs. Merriweather ushered her inside the Hotel Dining Room, where they were greeted by a man in stiff starched white uniform. He showed them to a long table. For twenty-five cents they could have all they wanted from the buffet. Cone shaped screens covered each dish to keep flies off the delicacies. A servant girl lifted the screen and ladled their choices onto their plates. Soon Molly was sitting down to a wonderful meal of fried chicken, biscuits, mashed potatoes, beans and even pie for dessert. She realized she hadn't eaten much in days.

When she thought she'd just burst, Molly asked Carrie where the toilet was.

"I'll go with you dear. It isn't safe for a young woman to be alone in a strange town."

No amount of discouragement from Molly could deter the woman. Then she was insisting that they hurry back lest they miss their boat. Molly felt close to tears. Not one opportunity had she had to escape. There wasn't even a chance to try and get word to Nathan.

Chapter 16

Nathan's exhausted horse was near collapse when he finally arrived at Molly's former home.

"Meyers!"

Nathan ran up to the door and pounded on it, rattling the whole door in it's homemade hinges. A frightened Winifred opened it just a crack. Nathan pushed past her to look inside.

"Where's Molly?' Inside Winnie's children stared at him from the table where they had been eating.

"She's safe with her Pa," Winnie answered.

"She's my wife. I want her back."

The look in his eyes made Molly's mother realize he was looking for answers, not just words. She hesitated between what Meyer's said and what she felt in her heart.

"I can't tell you where she is. I promised her Pa."

The aggressiveness in Nathan's tone softened.

"Please, Mrs. Meyers. I love your daughter. She wants to be with me. It's possible she's going to have a child."

Winnie's face quivered slightly.

"You shouldn't have just come and took her away like that. You didn't have no right, no right at all."

She tried to bury her face in her apron, but Nathan grabbed her hand as his steely eyes encountered hers.

"I'm sorry." He tried to remain calm.

" I'm asking your forgiveness, just please tell me where I can find Molly."

At the table, Earl could stand it no longer. He too had longed many times to be away from his abusive father. In his heart he knew the truth. Molly should be with Nathan.

"Pa took her to New Orleans," He blurted out. "Down to stay with Uncle Edward."

That was all Nathan needed. With one bound, he was out the door as fast as he had come in. After much coaxing, he urged his worn out animal to carry him to Preacher Brown's. Thankfully Preacher Brown and his wife understood more about the Meyer's family than anyone realized. Sympathetic and wishing to help Molly out all they could, the preacher jumped right in. Soon Nathan was swapping his horse for another and was on his way to St. Louis at breakneck speed. His jaw was set as he felt he had a direction to head in. Molly would be knowing he was coming after her, he just knew it. He found himself breathing prayers to the God he'd pretty much left alone. Those breathed out prayers were helping him more than he would realize for many years to come.

He intended to catch the first train out of St. Louis going to New Orleans.

Once in St. Louis, he wasted no time finding a stable for Preacher's horse. A strapping boy with freckles as big as raindrops was given instructions for wiping the horse down and feeding him. After paying the fees for the horse's board, he walked to the Post Office to dispatch a letter, letting the Preacher know where to find his horse and to get word to Frenchie to look after his place. Feeling that he was making progress made him more determined than ever. Next stop was the train station. He purchased a ticket and then sat on a bench to wait, his bed roll positioned behind his neck for comfort. It seemed like forever before his train came screeching into the station, steam flying beneath the wheels of the locomotive. "All aboard!" as the call was made, he picked up his roll and made his way into a car. Once on board he fell into an exhausted sleep.

Chapter 17

Jeremy Barnes watched as Molly and Carrie Merriweather boarded the boat. He noticed immediately that the poor girl was so forlorn. It was getting under his craw good that somebody would treat her like they did. He was determined to speak to Molly alone at the first opportunity. He wanted of course to explain about the satchel; then he wanted to get at the truth of her circumstances. She was so beautiful. Her long brown hair was clasped at the nape of her neck to keep it from her face. Her eyes were large deep pools positioned just right in her solemn face. Jeremy could just imagine how they must light up when she laughed. It was in his thoughts that he'd rescue her from her dilemma. Why he'd even offer to marry her. Raise her child as his. As he imagined the young woman as his bride, his face began to blush. Silently he admonished himself. He was way too young to even consider getting married. Fussing at himself, he turned back to his work.

Back in Mrs. Merriweather's room, Molly put her things all neatly in the satchel. Then she set it as near the door as possible without arousing her roommate's suspicion. Carrie was again talking a mile a minute. There was no escape at the moment so Molly had to be content with the lady's company for the time being. Time dragged ever so slowly. Finally Carrie announced that they should be getting ready for bed. Her assistance to Molly was unwelcome, but Molly curtailed her feelings and let the woman mother her.

"Where are your things, dear? I'm sure you'll be much more comfortable tonight not having to sleep in your dress. Now how did this satchel get way over here? We must have kicked it by accident. This room is ever so small!"

For the first time, Molly really looked at the room that was her present prison. That was just how she felt, caged and unable to break free. She had seen as they came back to the boat, that some folks were going on up towards the top of the huge boat, and others were walking where she and Mrs. Merriweather went. As rooms went it was small and cramped but clean and orderly. If circumstances were different, she would enjoy surveying the whole boat. Not to be, and anyway, women and men most likely stayed in different areas of the ship and she wouldn't want to get caught where she didn't need to be. She guessed she was glad her Ma had taught her a few things about life outside the farm.

Molly cringed as Carrie picked up the satchel and placed it away from the door. Soon they were both in their bunks. The noise of the crew seemed to be quieting down some. The lilting movement of the cabin should have made them heavy-eyed but Carrie Merriweather clearly wasn't going to sleep right away. The woman coughed and fretted while tossing and turning, almost as much as the river churned beneath them.

"I declare, this heat is just awful isn't it. I declare I'm so looking forward to being home again with my son and his family. Those big airy rooms are just superb in the summertime. The windows are big, there are transoms over every door, and when they're open the breezes just come right in across the bed nice and cool like."

After two agonizing hours, Carrie Merriweather finally settled in and slept. Cautiously Molly crept out of bed and retrieved the satchel. As she struggled to put on her dress, she heard the sound of the engines begin. The boat vibrated and the paddles began to turn. The noise caused Carrie to stir in her sleep. Molly held her breath for a moment, and then began to make her way to the door of the cabin. She'd have to hurry or the boat would be too far from shore to get off. Once she was out of the cabin she hurried to the deck. She gasped in disappointment and dismay. She was alarmed that they were further from the shore than she expected. There was no way she could leave the boat right now. Lord, help me she silently pled.

"Excuse me ma'am. Is there something I can help you with?"

Molly whirled around in anguish at the possibility of being found out but she quickly recognized the young man who had given her the satchel.

"I expected to get off the boat, but I guess it's too late."

"Aren't you scheduled to go all the way to New Orleans?"

"I'm not supposed to be here at all! I've got to get off this boat."

Hysteria welled up in her.

"The man who brought you here, was he not your father?"

Molly couldn't help it, she just had to tell somebody her predicament.

"Yes, he is my father, but he took me from my home against my will. I'm married now you see. He didn't exactly approve of Nathan."

Jeremy's disappointment was evident at hearing Molly was wed. His fantasies of being her knight in shining armor were fading rapidly.

"Where is this Nathan, your husband?" He queried.

"Why did he let your father take you?"

"He wasn't home when my father showed up." Molly was hoping this young man would listen and believe her.

"He must be worried sick. When will we stop again" Jeremy noticed Molly's furrowed brow in the moonlight.

"We'll be stopping in Memphis by noon tomorrow."

"Memphis. Then I'll just have to wait until then." Looking at the luggage, she continued,

"Oh, I didn't think to tell you before. This isn't my satchel. I didn't have any things."

"I knew it wasn't yours. Your father didn't leave anything. That satchel was left behind some time ago by another passenger. It wasn't missed and I doubt it will ever be claimed. You're welcome to it. I figured you could use the things."

"Thank you so much. There was some money too."

"Keep it. The previous owner had plenty. I'm sure you'll need it in Memphis."

Reluctantly, Molly turned and made her way back to the cabin where Mrs. Merriweather was making little tweeting sounds as she breathed in and out, her bosom heaving in the dim light. She tiptoed to the corner of the room and set down the satchel. Slowly she undressed, ever mindful of her roommates state of sleep. Then she reticently crawled back into the cot.

In the darkness Molly let her thoughts wander to her own cozy home with Nathan and tears begin to slide silently down her cheeks. She wondered what Nathan had thought when he came back from Frenchie's and found her gone. Surely he was looking for her this very minute. She silently prayed again that he would continue to look and not give up. She began to drift into a fitful sleep. Just as she could see Nathan's face coming close to her in her dreams she was jolted back awake by a bump and a shudder. Straight away, the throbbing of the engine stopped. Mrs. Merriweather was now awake as she sat up quickly and clutched her covers about her.

"Oh, dear me, are we sinking?" Voices and shouting could be heard above them. Through the mixed voices, Molly heard someone holler, "We're on a sand bar." She got out of her bunk and timidly peeked out the door. Through the dim light of the kerosene lanterns Molly could make out deck hands scurrying here and there. Mrs. Merriweather stood close behind Molly, peeping over her shoulder.

"Oh dear, oh dear me!" She mumbled fretfully. "What in the world are we going to do?"

Molly reached back for her hand in a comforting gesture. A memory verse learned from her Sunday School came to mind and she quoted it softly to the older woman. "Deuteronomy 31:8 And the Lord, He it is that doth go before thee: He will be with thee He will not fail thee neither forsake thee, fear not, neither be dismayed." Mrs. Merriweather hugged Molly and instantly calmness came over the two of them and they waited patiently for more news.

Chapter 18

As the train rumbled its way down the tracks in the night, each car swaying on the metal highway of tracks, Nathan slept soundly. The click clack sounds were restful to his mind. His worn out body desperately needed the respite both physically and mentally. He had been thankful for the marvel of modern transportation, especially one that could get him to his goal so quickly with no bother of the weather or having to sleep out on the ground in the damp of the night. By the break of day he'd be halfway to his destination. Preacher Brown had given him detailed instructions for finding Edward Meyers' place once he'd made it to New Orleans. In no time at all Molly would be out of harm's way in his arms once more. His heart soared and he vowed to himself and to God that he'd never let her out of his sight again.

Chapter 19

On the City of St. Louis, no one was sleeping. Captain Jack had felt the jolt of the sudden halt of the big boat and ran on deck, hiking up his suspenders and throwing his coat on as he went. He quickly surveyed the situation and began barking out orders.

"Let's get these anchors down! Pull the ropes tight against the capstans!" With that the vertical-axle rotating machine began applying tremendous force to the ropes, cables, and hawsers, those huge behemoth ropes used for mooring.

Jeremy hurried to do as he was told along with the other deck hands. The scene unfolded like watching ants working a mound, each one doing their part, separately and yet together. Experience had taught him, as well as the more seasoned hands, to follow Captain Jack's explicit directions. To deviate even slightly from such orders would never produce the desired results and anyway Jeremy knew he could trust his captain's knowledge. At the same time four heavy anchors were dropped, aft and fore, bow and stern. Each one made a deep thudding sound as they hit the water and spray flew high and wide. Strong young muscles pulled the ropes taut, wrapping them around the capstans. Molly and Mrs. Merriweather silently made their way to the Texas deck careful not to get in the way of anyone's efforts. They found chairs and sat close together, hands intertwined. Little did they know it might not be safe on deck, and everyone else was so busy they were totally unnoticed in the commotion. They were joined, one by one by the other travelers. Some sat on packing crates and all stared into the moonlit darkness trying to figure out what was happening. Soft murmurs of conversation made it difficult for Molly to clearly understand the shouted directions between the Captain and his crew. She finally made out that they were not sinking, but had merely "come aground". Hearing also about a sandbar, she figured out that come aground meant they were stuck. She patted Mrs. Merriweather's clasped hands and reassured her once more. As the cluster of huddled passengers realized that they were not in imminent danger, the conversation became less intense. Laughter could be heard here and there and the male passengers were voicing their opinions as to the best way to resolve the situation.

With the anchor ropes tight and the boat at a total standstill, the captain gave the order to fire up the engines again. Slowly the rhythmic churning of the paddlewheel could be heard as it began the reverse action. Sand began to shift under the magnificent power and slowly dissipate into the muddy current. The slightest movement of the big boat and the deck hands were quickly tightening the ropes. Each time the boat lurched, the passengers would huddle together express their fear, but in general both passenger and crew trusted the able captain's expertise and wisdom.

The moon was waning when at last they were free of the treacherous sand bar. Slowly, one after another, the passengers all made their way back to their cabins, thankful that the crisis was over. As Molly passed by the young deck hand that'd been so helpful, she paused.

"I haven't asked your name."

"It's Jeremy Barnes. I know yours is Molly. I heard Mrs. Merriweather talking to you."

"You've been so kind, Jeremy." She laid her hand on his forearm and he could see she was being sincere.

"I guess since I must wait until we get to Memphis, I should go back and try to rest. Do you think you might be able to help me then? I just know I'll never be able to get away from Mrs. Merriweather. She evidently promised my father that she'd look after me."

"Don't worry. I'll see that you get off the boat and on your way."

With that Jeremy tipped his hat and walked down the deck.

Molly went back to her room. Truthfully she was grateful for the opportunity to rest. She was feeling a little sick from the returned motion of the vessel. Maybe it was best that she hadn't been able to get off the boat in Paducah. It was late and dark and she really had no place to go and no real plan.

"That's it," she thought to herself as she drifted off to sleep, "I need a plan."

Morning came and Molly found herself feeling much better. The day was gorgeous as the sun gleamed across the water reflecting the azure skies above. The ship's paddles sent up a fine mist which kept the heat down. One would think on water it would always be cool, but unless there was a good breeze it got sultry. As she and Mrs. Merriweather made their way to breakfast, Molly looked around her at the beautiful paddle steamer that she was on. Molly could tell that all sorts of people rode these navigation machines. She thought of the cabin she and Mrs. Merriweather had been sharing and cramped was the word that came to mind, even though the cabins did have a nice bed and a door to keep out the riff raff who always traveled the rivers. People with less money or traveling only short distances would simply buy a ticket to stand on the deck. Those traveling overnight would "bunk in" on the cargo deck in any handy spot. Near the shore, turtles plopped from the logs where they sat as the boat slipped casually by. Birds were plentiful and their songs resounded in harmony. If you watched closely enough you could see a fish jump up occasionally. The boat had left the confluence of the Ohio River and was navigating the Mighty Mississippi River. The largest river in North America, the Mississippi River rises in Minnesota and flows almost due south across the continental interior to the Gulf of Mexico. But here, below the Ohio, is where the river was in its most grandeur. Molly had never traveled this far in her life, but stories of this river came to mind as her eyes spanned the enormous width of this churning waterway. Often a mile and a half from bank to bank, the lower Mississippi was a brown, lazy river. Memphis couldn't be far now. Not even Mrs. Merriweather's constant repartee could spoil Molly's mood.

"My, isn't it nice up here on the deck, dear. Why don't we just have our breakfast up here, like a little picnic? That way we can avoid that awful heat downstairs."

Molly couldn't agree more. She had stashed her satchel on the deck under some of the freight while Carrie had still been sleeping and she didn't intend to go back down at all.

The two made themselves comfortable on a molasses keg and ate biscuits with slices of salt cured ham that they'd taken from the dining hall. Every now and then they'd see a shanty boat tied off at the bank and wave at the occupants if they were outside. Funny how some folks could live right on the water. Here and there a house could be spotted high on a bluff above the river. Soon there were more and more houses. One particular house was a lovely mansion set back in the distance. Stately oak trees guarded it like sentinels. The stately country villa stood as a living reflection of its obviously wealthy builder. Recalling the home she was raised in had made Nathan's place seem so opulent and yet compared to that home atop the limestone bluff, Molly wondered who could live in such a fine place.

As the sun grew hotter and higher in the sky, the boat steamed around one more bend and the beautiful city of Memphis came into view. Molly could barely contain her excitement.

Mrs. Merriweather was delighted as well. "We must go ashore in Memphis. You've never seen the big city before have you Molly?"

"No ma'am, I haven't."

"Well there are certainly lots of things to see. So many shops, I'm sure we'll have time to browse a little."

Boat traffic was becoming heavier. Whistles blew and bells clanged along with voices shouting as they approached the port of the city. Docking here was taking longer than when they were in the small town of Paducah. Molly couldn't help but be impressed with all the tall buildings of the city. The air was filled with the soot and smell of the factories and the boats and when combined with the fishy, muddy smell of the river it was thoroughly unpleasant. Molly put her hand to her mouth and wrinkled her face to quell the nausea that threatened.

When the boat had finally docked, Molly tired to remain calm while she waited for the opportunity to escape the ever watchful eye of Mrs. Merriweather. That time presented itself soon enough when Carrie excused herself for a moment to return to the cabin for her purse.

"Shall I bring yours up, Molly?" She asked.

"Sure" as she hunted for her purse. "Thanks."

As soon as her companion was out of sight, Molly ran to her satchel. She grabbed it up and hurried to find Jeremy. As he had promised, he was waiting for her.

"Let's go," He urged, putting his hand under her elbow. "I'm due for relief. I'll go with you and show you around."

He hurried her up the dock toward the levee. Almost immediately they were swallowed up in the crowd of people milling around. Jeremy guided her to a place where buggies could be rented.

"Come on" he urged, "I'll take you to the train station."

Such elegant buggies there were. Fringes on some, velvet covered seats on others. Some were big enough to hold several people. There were covered ones and open air models. Molly was used to farm wagons. These weren't practical for anything except for fancy folks to ride around. She ran from one to another. Too many! It was hard for Molly to choose.

"You'd better decide which one," Jeremy laughed. "Or else someone else will rent them all and we'll have to walk."

At the thought of being found, Molly chose quickly and they were riding down the street. Molly was wearing one of the beautiful dresses from the satchel. The silk taffeta had crocheted buttons down the front. Someone had done meticulous work, probably not the intended wearer. Molly hadn't seen such fine hand stitching. Her own handiwork couldn't be compared to this, but she was still pleased that she could turn muslin into something that Nathan had admired. Oh Nathan.

Brushing thoughts of Nathan from her mind so as not to get sick at heart, she pretended that she was from the big house they'd seen from the river. People who lived in a house like that probably rode in grand surreys with fringe on top and fine dresses every day.

Finally at the train station, there was more noise and clanging and steam noises. More people than she could imagine, men in suits, sporting canes and women in even finer attire. Jeremy guided her up to the ticket window. When Molly went to pay for her ticket, she couldn't find the little purse with the money. Frantically she searched through the satchel again and again.

"I must have left it on the boat." She was pale and getting nauseated again.

"I'd buy your ticket, Molly but I spent what I had on the carriage. We'll just have to go back and find it."

"No," Molly said firmly. "I will not go back to that boat. I'm off and I'm going to stay off."

Jeremy could tell she was resolute and he couldn't blame her, not one bit.

"I know someone who might help. I have a friend here in town. Her name is Ruby Mitchell. Come on let's find Ruby."

With that Jeremy took her arm and herded her down the street. Molly was surprised at Ruby's place. The outside was quite ornate. Gingerbread trim decorated the cornices and heavy velvet drapes covered the tall windows which gave no opportunity to sneak a peek inside. It appeared to be a hotel for girls but nobody seemed to be up though it was well past noon. Jeremy knocked at the door repeatedly until finally a sleepy eyed young woman opened it up just a crack.

"Whadda you want? Can't you see we're not open yet?" She rubbed her eyes indifferently.

Jeremy had the grace to blush at the question when Molly looked at him inquisitively. She turned back to the girl at the door only to wonder at the clothes she was wearing. Molly realized the sleepy young woman was in a nightgown and a thin one at that! Hardly the attire to wear when you answered the door. Slowly a red stain of embarrassment spread up her neck and face as she suddenly realized that Jeremy had brought her to a house of ill repute.

"Your friend lives *here*?" She stammered.

"Maybe this wasn't such a good idea." Jeremy whispered under his breath. "I'm gonna run back to the boat and find your purse. You stay here with Ruby and her girls until I get back."

He pushed her in the door. The young woman inside stared rudely at Molly, and then glanced at the grandfather clock and heaved a big sigh. As soon as Jeremy was out of sight she pushed Molly back out the door. She had already sized the stranger up and down, and thought Molly was competition she had no intention of allowing around here. After all she had her clients to look after.

"Ruby ain't here right now."

Her eyes meandered slowly to the wicker settee on the veranda and came back to rest with apparent repulsion, on Molly.

"You wait on your friend outside." With that the underdressed "girl" disappeared back into the darkness and closed the door with a quick resounding thump. Alone but in the shade, Molly looked hopefully down the street to see if Jeremy was in calling distance, but the buggy and Jeremy were already gone. As she stood there waiting, a drunken disheveled man came around the corner and started up the walk.

'Hey there missy, Hows 'bout having luncsh with me?" He staggered in her direction and gave a toothy grin. His voice told his condition. Panicky, Molly turned her back to the man and trying to avoid him she went off the portico on the side. He called out again, and she picked up her pace as her heart was beginning to pound so it felt like it was going to beat clean out of her dress. She glanced back at him. He seemed to be gaining on her. She began to run. She turned a corner and ran even harder.

Chapter 20

After a few minutes Molly just had to stop to catch her breath. She dreaded to look again. The man was no longer behind her. She found herself on a busier street now. There were people all around. Her fright began to subside and she could breathe easier. She started walking at a more normal pace and tried to get her bearings. She had no idea where she was.

Molly walked and walked. Sweat began to pour down her face. She hadn't had lunch yet and wasn't sure about the time. The day was proving to be quite warm and the sky had taken on a copper hue. That sick stomach feeling was coming back. Where was Jeremy? Which way was the river? Molly scanned the scenery for a place to sit down. Her legs were feeling shaky. Ahead there seemed to be a little park. As she got closer, she saw huge oak trees with boughs hung low like friendly arms beckoning children to come aboard. There were also fragrant flowers and here and there were little stone benches. It looked so peaceful. Molly hurried over and sat down on one of the benches and found it to be cool and restful. She would have passed out if she'd gone one step further. She leaned over slightly to try and let the blood go to her head a little.

"You sick, chile?"

Startled, Molly looked up. A lovely black woman sat down beside her and offered a handkerchief.

"You look like you 'bout to be passin' out. You alrat? Lemme get you some water."

"Thank you," Molly murmured.

The woman brought Molly a drink. She poured a little water on the handkerchief and washed Molly's face with it.

"You need to be out of this heat," waving her hand towards a row of storefronts, she beckoned "Come on over here. My missus' dress shop's right over here. You can cool down a spell."

Molly followed her gratefully. Inside the dress shop it proved to be much cooler. The drapes were heavy but they were opened slightly. There was a beautiful silver service on a table. Near the table were lovely velvet chairs, three of them. There were also four floor length mirrors on stands. Just to the corner of this room there was also a little platform with mirrors on three sides of the back. A beautiful dress lay draped across a bench on the stand. It looked as though women might walk around and look at the back of their dresses. On a shelf just next to the stand were several beautiful hats, some with feathers, some with lace. Over by the window was a desk with white slips of paper stuck on what looked like a nail.

The woman noticed that Molly was taking it all in. "that's Miss Priscilla's idee. She says the womenfolk done like lookin' at dereselves so much, she would fix it so'ns they cood look more! I declare it 'bout makes me bust ev'time sumbuddy comes in heah." Thinking she might have overspoke herself, the black woman took Molly to the back sewing room and sat her down.

"Now, what yo' name, gil?"

"Molly Smith," she really didn't want to tell her, but the woman's sing song voice just lilted with friendliness.

"Well, I'm Rosella. I sews for Miss Priscilla Canton. This here's her dress shop. Can I go and git somebody fo you?"

Molly had no idea where to send her. If she tried to send Rosella to the boat looking for Jeremy, then she would surely be confronted by Mrs. Merriweather who would follow her and insist that Molly get back on board.

"No, I'm here alone."

"Young thing lack you, 'lone in this heah city?" Rosella was flabbergasted. 'That won't do none t'all. I'm goin' ta fetch Miss Priscilla.'

Rosella returned quickly and the woman she brought to Molly was quite elegant. One look at Molly's peaked face brought out her most gracious concern

"Rosella, get this poor child something to eat. She looks half starved."

"Yes'm. I'm just thinking that myself."

Rosella left the room in a flurry to find lunch and Priscilla sat down beside Molly. By the clothes that Molly was wearing, it was assumed that she was the daughter of a wealthier resident of Memphis.

"Who are your folks, Molly?"

"I'm not from around here, ma'am. I came down on a river boat. My Pa was trying to send me to my uncle's place in New Orleans, but I have a husband back home and I want to go back. He doesn't know where I am."

Priscilla didn't for one minute believe that. She figured Molly for a run-away. Come to think of it, the dress she was wearing had a familiar look to it. Priscilla searched her thoughts trying to recollect. Of course, this was a dress she had made for Sally Thornberry. How did this young woman come by it?

"Where is home?", she queried the young disheveled girl.

"Springhill."

"I don't believe I know where that is? You came on a river boat? Which one?"

Molly hesitated. She did not want this woman to take her back to the boat. "I don't remember," she lied.

Priscilla saw through it. She decided that perhaps she should just keep Molly put until she could find out who she really was. Rosella came swishing back into the room carrying an elegant silver tray with food, cutlery and a small vase holding a delicate rosebud. Catching the sweet smelling aroma the rosebud gave off, Molly gratefully accepted the potato soup and the hot buttered corn bread.

She was so hungry she barely noticed as Priscilla motioned Rosella into the other room.

"Rosie, will you go down to the Constable's office for me? I want to find out who Molly really is. I'm sure her folks must be frantic. I don't for one minute believe that a young girl like that came to Memphis on a river boat by herself. Or if she really was going to New Orleans, someone must have been accompanying her. She must be running away. Did you notice that dress she was wearing? Didn't you make that up when you were helping me with Sally Thornberry's summer things?"

"Yes'm, Miss Priscilla. It do look like Miss Sally's dress. I'll go and see what I kin find out."

"Thank you, Rosie."

Priscilla went back into the room where Molly was eating.

"There now, are you feeling better?"

"Yes ma'am," Molly answered. She finished her meal and stood up. "I'll be glad to take the tray back to the kitchen if you'll tell me where it is."

"That's all right," Priscilla responded. "We'll just put it here on the sideboard and Rosella can get to it when she gets back."

The kitchen was too easy an access to the street and Priscilla had a feeling that Molly would bolt like a deer at the first opportunity.

"Why don't you lie down for a spell? I think this heat has just been too much for you." She led Molly into an adjacent room where there was a small cot. As much as Molly wanted to leave, fatigue caught up with her. Maybe just five minutes she told herself. Then she'd go and find Jeremy.

When Jeremy Barnes returned to Ruby's place, Molly was nowhere to be found. The girl they'd talked with earlier refused to give him any information at all. She insisted that Molly had decided not to stay and had left of her own accord.

"She said she remembered a friend. Told me to tell you not to worry." She was tired of being questioned about that girl.

Jeremy was perplexed, but he didn't know what else to think. Surely she wouldn't have wandered off down the street in a strange city, unless perhaps she did remember a friend. He walked around a while, checked out the park and finding nothing went on back. When Carrie Merriweather questioned him about Molly, he told her that Molly evidently knew someone in Memphis and had decided to stay and visit with them. He had a nagging feeling it wasn't the truth, but he'd have to be back on duty soon and for now he'd just have to let it be.

Chapter 21

Once in New Orleans, Nathan was glad to be off the train. He hadn't realized that even traveling in comfort could become tiresome after a while. Being confined to the seat for so many hours had made him stiff. Even though he could have used a hot bath and some food, he wasted no time finding the place where Edward Myers lived. Edward seemed to be more cordial than his brother.

"Yes," he admitted, " I did receive a letter from my brother saying his eldest girl was coming. Don't expect the boat 'til this evening sometime. Who might you be?" He questioned.

"I'm Nathan Smith. I'm Molly's husband and I've come after her."

"I didn't know she was married. Letter didn't say anything about a husband."

Nathan hesitated as he thought how best to answer this man.

"Well, I guess Molly's Pa thought she was a bit young to marry, so he was hoping a separation might make a difference. Truth is, we are already married. I brought our marriage papers with me." He pulled the paper from his pocket and showed it to the man.

Rather than admit he couldn't read, Edward Myers took the paper and peered at it thoughtfully. He hadn't wanted the responsibility of another mouth to feed anyway and this young man sure seemed like a nice sort of fellow. It'd be nice if his daughters would find the likes of him and get married. He handed the paper back to Nathan, scratching his chin thoughtfully.

"Seeing as how you got the paper showing you to be Molly's husband, I don't see as how I should stand in your way of taking her home. You can meet the boat if you want."

Nathan was pleased that the man was so agreeable. He wouldn't have any problems here. He thanked him and left. He'd find a place to clean up and eat, so he'd be refreshed when Molly's boat arrived.

Chapter 22

At Priscilla's dress shop, Rosie arrived with the constable. Quietly Priscilla talked to the man then she led him to the room where Molly slept unknowingly spied on.

Ben Harrison stared thoughtfully at the young girl's face, and then he motioned Priscilla back into the other room.

"I don't recognize her as being from around here. Nobody I know has reported a missing girl. Maybe she was telling you the truth. I'll keep an ear open for any news, but I wouldn't worry too much."

"But, that dress she's wearing. I'm sure it's one that I made for Sally Thornberry. I can't help but wonder how she came to be wearing it."

In the other room, Molly stirred as she heard voices. Miss Canton was talking with someone.

"Well, if you say it's Sally Thornberry's dress, you're probably right. You've always had a keen eye for the clothes a person wears." The man gave a slight chuckle. "I know you're constantly on me about what I'm wearing."

"Or not wearing," The woman returned a soft quiet chuckle.

Molly sat up in the bed with a start. She heard Miss Canton say she recognized the dress as belonging to a client of the dress shop. "They'll think I stole it." Molly got up quickly and put on her shoes as quietly as she could. Then she grabbed the bag and went to the window. Although it was a tight squeeze, she managed to get through and cautiously made her way to the street. Dusk was falling. Molly hadn't realized she'd slept for so long.

Back in the dress shop, the conversation continued.

"If Sally gave her the dress, then chances are she will know the young woman. Will you check with the Thornberry's for me? This girl seems to be too young to be out on the street like that."

"Yeah, no problem. I'll check with them first chance I get. For now, why don't you just let her stay here? If someone comes looking for her, then she'll be easy to find. Maybe she'd be willing to stay and help out a little."

"I was thinking that myself. I tell you, the way business is growing I'll have to take on another full time seamstress before long anyway. If she's got no place else to go, maybe she'd be willing to help out a while."

The two continued with their conversation, totally unaware that their subject of the conversation had already disappeared into the night.

Chapter 23

Nathan anxiously watched as the City of Louisville slowly came down the river towards the dock where he stood. She was 300 feet long and had a capacity of 160 passengers. A White Collar Line steamer, she was marked by a pair of white bands around the top of her smokestacks. A white fence edged the perimeter of the lower deck and passengers had gathered there to watch the boat land. On the shore, busy people stopped to observe the beautiful packet as she slowly, engines reversed to ease approach, made her way to the designated dock. At long last the crew was making the boat fast and he could go up to it. A few passengers on board were making their way to the exit and he searched each face. People were taking their time, talking with one another or stopping mid exit to wave and yell at someone on shore. Molly wasn't among them. Thinking she was still on the boat, he started to board. A young deck hand approached him.

"Can I help you sir?"

"Are there any more passengers on board?"

"No, sir, everybody's gotten off already. Were you expecting someone?"

"Yeah, I thought my wife was on board."

"Your wife, sir?" suddenly Jeremy's suspicion was aroused. "What was her name?"

"Molly. Her name is Molly Smith."

So this was Molly's husband. A pang of jealousy surged through Jeremy and a flush crept up his face.

Nathan noticed the change in countenance.

"Was Molly Smith on this boat?"

"Yes sir, Molly was on this boat."

"What do you mean was? Where is she now?"

Seeing the tension rising in Nathan, Jeremy thought the man might strike him. He hesitated, wondering if this man would be abusive to sweet Molly. Then he remembered her face when she talked of him. Her strongest desire had been to return to him.

"She got off in Memphis. She wanted to get back home to you, sir. I helped her as much as I could."

"She's alright then? You saw to her?"

"As best I could sir. She was alright the last time I saw her."

"Where in Memphis is she?"

"I don't know for sure. She said she had a friend there."

Jeremy still wasn't sure that was true, but he wasn't about to admit to Nathan Smith that Molly had disappeared in that big city all alone. He felt guilty that he hadn't done more. Couldn't do more.

"I wasn't aware that she knew anyone in Memphis." Nathan was trying to conjure up some memory that would lead him to anyone Molly had ever talked about. "Did she mention any names? Did you take her there?"

Sweat beaded up on Jeremy's upper lip as he lied to Nathan. He just wasn't sure what the reaction would be when Nathan realized that Molly could be lost and alone.

"I believe she said her friend's name was Mary or Myrna or something like that. I put her in a carriage and she told the driver the address. I don't quite remember what she said. It was somewhere in the eastern part of town."

At least Jeremy could steer him in the direction where he had left Molly.

At this, Nathan frowned. He had been in Memphis before. The eastern part of the city was the less savory district. Who on earth could Molly know there? Well, it gave him a starting point. He stuck out his hand to shake with the young deck hand.

"Thanks for your help. I'd best get the next train to Memphis." He turned and strode away.

Jeremy breathed a sigh of relief. The man was much nicer than he had anticipated and had a fearsome concern towards his wife. He'd find Molly. She'd be alright soon and Jeremy wouldn't have the burden of concern for her welfare. Grabbing a chain, he went back about his business.

Chapter 24

Molly's nap and the meal at Miss Priscilla's had refreshed her but once again she was faced with the prospect of no place to go and no money. The streets were getting darker as she rushed further and further away from the place where Jeremy Barnes had taken her. Ahead of her a sign proclaimed, "Rooms for Rent" with the additional by the week or by the month. Underneath, a smaller sign proclaimed, "Help Wanted". She stopped and read the sign again thoughtfully. Suddenly she could just see Sister Prudence Brown talking to them in Sunday school. "The Lord always looks after His children. If you're afraid or alone, all you have to do is ask and you'll receive." At that moment she just knew that the Lord was looking after her even though she had forgotten to pray. Hadn't he given her Nathan? Hadn't he provided, first Mrs. Merriweather, albeit she had been more than helpful most of the time, and then Jeremy Barnes to help her? Right then and there Molly decided that she was not going to be afraid anymore. An incredible rush of the most blessed peace she'd ever felt came over her as she knew in her heart that God loved her and Nathan loved her and things were going to be alright. Sister Prudence's seed of faith was taking hold and beginning to grow. With a refreshing resolve, Molly turned and walked up to the door of the boarding house. Her knock brought the proprietor to the door.

"I'd like to ask about the job."" Molly turned and pointed to the sign.

The door opened wide and Molly was invited in. The proprietor, Dorothy Hinson, gave her a quick appraisal as she came in. The hands were small but calloused. Used to working, no doubt.

"You're out kinda late, ain't you?" She queried.

"Yes ma'am," Molly admitted. "I've come in from out of town. I could sure use the job."

"When would you be able to start?"

"As soon as I'm needed, if you don't mind."

"Where you staying?"

Molly hesitated. She wanted to make the right impression, but she needed to stay here if at all possible.

The woman sensed her hesitation. Street kid, she thought. Nice dress for a street kid. Probably wouldn't stay long, but she looked like a decent sort.

"You say you're from out of town?"

"Yes ma'am."

"You ain't got a place to stay have you?"

Molly's face blushed crimson and she looked down at her feet. "No ma'am, I don't. I was hoping you'd let me work for board."

The woman pretended to look tough. She crossed her arms over an ample bosom. Keeping help wasn't easy. They came and they went. Thinking of the rather large pile of dirty dishes in the kitchen, Dorothy knew she'd give this girl a chance.

"I tell you what. If you're willing to start tonight, I'll give you a bed for the night. We'll decide in the morning how it'll go."

Molly lifted her face in gladness. "Oh thank you. I'll be glad to start tonight."

She turned to the door and fetched her little satchel.

Dorothy wasted no time leading her to the kitchen. "For starters, what's your name girl?"

"Molly, Molly Smith."

"Well, Molly, I'm Miss Dorothy. If you'll clean up the kitchen, then you can sleep in this room here." She pointed to a door to the right of the kitchen. "I'll wake you in the morning to help with breakfast." With that Dorothy left her standing in the middle of the kitchen and left the room.

She was tired and had been dreading the kitchen chores. She went straight to her room and got ready for bed.

Molly stood in the silent kitchen and surveyed the task before her. Well, God may have provided her with a place to stay, but it was time to earn her keep. She set the satchel by the door and rolled up her sleeves. The stove had a water tank that was filled with hot water and the soap was on the counter. The mound of dishes looked like a mountain to her. Filling a dish pan with soap and hot water, Molly began to wash each one. The despair had lifted from her heart and she actually began to hum as she worked. As she finished cleaning up she looked around for a bite to eat. She helped herself to some leftover bread and a slice of ham for a late supper. She had no idea what the hour was. The whole house was quiet except for the ticking of a clock in another room, as everyone slept and Molly, with a renewed faith in God, at last made her way to the tiny room allotted to her. Crawling into the dirty little cot, she closed her eyes and fell into a restful sleep.

Morning came quickly and Miss Dorothy appeared in the kitchen. She stared in amazement at the gleaming spotless kitchen. It hadn't been that clean in months. That girl would be worth keeping. She went and knocked on Molly's door.

"Wake up Molly, time to get breakfast.'

Molly was getting used to waking up in different places. It only took a few seconds to remember the boarding house and Miss Dorothy. This was like when she was still at home with her Ma, getting up to help with breakfast. By the time she had dressed, Miss Dorothy had already started coffee and was patting out biscuits on a well worn board. A rasher of bacon and a slab of ham sat on the table ready to be sliced. A canister of grits and a bowl of eggs were also waiting for attention. Molly needed no direction. She just pitched in and did what required doing. Dorothy was immensely pleased with her new employee. She kept Molly hopping all morning with cooking and cleaning. It wasn't until after the noon meal was finished and cleaned up that they even had time to talk other than the snatched conversation of the busy morning. When they did stop, Dorothy invited her to sit down in the parlor.

"Now, I told you last night that this would be a trial. I just want you to know that the work you did this morning was just fine and you're hired on if you're willing to stay.'

Molly decided to let her think she was interested in staying on. If Miss Dorothy knew she was just trying to get enough money to go home, she almost certainly wouldn't have offered the job.

"Yes ma'am, I'd like to stay. How much does the job pay?"

"Well, your room and board is part of your pay understand. I pay fifty cents a week plus room and board."

Molly knew it would have to do. It would take a while to accumulate train fare at that rate but at least it was something. She shuddered as she remembered the scantily dressed girl at the other place and the drunken man showing up. Thinking again of Nathan, she knew she should try and get word to him and then just stay put.

"That'll be fine with me. Miss Dorothy, do you have some paper and pen so that I can write to my folks and let them know I found a job and I'm okay?"

"Sure, hon. Just look through that desk there and get what you need. When you're through just lay it on the corner there and I'll post it for you. I'll be out back doing some laundry. You can just go ahead and start supper when you're through here."

Molly found some paper and sat at the desk and began to write.

"Dear Nathan,

> I guess by now you have learned that Pa paid us a visit while you were at Frenchie's. I'm so sorry to have worried you, but Pa didn't give me a chance to explain. I'm not holding it against him. I used to hate the sight of him, but I think now that he's to be pitied and just needs God in his heart. I've been thinking about God a lot these past few days. He's watching over me and I'm alright, but I'm missing you terribly. I'm at a boarding house somewhere in Memphis. I'll tell you more about it when I can. I'll

just stay here and work until you can come for me. I'll be praying until I see you again.

Your loving wife, Molly
P.S. We will be having a child sometime next winter."

Molly reread her letter to be sure it was satisfactory and then she addressed it to Nathan in care of Jake's Mercantile in Springhill. Then she laid it on the corner of the desk and went back to her chores dreaming of Nathan as always. She removed the bedding from the little cot and carried it to the back yard where Miss Dorothy was stirring the wash, with a big wooden paddle, as it boiled in the big iron wash pot. Molly took her bedding to the wash tub with the soapy water and began to scrub it on the scrub board. By the time Miss Dorothy had scooped out her pot of laundry, Molly was ready to put the next load into the boiling water. Miss Dorothy silently observed how hard the young woman worked and the fact that she needed no direction to know what was needed. When the laundry was finished and hanging smartly from the clothes lines, the two women headed to the kitchen to start the evening meal. Molly was tired beyond belief, but she tried not to show it. The older woman noticed.

"While this food is cooking, you can rest a bit." She told Molly. "I'll call you when it's time to start dishin' the meal up."

Molly was so grateful that she didn't protest. She went to her little room and lay down on the cot. She felt like she'd barely closed her eyes before Miss Dorothy was calling to her.

Chapter 25

At the train station in New Orleans, Nathan was not pleased to learn that he'd missed the last train out. Too anxious to wait for the morning train and too restless, he headed for the livery stable. If he could get a good horse, he could ride all night. If Molly was with a friend, then surely she'd be safe. The train would be faster, but he had to feel that he was doing something to find his precious little bride. He proceeded to spend a good portion of the money he had left on a horse with a saddle and bags. Heading into the darkness he followed the road that would surely lead him to his Molly. Night was never quiet in the summer. Little creatures turned up the evening volume, one after another as you could just see some scurrying away through the grass as the horse's hooves disturbed them. An owl could be heard calling out to a mate before he swooped to catch a noisy little rodent. Water could be heard running somewhere across smooth stones in a nearby brook. In the early hours of the morning, Nathan stopped near a murky creek to rest the horse and let him drink. He found a mossy spot and settled down against a rock to rest a bit himself. His eyes slowly closed and sleep descended heavily upon him. In his dreams, he could hear Molly's soft voice telling him that everything was going to be okay.

In the pre-dawn darkness, when the moon had gone over one horizon and the sun had not yet peeped over the other, two men came riding down the road, near where Nathan slept. Nathan's horse whinnied at the sound of someone coming, but the dog-tired Nathan slept on, unaware that danger approached. Hearing the horse, the two became cautious and crept in toward where Nathan lay propped against a rock sleeping the sound sleep of an exhausted and troubled mind. The two men quietly led Nathan's horse away carefully avoiding leaves and sticks, watching Nathan closely as they did. After they were sure he still slept they crept back on foot and attempted to lift the tired man's wallet. Startled, Nathan jumped to his feet only to receive a blow square in the middle of his face. There was a crunching feeling in the vicinity of his nose and a blinding flash as he blacked out and went to the ground. The two men quickly searched him, took his money and a pistol that he carried and hurriedly made tracks away.

Nathan was looking across a cool green pasture at the milk cow munching fresh grass. He saw his Molly laughing and dancing and what appeared to be a small child by her side. The methodical sound of the cow's bell got louder and louder and Nathan came to, realizing that it was only a dream. He tried to sit up but the throbbing in his head stopped him momentarily. He put his hand to his face to rub his eyes and felt the crusted blood and dirt and the swollen and painful nose. Then he gingerly ran his hand over the back of his head and felt the large knot where his head had hit the rock he had been resting on.

"Hey, mister, are you hurt?"

He started as he realized he was not alone. Through swollen squinty eyes he glared up at the two young boys who stood directly over him. Near them, a brindle cow shook her head impatiently and pulled at her rope causing the bell to clang even louder. It was time for her morning milking.

The taller of the two boys spoke again,

"Hey *mister*, are you alright?"

They stepped back a little as Nathan slowly pulled himself to his feet. "I'm okay, I guess. Can't remember what happened."

"Looks like you been in a scrap with a bear and he done won," the other boy said.

"Yeah, somebody beat you up real good." He spat on the ground as though he was impressed.

"Fight?" Nathan remembered no fight, trying to clear his mind and remember what he was here for.

"Can you walk, Mister?" The older boy reached out to him. "My Ma can fix you up. She's good at doctoring folks. Feed you breakfast too if you want."

"Sure," Nathan mumbled. He turned to go with the boys, his confusion mounting. They turned away from the creek down a well worn path leading the cow and Nathan through the woods.

"We just live about a mile down here. Mister you shore are lucky we had to come find Bessie this morning. She gen'ly comes to the house by herself. But for some reason this morning we had to hunt her up and there you was just laying there moaning and all beat up."

The boy was talking a mile a minute and Nathan scarcely paid a mind to what he said, only to the throbbing in his skull. Suddenly they stopped in the trail and the boys were looking at him expectantly. He realized they were expecting an answer, but he wasn't sure what the question was.

"I said, what's your name, Mister?" the smaller of the two boys put his hand on his hip. Nathan looked at him. He was red haired and blotchy freckles were peppered along his cheekbones. His clothes were worn but clean, bib overalls without a shirt and his feet were bare. Cute little fellow, must have been nine or ten. The other boy, as dark as his brother was fair, dressed much the same joined in.

"Don't you even know your own name?" He seemed to find the idea incredulous. "Did you hit your head so hard you can't even remember your own name? I heard of that happening but I ain't ever seen it for real! I hope you ain't no outlaw or nothing."

Outlaw reflected Nathan. He reached into his pocket. No wallet.

"No," He told the boys. "I'm not an outlaw, but I think whoever beat me up was. I think they took my money and my horse."

"Well, if you can remember that, then how come you can't remember your name?'" The little one said disgustedly. They continued walking down the trail kicking dirt clods towards each other and laughing as first one jumped out of the way and then the other.

"It's Nathan," He finally responded bewilderedly. "My name's Nathan. Now who might you fellows be?"

"My name's Sam, but most folks call me Red. Wish they didn't though. Don't like being called Red."

"Fine," Nathan responded. "I'll call you Sam then. How about you?" He asked the other boy. "What do they call you?"

"Charlie. They call me Charlie and I like it just fine."

The chattering continued as they walked along the trail. The sounds and smells of the summer morning were all around them. The cow bell tinkled again, birds chirped above them and insects buzzed at their faces. Honeysuckle permeated the air like sweet perfume and ripe plums squished under their feet occasionally where they had dropped on the trail.

As they neared where the boys lived, the cow mooed anxiously. Sam let go of the rope and she trotted on ahead to the barn. Then he ran toward the house.

"Ma!" He called loudly. "Ma!"

A woman leaned out the back door.

"Red, you get washed up before you come in here. Breakfast is ready." Then she noticed the stranger with the boys. One look at the bruised and swollen face and she was out the door like a mother hen. "Land sakes, what on earth. Where'd you boys pick this fellow up at?"

"Found him on the creek bank, Ma," Charlie answered happily, as though he'd found a treasure. After all it wasn't often a rank stranger showed up around here. "Somebody beat him up real good and robbed him. Name's Nathan."

"Charlie, go get your Pa. That cow can wait. You better come on in and sit down, Mister. I'll get a basin so's we can wash your face and see better what kinda damage has been done."

Nathan felt weak enough to appreciate the attention he was getting. In a few minutes, a man came in from the barn. He was tall and dark haired like Charlie.

"Charles," the woman called. "Come look at this poor man."

The man was by Nathan in an instant.

"Say, fellah, what happened to you?"

One thing was for sure. This had to be the nicest family he had come across in a long time. All this concern for someone they didn't even know. Nathan told them what he could. He did remember his name, but there was a whole lot that was real fuzzy. One thing for sure, he had no idea where he was or how he came to be there. That trail he had just walked, the wild flowers he saw, the humidity that hung so thick in the morning air. He was sure this was the deep south. He'd been south before. He figured he was a long way from home since these folks weren't familiar and their drawl was different than he'd heard in a while. They'd told him he was in Mississippi. Mississippi? Why had he come to Mississippi? Well, he'd think about it when his head stopped hurting. After, Mrs. Turner had washed his face and clucked her concern over his apparently broken nose, he was brought to the table for breakfast. He was terribly hungry and eagerly picked up his fork to take a bite of scrambled egg, when he felt four pairs of eyes on him. Slowly he lowered his fork back to his plate. The family joined hands, then shyly, Sam on one side and Charlie on the other, reached to take his hands. He took the two small hands in his and bowed his head when they did.

"Lord," Charles Turner began. "Bless this food we are about to partake and bless this man, Nathan, whom you have sent to us, in Jesus name, amen."

Nathan was pensive as he ate his breakfast and watched this family as they ate their meal and enjoyed one another's company. Something in the back of his mind studying this picture, made him miss someone…his home? His head throbbed again and he shook the thoughts away and kept eating. The meal was good and this family was palliative. After breakfast, Charles invited him to walk to the barn so they could talk, just the two men, while he milked the cow. The boys got up from the table and scurried about helping their Mother. She tousled the little redhead's carrot top and he smiled up at her warmly.

In the barn, the two men talked and worked together. At least Nathan tried to help, even though his face throbbed as though he'd been kicked by a mule. There was the milking, mucking the stalls and all the usual morning chores necessary on a small family farm.

"I guess when you hit your head on that rock it affected your memory a bit. You're welcome to stay around here for a while until you get your bearings and are feeling some better. You must have had a reason for coming to Mississippi in the first place. It'll come to you in a few days more than likely."

Nathan agreed that it would, but he sure couldn't think of any reason at the moment to be in Mississippi.

Chapter 26

At the boarding house in Memphis, Molly worked hard right along side of Miss Dorothy. Miss Dorothy's good down home fare had Molly feeling so much better. No more fainting feelings or nausea. Molly even thought she could see her stomach beginning to stick out a little. She was so curious about the new little life that was growing inside her. A little life created from their love together. Thinking about her own raising, she knew in her heart that Nathan would never be a gruff pa to their children. A sense of deep peace again invaded her heart as she daydreamed about life on their farm. She thought about her letter to Nathan. Would it take long for the letter to arrive at Jake's store?

She decided to write another now that she knew the name of the boarding house. That was information Nathan would need to come and get her. Before long a week had passed and she put aside her first earnings from Miss Dorothy. Then the week stretched into two. Molly wrote again. Her thoughts were constantly of Nathan. Why hadn't he come for her? She never cried in front of Miss Dorothy, but at night the tears came freely. One night as she lay there unable to sleep she felt a small flutter in her stomach. In an instant her sadness changed to joy and she laid her hand tenderly on the spot and waited. Sure enough she felt it again. The baby was moving! Once again God was speaking to her heart and using a small unborn child to do it. Her faith blossomed. Everything would be alright. She simply had to be patient. Pulling her joy over her like a blanket, she finally slept.

With morning light Molly was up with more of a lilt in her heart and Miss Dorothy immediately noticed the change in Molly's mood. Molly was always a willing worker and good at everything she did, but this change in her demeanor made Miss Dorothy like her all the more. She took a good long look at her young employee. No longer did Molly look emaciated and childlike. Her cheeks were rosy and filled out. Her figure had matured seemingly overnight.

Suddenly it dawned on Miss Dorothy why this girl had begun to look so grown up. Molly had only told her bits and pieces about her life, but Dorothy knew from the letters that she posted each week that Molly was writing to someone named Nathan. It was time to have a talk with that girl. Dorothy dusted off her apron and made for the kitchen.

Molly was busily washing dishes when Miss Dorothy approached her.

"Molly dear, when you're through with those dishes, let's go into the parlor and talk just a bit."

Molly hesitated for a second, a slight blush creeping up her cheeks. Uh oh, something was up. She brushed her hair back from her face in an effort to hide her embarrassment.

"Sure Miss Dorothy. I won't be long."

When she had finished she hurried to the parlor trying not to be nervous. Miss Dorothy offered her the rocker.

"Sit down for a minute, Molly." Molly did as she was bid.

"Are you still writing to your young man?"

"Yes Ma'am." Molly whispered a response.

"But you still don't have an answer do you?"

"No Ma'am." Even Molly was wondering what was taking so long.

"Does he know about the baby?"

Molly dropped her head and a silent tear rolled down her cheek. Miss Dorothy waited patiently for her answer. At last Molly raised her head and looked at Miss Dorothy.

"If he's gotten any of my letters then he knows."

"Will he do right by you?" Molly could hear the stern disapproval in Miss Dorothy's voice.

Molly was startled by the insinuation, but then realized she'd never given the woman any reason to think otherwise.

"He's my husband ma'am. We were married last spring."

"You're already married? But why, I mean how? I'm sorry Molly, I don't mean to pry, but how could he just let you come off to this place without even knowing how you was getting along or anything?"

Sweet Miss Dorothy. How could Molly have waited so long to confide in her? The whole story came pouring out like a torrent as Molly opened her heart up to this woman who had befriended her when she was so alone and afraid. How horrible, Miss Dorothy thought to herself, incredulous at how this girl could survive such a travale. Her motherly instincts took over and Molly was in her arms and the lady just let the woman child cry.

As finally Molly's tears began to lessen and her shoulders began to rise, Dorothy took her face in her hand, "If your young man is all you say he is, sweetie, then he must not have gotten those love letters yet because he's not here. I got a good feeling he's worried sick about you and probably hunting high and low. Is there anyone else you can write to?"

Molly thought a moment, the old panicky feeling returning as she wondered if there was anyone else in the world she could trust. A light dawned! "Oh, my brother Earl, maybe. He's a year younger than me, but I'm sure I can trust him."

"Very well, then!" Miss Dorothy was feeling the same excitement she saw on Molly's face, that of hope and purpose. "You go ahead and write to your brother. I want you to just take the rest of the afternoon off. You work plenty hard around here. Oh yes, and I've got something for you. You just wait right here."

Molly was working on a letter to Earl when Miss Dorothy came back. In her arms she had a pile of neatly folded, clean white flour sacking and some other bits and pieces of material, good sturdy pieces along with some softer delicate ones. Molly touched the gift and gave thanks to the Lord for yet another good turn of events.

"You better get started on your layette, dear. You're going to need some things. I figure if that baby is moving around you are more than five months along. These flour sacks will do just right for diapers. That's one good thing about running a boarding house", she smiled at Molly warmly. "I use an awful lot of flour. And look here! These flannel pieces from last winter's night clothes will make several baby gowns. Shaking out a nice square length, Miss Dorothy shared, "Why this piece here is big enough for a blanket. You can go through all this stuff and use what you need. None of its really big enough for anything but quilt scraps no how."

Molly was overjoyed with her gift for this baby underneath her heart! She took the box of scraps out onto the front porch and started sorting through them. She lovingly smoothed several pieces of flannel across her lap and began to plan how to cut and stitch. It wasn't long before one of the boarders, Mr. Kingston, came out and sat near her. He worked at the cotton mill along with a couple of the other boarders. The pay was good but the work day was long. He'd leave every morning by 6:00 and walk to the mill. Work started at 7:00 and the foreman didn't tolerate tardy workers. Jobs like that were hard to come by so everyone who wanted to work made sure they were punctual, especially Mr. Kingston. Regrettably, the lint constantly produced at the mill caused him to cough and snort but Molly enjoyed his company. He made small talk while she stitched on tiny little patterns. She was barely listening to him when a resounding slap startled her. She looked up to see him slapping fiercely at three buzzing mosquitoes around his face.

"Danged skeeters!" He exclaimed pulling out his pocket watch as though he needed to check the time. "Never give a man a minute's peace. I guess I'd better get back in. Molly, don't hang out here too long. Girl like you don't need skeeter bites giving her grief." With that said he jangled the loose change in his pocket, got up and walked into the house. As the screen door screeched shut, Molly realized she could hear the soft hum of the mosquitoes getting louder and louder. She could tell by the sun that it was time to go help Miss Dorothy with supper. Reluctantly she put her delicate presents back in the basket and followed after him through the door. For some reason mosquitoes never did seem to give her much bother.

That night, as she lay in her little cot, she could again hear the incessant drone of the mosquitoes, along with the tree frogs, bull frogs singing from a nearby pond and the occasional cacophony of toads. Fortunately, the sheet she had tacked up over her window was doing a good job of keeping the pesky critters out of her room.

The next morning was Sunday. Miss Dorothy had invited Molly to church and she was feeling so much better that she accepted. After cleaning up from breakfast, they were both ready. Mr. Kingston was ready. Another boarder, Frank, was sitting on the porch as they were leaving.

"Going with us today?" Mr. Kingston nodded towards him. Every Sunday he would ask Frank to go along. He always received the same answer.

"No thank 'e. Maybe some other time."

"Alright. See you when we get back."

As the unlikely trio walked down the street, Molly noted that there seemed to be a lot of churches. One of the store clerks had said the other day that two vital strains ran through the city of Memphis. One was it being a rowdy river town, and the other was its Churches. Unlike the small rough hewn meeting houses back home, which served as both school during the week and house of worship on week-ends, these Memphis churches were a sight to behold. It seemed that there was a great sense of pride and grandeur in the stone that was used, in all the architectural elements, the balance and composition. Molly didn't know much about things like that, but she knew it was different than home.

Molly also marveled at the beautiful enormous stained glass windows, especially in the bigger buildings, which seemed to symbolize, through color and pattern and imagery, a congregation's striving toward the beauty and harmony of spiritual enlightenment.

As the smells from the canals running alongside caused Molly's nose to wrinkle, she took her handkerchief from her pocket and pressed it against her face. The sewage canals, running here and there alongside the street and sometimes right through the middle, were the hot topic of the day. This rudimentary system for carrying waste away from homes and businesses was both unsanitary, although most people didn't realize it at the time, and unpleasant. The Memphis Appeal was full of commentary on the debates of the City Fathers as they discussed and fumed and argued out the problems that were the result of the open sewage. The water supplies were inadequate for the flood of newcomers and with the growth of the city due to the mills, something needed to be done.

As Miss Dorothy lead them to the pew, the rich resonance of the pipe organ trailed off to the opening prayer. As always, the preacher, or Reverend as they called him here, gave a message that was both charging and uplifting as though God had a battle plan and the congregation were soldiers in the army. And the singing, while a bit off tune here and there, sure made Molly homesick for Preacher and Mrs. Prue. "Precious

Memories, how they linger…" For the most part, people seemed to be friendly and Molly enjoyed the respite from work. Miss Dorothy, now feeling that Molly was like her own child, warned her that some of the ladies could be a bit pompous but not to take anything someone said to heart. Good folks most of them.

After service, the women talked over new bonnets and the latest styles, chatting under their breath about first one and then another while the men stood around in groups discussing the city's plight.

"Need to clean this place up." Someone said, tapping the pipe he'd put in his inside pocket.

Need more water." Said another pointing towards the river, unseen from this vantage point.

Molly smiled shyly at some of the ladies from the congregation. One lady eyed Molly's figure suspiciously.

"Married, you say?" She asked, look down her nose from her spectacles, holding them with her fingers.

Molly's face reddened as she realized what the woman was insinuating. "Yes ma'm"

She answered firmly.

"Where's your husband?" The woman continued. "Not a Christian man?"

Molly was surprised at the woman's bluntness. Miss Dorothy stepped right in.

"Molly's husband has had business away just at the moment." She pushed Molly in the direction away from the stern faced woman, flipping her shawl up higher over her shoulders. "Well, we'd better be on our way, dear, we've got to get dinner for the boarders." She patted Molly on the arm as though to wipe away the hurt and dismiss the affront.

Molly meekly followed Miss Dorothy toward the street. She felt embarrassed that Miss Dorothy had to defend her.

"Don't worry about that old busybody, Molly. She thinks it's her personal responsibility to keep everybody on the straight and narrow. She might want to work on herself a little harder. Makes me wonder sometimes if they even hear Reverend Meeks' words "

For the rest of the week, Molly worked harder than ever. She tried not to think of the woman at church but it did hurt that the woman had questioned her morals.

By Friday the heat was unbearable and the mosquitoes were relentless. The rain, scant as it was, only seemed to fuel the heat and the insects.

Mr. Kingston didn't come down for breakfast the next morning. When Molly inquired about him, Miss Dorothy went to check. She came back into the kitchen, retied her apron and resumed her chores, wiping her hair back and pinning it out of the way quickly.

"Says he don't feel so good this morning." She shrugged, as though she was shaking off something, "He's complaining of a headache. I just hope he wasn't out drinking last night. If he was, it'll serve him right."

"No," Molly remembered. "He was right here last night. He talked to me for a while before supper and he seemed fine then."

"Well," Miss Dorothy countered. "It's a good thing it's Saturday, because down at the factory, there's not a headache bad enough to excuse missing work."

By afternoon Mr. Kingston felt worse. Miss Dorothy checked on him again and found him to be feverish. Fever in those days was an ominous sign. As it wasn't decent for a young woman to go into a man's room, Molly was forbidden to check on him.

"You just make him some soup," she told Molly, "I'll make sure that he eats it." Although the tasty soup was hearty and substantial, it didn't help much. By the next morning, the man was suffering from the most awful chills. He was aching all over, trying to grab more heat from the covers, while drenched in sweat and red from the suffering; he no longer had the strength to get out of bed.

Miss Dorothy had seen how sickness could spread so she was real careful with the slop jar and making sure things were carefully cleaned. She was a firm believer in adding vinegar to the cleaning water or just using it straight. Vinegar would leave anything sparkling clean. She instructed Molly to brew up some cow chip tea for the patient and then she sent for the doctor. Molly knew that although cow chip tea was never very appetizing, the herbs that the cows ate could provide good medicine. When finally the doctor arrived, he flew in the door, rumpled and unshaven. "Lots of folks are sick and I'm about worn out!" Miss Dorothy offered him a cup of coffee but he refused.

Doc Madison went in to find that Mr. Kingston was now out of his head. The black vomit in the bucket was a telltale sign and the news was grim. Yellow fever was the diagnosis.

"I was here in 1873 and it was awful. I hate to make assumptions, but I am seeing far too many of these victims again. God help us if we have another outbreak." Before he left, he posted a quarantine sign on the boarding house door. None of the boarders could leave and certainly nobody else could come in.   This was serious business. Memphis was suffering. The summer heat was oppressive. The hospital was full of those folks who could afford to go. The few doctors in the city were stretched mighty thin trying to keep up. Anyone who wasn't sick was doing what they could for the folks who were.

Afraid for their families, many people loaded up their goods and headed for the country. Virulent fevers rocked the city, and thousands of fleeing citizens took the fever with them to towns all over West Tennessee — staggering losses were beginning to be experienced.

The newspaper reported that city leaders were having fierce debates on just what caused yellow fever in the first place. Armed safety patrols were being set up to keep people from leaving. Everyone, young and old, rich and poor, knew one thing was for sure, the ditches and drains around the city where the slop jars were routinely emptied were creating a mighty stench. Before anything could be done about the yellow fever, something had to be done about that problem. City fathers gathered with engineers and workers to plan a modern sewer system; something the city had needed for a long time. The fight for more clean drinking water was also begun. When workers discovered an artesian well, the city knew it was on its way to recovery. There would be plenty of jobs for the new sewer and water system.

Chapter 27

Back in Springhill, young Earl Myers noticed that fall was approaching. He kicked at the leaves in the road as he walked down to the Mercantile. It was the first time he'd come to the store by himself in a long while. He usually had a brother or sister or two with him. Since Pa had come back he'd been keeping Earl real busy. At least it helped him not to worry so much about Nathan and Molly. He'd still heard nothing and he knew his Ma was depending on him to get news of the situation. Deep down he knew Ma trusted Nathan even though she hardly knew him. She was sure he'd find Molly and bring her safely home. Still she'd heard nothing and that just wasn't like her girl. Sending Earl to the store alone would be the best way to get news, if there was any.

As he walked into the store, Jake looked up, pleased that the young man was by himself. He was cleaning some shelves and noticed that Earl was alone. He'd been waiting for this opportunity so they could talk.

"Hello, Earl." He spoke warmly but in a hushed tone as he felt he had spies all around.

"Hey Jake, what's up?"

"I've got something for you." Jake was trying not to appear too excited, but this was news that was about to bust his britches!

"You have? I ain't expecting nothing." It dawned on him that there might be news and his heart jumped in anticipation that it would be something from Nathan.

"It's a letter from Molly." Jake held the paper envelope in his hand like it was something reverent. "From Molly? For Me?" Earl's eyes widened in both relief and joy.

"Yeah, she's been sending letters to Nathan for some time now, but I haven't seen him to give them to him. I've been holding yours, hoping you would come in without your Pa."

Earl ripped open the letter and read it while Jake waited impatiently. Quite frankly Jake had really been worried when Nathan didn't come back. Obviously he was having a hard time searching for Molly or he would have heard by now.

"What'd she say?" Jake finally interrupted not being able to wait any longer.

"She's in Memphis. At some Boarding House. Seems she works there. Nice lady. Good place to stay. Oh, and she wants to know if I've seen Nathan."

Looking up to Jake for an answer, Earl felt unable to help his sister. "I thought Nathan went looking for her. Have you heard from him?"

" No, I haven't. Not since he left to find your sister. What do you think we ought to do?" Jake felt a shudder of concern as he realized again how long it had been since he'd seen his friend.

"Gee, I don't know, Jake." Earl was clearly agitated. "Dang if I had the money to go to Memphis, why I'd go get her right now."

"Maybe that'd be a good idea, Earl." Jake opened the till and began to count out a couple of bills and some silver coins. I'll loan you some money. Maybe you can catch a south bound boat."

"You'd do that for me?" Earl asked looking into the man's eyes, his hopes rising.

"Nathan's my friend. Molly too. How soon do you think you can get away?"

"I'll sneak out tonight. I gotta tell Ma. She's been awful worried about Molly."

Earl turned to leave but Jake called him back.

"Earl, was you after something when you came in?"

Scratching his neck, he replied sheepishly, "Yeah, I almost forgot. Ma needs some baking powder."

When Earl got back home, he strode up to his Ma.

"Ma, here's your baking powder." His tone of voice made Winifred turn from the stove to take the powder and look him in the eye.

"Thank you Earl," Her voice trailed off as she saw that Earl had a letter in his hand. "What's this?"

"It's from Molly, Ma. I know where's she's at. I gotta go to her. Jake at the store said he'd help me. Ma, you can't tell Pa." Earl was whispering hoping his Pa was nowhere around.

Winifred's hand shook as she took the letter from Earl. "What's the letter say, son?"

"She's doing okay, Ma. She just wants to come home. Nathan ain't found her. She's been writin' to him too, but she ain't heard from him and he ain't been back to the store since he went looking. Jake says he knows Nathan and he won't quit till he's found her. First I'm going to bring her home and then I'm gonna find Nathan."

"When are you going, son?" Ma was inwardly thanking God that somehow her prayers were being answered. Wasn't much out loud praying allowed around the farm, but nobody could keep her from asking and asking something from God for her kids was what she did most.

"I'm going tonight. And, Ma", he said, eye to eye, for he had grown tall in the last few months, "Please don't tell Pa. Just let him think I ran away or something."

"Do what you gotta do, son."

A tear ran down Winifred's cheek and she reached out and touched Earl's face. Her children were growing up. First Molly and now her dear oldest son. If Earl left now, he probably never come back home. She'd known they'd leave someday. All young'ns leave home eventually, but hers would go at first chance. One by one they'd go and when they were all on their own, she'd leave too. Until then she'd do what she could to hold things together. One thing though, she was sure proud how they were turning out. Her brood was gonna do alright. She turned away from Earl then, stuffed the letter in her apron pocket and went back to preparing their supper.

Meyers came in from the barn and never even noticed that Earl and Winifred were much quieter than usual. He was tired and as usual he ate his supper without talking and then went off to bed early. It was just the opportunity that they needed. The younger children were told to do their evening chores and get ready for bed. Earl quietly gathered up his few clothes and stuffed them in a flour sack. Ma put some tack and cornpone in a lard bucket. If the other kids noticed, they didn't say a word. Finally Earl was ready to leave. He stopped at the table where the others were doing their schoolwork.

"I'm going to find Molly," He told them softly. "Now I know it'll be harder on you guys if I'm not around, but I want you to help Ma as best you can. I'll be back before you know it."

Then he slipped out of the house careful to miss the squeaky board near the door and not to let the screen slap behind him. Winifred stood watching as he disappeared down the road. She was both wistful and hopeful – wistful that her boy man was leaving and hopeful that soon all would be set right for her girl Molly. Another prayer sprang up in her heart.

Jake was waiting for him when Earl returned to the mercantile.

"Sleep here tonight. Then you can be on your way early in the morning. I'll get you up before dawn just in case your Pa catches on and tried to come after you." Earl felt a stab of concern for this man, his friend, and how Pa could be if he thought somebody crossed him. The two of them made a good team when it came to helping friends.

Chapter 28

It was Sunday morning and the Turner family was headed for Sunday meeting. The kids were fresh starched and the horse and buggy stood ready to take them down the road.

"Nathan, I sure wish you'd go with us this morning."

It was the same thing Charles had said to Nathan every Sunday morning since he'd been with them and Nathan's answer was the same as it always was.

"Not this time, Charles. Maybe next time."

Nathan had gone to church with his folks as a child, but there had been no church near his cabin and he hadn't been in the habit of going. The two boys went along with their parents as always but their wistful glances back left no denying that they wished they could stay home as well. It was obvious that they'd rather be with Nathan than going off to church. For the first time, Nathan felt a twinge of guilt for the influence he had over the boys. These folks were good people and he'd never seen any Ma and Pa do better than them at raising their boys right. Charles was about as good a man as he'd ever met and the obvious love the couple felt for one another reminded him every day that something was missing in his own life.

Nathan studied as to kind of a father he'd be someday. For some reason thinking about that disturbed him. He felt his skin crawl and a momentary panic set in and a shadow of memory tried to come in. He searched his mind for a reason for feeling the way he did, but nothing was revealed. He shook his head to ward off the strange feeling and went back to what he was doing. He took clean white strips of oak and worked it into the basket he was making for Amanda Turner. Occasionally he swatted at a mosquito buzzing around his face. Dadburn mosquitoes! Here it was the fall of the year and they were still causing trouble and trying to bite whatever meal they could find.

The weather was still hot here in the delta. Now back home in Kentucky, by now it would be cooling down. The leaves likely were already turning and he'd be getting his traps ready for the winter's season. It had been okay to spend the summer with the Turner's but come winter, Nathan would rather be on his own place. He'd worked for Charles Turner all these weeks even though Turner couldn't pay him much. But, he would be willing to provide supplies for the trip back home. Nathan worked on the basket some more and felt increasingly homesick. He'd have to let the Turners know when they got back from evening church that he would have to be leaving soon.

Chapter 29

Back at the store, Earl was up and raring to go. Jake already had coffee brewing and some bacon in the skillet.

"Morning, Earl. Have some breakfast before you go."

"No time, Jake." As he gingerly guzzled the hot brew, "I need to be long gone when Pa shows up."

"You've got time to eat." Jake answered. "And I've made up a bed roll for you. You might have to sleep under the stars a night or two."

In no time at all, Earl was bounding down the trail toward the river. "Keep your pace old boy he muttered to himself. Don't want ta' wear yourself out. You got miles to go."

He paid no attention to the sleepy chirps of birds announcing the dawn. Here and there squirrels were barking back and forth and occasionally they'd jump high above from one tree and then to the other.. He had too much on his mind to pay much attention to the wild critters. Behind him from the east, the sun was peeking just above the horizon. By the time the light of day was in its full glory, Earl could smell the distinctive muddy odor that told him the river was near. He stepped out onto the river bank and surveyed his surroundings. He smelled wood fire and he thought he could hear the faint sound of laughter in the distance. That was probably the wood hawk camp. Those men knew Pa so it was probably a good idea to go on down river so as not to run into any of them. To do so would risk the chance of missing a boat, but Earl felt it was too chancy ; he didn't want to give his Pa any hand up. Besides, he knew that if his Pa caught up with him he'd be stopped before finding either Molly or Nathan.

He followed a deer trail just out of site of the river. His legs were strong and used to walking and soon the smoke and voices trailed away and were no longer a threat.

The morning passed quickly. By the time the sun was mid-high, he was ready for some of Ma's lunch and a good cool drink of water. River water would do if nothing else was available but Earl kept a lookout for a cove. Usually that was a sign of clear cool water flowing into the river, carving out a quiet little spot for animals and people alike to take advantage of.

Unexpectedly a gust of wind blew towards him and there was again the smell of wood fire. Surely there wasn't another wood camp this close to the last one. Earl stopped. Then he cautiously and softly eased down the trail to get a better look. Relief flooded his soul as he spotted the source of the smoke. It was the mouth of a creek alright and there tied to a tree out of the current of the river was a shanty boat. Not the wood hawks, thankfully, just some river folk camping out for a spell on their way south for the winter.

On the creek bank, a woman was bending over scooping up fresh clear creek water into a bucket. When she heard Earl approaching she straightened up and faced him.

"Howdy," she greeted him.

"Hello," he responded, stopping respectfully a short distance away.

"James!" she turned and hollered toward the boat. "We got company"

A man stuck his head round the side of the boat. For a moment he said nothing, just spat a tobacco stream behind him toward the bank.

"Where you headed, young feller?" He finally asked talking as slow and lazy as the river they were traveling on.

"Trying to get to Memphis," Earl answered. "You folks seen any tow boats around here lately."

"You just missed the Norman. She went through here late yestady." Earl was disappointed but ventured on with more questions hoping they had more information.

"Got any idea when the next one comes along?"

"They don't usually run that close together." James replied. We're fixin' to head on down river. You're welcome to ride along with us."

Earl stood there for a second unsure what to do.

"I'd be appreciating it." He finally said.

"Come on board," The woman invited with a somewhat crooked smile. "We're just sittin' down to have a little dinner."

Earl followed her as she stepped on a little board plank and went onto the boat. It was small as shanty boats went, only one room and a tiny porch. Inside a fire burned in a little pot bellied stove just the right size for the little river home. Potato soup was simmering and the woman took a rag and lifted the lid from the cast iron pot. She stirred the soup with a wooden spoon, mashing a potato to see if it was tender. Soon three bowls of hot soup were placed on the tiny table. Earl sat down with his hosts to share their meal. Three heads bowed and the man offered a brief prayer. "Lord we thanks ye for what ye provided."

Afterwards the woman, who had introduced herself as 'Sary', cleared the table. The dishes were washed in a pan of the clear creek water from atop the stove. Earl dried each one with a dish cloth and put them neatly in the wooden box that served as a cupboard. Then Sarah began to stow their meager belongings in preparation for cast off.

Earl followed James outside and following his lead, helped to gather up supplies on the bank. A johnboat with oar locks for two rowers was pulled off the bank and secured by rope to the front of the houseboat. The water barrel was patiently filled, bucket by bucket with the clear creek water. The fish lines and the bucket used as a live well were pulled up and stowed in their proper place. At last, when Sarah had indicated that everything inside was secured, James got into the johnboat and motioned to Earl to untie their meager water home from its moorings. Earl threw the main rope to Sarah then stepped into the water and joined James in the johnboat. With steady pulls on the oars by the two strong men, the little boat shuddered and left the shallows of the creek mouth. Before hitting the current, James expertly brought the boat back near the river bank. In no time at all the johnboat was secured on the back and with a long pole the shanty boat was pushed into the gentle current. Earl had never been on one of these before and he curiously glanced around to take in the tiny home. On one side, a frame was fastened to the wall. Strong rope crisscrossed the bottom and a straw ticking could be observed through the latticed rope. It would let down at night for the bed. The only other furnishings were the cabinet near the stove to hold the cooking utensils and supplies, a small table and four rickety cane bottom chairs. He spied a small rocking chair that must have belonged to Sarah tied in the corner. On the deck a small trap door appeared to open to the river but it was actually a hold for storage in the hull of the boat. A door at one end led to the porch and a window at the opposite end let in the light. A ladder from the porch gave access to the flat roof where fresh ropes, poles and other equipment was lashed down.

Earl was shy and not given to much talk, but he needn't have worried. James talked non-stop as the little boat floated along. Earl was learning everything there was to know about river living.

Chapter 30

Molly and Miss Dorothy worked hard to tend the sick at the boarding house. Each day Mr. Kingston's condition grew worse. And now, another boarder, Frank Miller, was sick. Molly liked Frank. He worked at the factory too, but he was never too tired to lend a helping hand. He would empty the heavy flour sacks into the flour bin so that Molly wouldn't have to pick them up. He didn't mind moving the furniture out of the way so that Molly could sweep under it. She was thankful for any help with the heavy things around the place as it was getting harder and harder for her to keep up the pace in her condition.

Each morning she hemmed her day in prayer as steadily as she hemmed the pieces of cloth for her little baby. She prayed first for Nathan, and found that even with them apart, her love was growing daily. And then her family; particularly, her Pa. It was strange how her feelings had changed. Although she still wouldn't trust Pa, she knew praying for him was a tonic for herself and her unborn child. She prayed for Earl especially. She knew her brother was getting to the age where he'd be wanting to leave home and she hoped fervently that she would get to see him before he made his way into the world to find his own way. It was comforting to know that the same God who watched over her was watching over those she loved. She prayed for Frank and Mr. Kingston. She prayed for strength and healing and forgiveness. She just knew that somehow sooner or later her prayers would be answered. She waited patiently, but kept busy all the while. And in spite of it all, her faith did not waiver, but rather grew stronger. All the lessons she'd learned as a young girl from Miss Prudence came back to her. It seemed that if anything was bothering her she would recall a verse from the Bible that just fit the situation. Her favorite one was the one about all things working together for good. That one always gave her much hope and such joy. Knowing that somehow everything was going to work together for good made the days seem just a little shorter and the nights just a little more restful. Miss Dorothy had turned out to be such an excellent friend. Her strength and take charge attitude was encouraging. Molly would find herself wishing that her own Ma had some of the tenacity that Miss Dorothy had. Well, one thing was for sure, Molly was learning to be strong watching Miss Dorothy from day to day.

Reports kept coming in that more and more folks in the city were falling ill. The two at the boarding house were not showing any signs of recovering, and their rooms were off limits to any one but Miss Dorothy. She said she'd had yellow fever when she was a girl.

"If ever you live through it," she said, "You won't get it again." Molly felt bad about Mr. Kingston and Frank. They were in her prayers the same as her own family. Miss Dorothy still refused to let her into the sick room. She insisted that Molly follow her strict orders. Hands must always be washed with strong lye soap. Molly had washed her hands so much that they were getting rough and chapped. Molly had to leave the laundry alone that came from the sick room as well. Miss Dorothy scrubbed and boiled those things herself. Dorothy had moved Frank in with Mr. Kingston and had cleaned Frank's room thoroughly, washing everything down with lye soap water – mere vinegar wouldn't do.

She sure was tired from tending to the men as she did. Blessed little Molly had taken on so much of the responsibility for the rest of the house. Every morning the girl would slip a piece of paper under the door with a list for the delivery man and every evening the filled order would be left on the porch. The quarantine made it so hard. They were totally isolated from the outside world.

Dorothy was amazed at how Molly was maturing. When the young thing had first appeared at her door, she had seemed like a scared little rabbit. Now she was becoming self confident and womanly. In spite of the circumstances, she would go around the house singing and smiling as if she didn't have a care in the world. She worked hard cooking and cleaning while Miss Dorothy took care of the sick men. Whenever Dorothy questioned her about it she would always answer. "Well, it says in the good book that a merry heart is as good as a tonic. I guess it's the truth."

One thing was for sure. Dorothy certainly felt better just being around her. She had come to love her like a daughter and she dreaded the day that Molly would leave her. Surely her brother would show up for her any day now. Until then, the work had to go on. If the sickness didn't leave this house then Molly couldn't leave even if her brother or her dear Nathan did come for her.

Days went by and Frank began to feel some better. Unfortunately, Mr. Kingston wasn't faring so well.

Before they could catch their breath though, the sickness came back on Frank and this time with a vengeance. The doctor was called again. After he examined the two men again, he told Miss Dorothy that there was just no hope. She saw the resignation in his eyes and heard it in his voice. It looked to her like he'd aged years since he'd been here last.

"People are sick unto death all over the city." He stated matter of factly. "There are more folks leaving on the trains and boat than people coming in. Everybody's afraid of catching the fever. Then there's the people who are afraid for anyone to leave. Seems the sickness is spreading everywhere up and down the river."

He sighed and picked up his bag to head to the next stop. He was tired of all this sickness. Everyone was. As Miss Dorothy recounted to Molly what the doctor had said, they both began to weep.

"We'll just have to pray harder," Molly cried. "God will heal them both."

"I know God *can*," Dorothy affirmed. "He sure healed me of the fever when I was a girl. That's why I'm not afraid. I know a body can't get the fever again. But I've seen people who didn't get healed. I am not sure if God is going to spare these two. But if they're putting their trust in the right place, then God will welcome them both home for sure."

Miss Dorothy headed back to the sick room to check on the men. She knew if either of them died, it wouldn't be because she hadn't done right by them. Mr. Kingston had been ailing the longest. Now he lay quiet, his body weak and worn as the fever was wearing him down. As Miss Dorothy dipped a cloth in the pitcher and pressed it to his forehead he opened his weakened eyes and seemed to look just past her.

"Did you see them?" He asked. His voice was surprisingly strong.

"Did I see who?" Dorothy responded, wondering what he was talking about. There was no way anybody got in this room without her knowing it.

"Those two men that was just in here."

Not knowing what to say, she gently mopped his face some more. He was so confused, she didn't know whether to play along just to comfort him or to be truthful and tell him there were no men.

"I guess they must have left," she told him gently.

"They'll be back," the old man said firmly in a way that belied his condition. "They're taking me home."

"Home, Mr. Kingston? You *are* home. You've lived here for years."

"No" the man stated with conviction. "They said they were taking me home. They said my ma and pa were waiting for me. I can't wait to go."

Miss Dorothy got a sudden catch in her throat as tears welled up. She whispered a quick prayer. Could those men he saw be angels come to take the man home to heaven? Just then a warm rush of wind went through the room, fluttering the curtains at the closed windows and brushing past her face.

Frank sat up in his bed across the room.

"Where did that light come from?" He asked in amazement.

"What light?" Miss Dorothy ventured.

"It was a real bright light, just came right into the room and washed right over Mr. Kingston." Frank's face was in awe as he looked towards the bed of his companion in illness.

Miss Dorothy looked back down at the worn out face she had been bathing. A sweet expression had replaced what just a moment ago had been weariness. She realized, too, that breath came no more. Tears began to roll down her face. Frank didn't know what to say. In a weak voice he asked if Mr. Kingston was gone.

"Yes," Miss Dorothy replied, holding back tears, "But somehow I know it's alright. I think God's heavenly angels just came and took him."

Frank's hands trembled as he fumbled with the quilt that covered him. "Am I going to die too, Miss Dorothy? Are the angels going to come for me? What if I ain't been good enough to go with the angels? What if..... what if I'm going to that other place?"

Miss Dorothy turned from Mr. Kingston and took both of Frank's hands in hers.

"Why Frank. I know you always shied away from going to church with the rest of us, but you know all about the Lord Jesus don't you?"

"Yes'm I do," he replied, " I went to church with my folks when I was younger, but the preacher's always yelling about our sins and how we was all going to hell. To tell you the truth Miss Dorothy, church always has scared me something awful."

At this point, Frank was pitifully choking back the tears. Fear was etched on his thin face.

"Oh, Miss Dorothy, I'm going to die from this yellow fever just like Mr. Kingston only ain't no angels coming for me. I done a lot of bad things, bad things." He shook his head and fell back on the pillow, now spent from the sudden feeling of panic. Miss Dorothy wasn't one bit afraid to pull that emaciated body into her arms and just hug him.

"Frank, there's not a bad bone in your body. Why I've seen you hurry to help Molly with chores when you were so tired from the factory you almost fell asleep at supper. Besides that, there's not a thing in this world we can do to save ourselves."

Frank leaned his tear stained face against her bosom.

"I don't know what you mean, Miss Dorothy. Is there hope for me?"

Miss Dorothy gently disentangled the thin arms from around her and laid the man back against his sweat drenched pillow.

"Now, you listen to me. Jesus did all the work for us when he died on that cross. All we have to do is accept His sacrifice. He did it all for us. Ain't none of us got no hope without Him. It's like this - If I was to offer you a free gift, would you take it?"

"Yes'm, I guess so." Frank had begun to settle down and wasn't shaking anymore.

"Well, that's it. Jesus offers us the free gift of salvation. We just confess to him that we are sorry for our sins and ask him to come into our life. Salvation is a gift and all we have to do is accept it."

"You mean, just accept it?" Frank's expression showed his confusion.

"Why, Miss Dorothy, that's kinda what I learned when I was just a little boy. My Ma always told me about the Bible and she always told me I could trust every word of it."

"Well, if you believe that, can you believe that his death on the cross was for everybody, including you?" Understanding began to brighten up his yellowed face.

"I do, I believe that."

"Then lets pray." Sunken eyes closed and tears flowed as Frank repeated the sinners prayer each word just as Miss Dorothy said them, "I'll go with the angels just like Mr. Kingston, won't I?"

The man seemed to grow stronger as the conviction of his heart was settled. "Oh, Frank. I'm so thankful what God has done for you! There's a lot of praying going on in this house. You hang on. You fight this ailment. I don't believe for one minute that Jesus saved you just to take you on. I believe you're going to recover. God's got a work for you to do."

Miss Dorothy couldn't believe that joy for Frank and grief for Mr. Kingston could both be coming out of her heart at the same time.

"Now, Frank, you just rest here and think about your new life and I'm going to go and get you some nourishment and this time I just know you're going to be able to keep it down."

In the kitchen, Molly looked at Miss Dorothy as she walked in. The woman's fairly shown and she seemed to be walking a little less tiredly. Molly knew something had happened in that sick room.

"Is everything alright?" She asked.

"Well, the Lord took Mr. Kingston on home, but I'll tell you, it was something. That room was filled with the presence of God, and oh, Molly, Frank saw the whole thing! He even made his own heart right with God. Mr. Kingston must be singing in heaven over all this. Pour up some soup for me to take to Frank and then go next door and tell the neighbors to send someone to the funeral parlor about Mr. Kingston."

Chapter 31

Night came creeping coolly to the river, as the fog started rising and making shapes along the way. James began to look for a secluded spot on the bank to tie up the houseboat. Around a bend a washed out cove with a sandbar that would serve as a little beach came into sight. Gentle guidance with the long pole edged the little houseboat closer and closer. Earl watched carefully for a chance to jump for the bank. Sarah threw him a line and in minutes it was secured to a sapling growing in the shallows. By the time the sun disappeared completely beyond the western sky, everything was secure. Earl helped Sarah gather a few pieces of driftwood still visible in the soft lamplight. Sarah fried salt meat and made flapjacks for supper. With satisfied stomachs, James and Earl sat on the tiny porch and dangled fishing poles into the water by the light of the moon. Tomorrow there would be fresh fish to eat. Inside the tiny cabin Sarah squinted in the lamplight as she stitched on quilt squares holding each piece as though it were made of the finest silk.

Once their catch was secured in a screened bucket lowered into the river to keep them alive until morning, Earl and George made preparation for bed. Earl was shown a comfy spot on the roof of the cabin where he could spread his bedroll under the stars. Inside the cabin he could hear as Sarah and James moved the little table and lowered their bed frame from the wall. At last the fire in the little stove was banked and the lantern was blown out. The boat rocked gently against the cove as the water made lapping sounds on the hull. There was the serenade by frogs who harmonized up and down the bank. There was the occasional fish dancing around in the water. Turtles could be heard as they lazily slipped off logs and into the black water. Though his mind was on locating his sister, slumber came swiftly. Morning would come soon enough and he'd be one day closer to finding Molly and Nathan.

Chapter 32

On a Mississippi farm, the work is never ending. No matter how many times the chores were done, they were always to be repeated. Peas and corn had to be picked. The cow had to be milked. Vegetables were picked as they ripened so they could be put up. Sweat poured down Nathan's brow as he led the mule to the creek. He used a damp handkerchief, pulled from his back pocket, to mop at the salty water that had turned the dust on his face into streaks of mud. While the mule lowered his head for a cool drink from the creek, Nathan followed suit, stooping to splash the cool water on his face. The bucket was untied from the wagon and laboriously he filled the water tank that was there in the buckboard. As he was filling the tank, the mule was edged more and more into the cool creek. When the tank was full, Nathan pulled at the mule's lead to turn him back toward the fields.

"Come on Jack!" The stubborn animal had no intention of leaving the oasis of cool water lapping at his belly. He lifted his head and brayed loudly then shook his head spraying Nathan with spittle and water.

"You stubborn old mule!" Nathan exclaimed half laughing. A couple of slaps on the rump and man and beast reluctantly headed back to the field.

Nathan and Charles had become fast friends as they tended the fields and cared for the livestock together. Nathan was far happier when chores included repairing things around the barn and house than he was fighting the never ending battle with thistles in the fields. One day they'd be just a bump in the grass, next day it seemed they were tall as a man. It was funny how something so pretty, with the purple topknot of bloom, could be so much trouble. Leave it one extra day and three more would be growing around it. August's dog days of summer were spent trying to coax a few more tomatoes from the withered plants as well as cutting okra from high grown stalks that were looking more like stick figures. Any potatoes dug from under the shade of the plants were put aside to store in the root cellar. Evenings were just as hot so they were spent on the porch shelling peas and snapping beans for Amanda to put up. There was nothing Sam and Charlie hated worse. Audible sighs were heard until their father glared in their direction. At last the boys were given permission to run to the creek for an evening swim.

"You boys watch for snakes and snappin' turtles. Don't need you losing any toes!"

Charles would laugh with his wife and the boys would look at one another quizzically, then one or the other would holler "Go!" and off they'd race to their favorite spot, dust flying behind them.

An old tree with a long limb hanging over the bank was the perfect place for a rope. The clay on the bank was slick and smooth where the boys climbed holding the rope and then swung out over the deep spot letting go with shrieks of laughter. It wasn't just for play though. Soap was taken along and when it was certain that no prying eyes were hiding out anywhere, it was time for a good bath. They'd come back a little more subdued. Between the day's work and the evening's fun they were tuckered out. When finally the night would begin to cool and mist began to rise in the fields the boys would settle in for the night. This was the time of the day when Charles and Nathan would head to the creek where a private spot was found for a refreshing bath as well. Amanda envied the freedom of the male species for this wonderful summer ritual. Bath time for her meant wrestling the washtub into the kitchen, pouring in several buckets of water and then emptying the kettle from the stove for warmth. It was a hurried affair between putting the boys to bed and the time the men came back from the creek. Later she'd sprinkle the bed sheets with a little rose petal scented water making it so that it wouldn't be so unbearably hot for sleeping and the scent seemed to make things cooler as well. Nathan slept in the barn where night breezes blew through the large cracks in the barn siding. Each day was greeted with the warm sun rising like a flame and work would begin again. The only relief to this heated workday was Sundays when only the things that were absolutely necessary were done. The boys could play and swim the whole afternoon long. Sometimes the church folks would hold all day singing and dinner on the ground. Those sultry days of summer were what memories were made of.

Chapter 33

Floating down the river with Sarah and James seemed terribly slow to Earl. In his bed roll on the roof of the river cabin, the nights were just starting to hold a chill in the breeze. Sarah offered him another quilt when the first frost fell. They woke up to the trees along the banks showing brilliant colors overnight and the urgent echo of barking squirrels could be heard from the forests as they scurried to and fro gathering up their winter stores. A couple of days were spent tied up on the river so that James and Earl could go squirrel hunting. The fresh meat tasted good after Sarah dusted it in flour and fried it in bacon grease.

At last they were nearing Memphis. Just like Molly had seen when she first arrived, the river traffic became thicker and gossip was traded as people shouted from one deck to another. One night a man from another houseboat rowed over in his johnboat to join George and Earl in a game of cards. He brought news of the yellow fever raging in Memphis.

"Lots of sick folks." He told them. "People can't hardly get out of that city fast enough. Everybody's looking for a boat out of town, but I tell you, I don't intend to get close enough for anybody to even try and get near my boat. Besides that now they're all starting to panic, cause word is coming in of more fever down the way."

News of the fever made Earl heartsick.

"Mr. James, I gotta go. What if she gets the fever?"

"Well, boy," James told him, "I think me and the missus will just float right on by. I've got no intention of catching my death."

Earl was determined. He wasn't concerned about the fever. He just knew he had to get to Molly. He would get her home where she would be safe from the fever. At a spot where a well worn trail came down to the river bank, he had James row him ashore. With his bed roll on his back and food in his lard bucket, Earl turned and waved to Sarah and headed up the trail. He would walk all the way if he had to.

Following along a well worn path, Earl hadn't seen a living soul. Little whirlwinds tossed brown leaves across the forest floor. Even though the sun was warm on his head, he knew the approaching night would bring a chill. In the early afternoon, he rested by a small spring. The water that bubbled across a smooth stone was cool and sweet. A cold roasted potato and some fish leftover from last night's supper made a tasty lunch. Soon he was on his feet again his long legs striding forward, his anxious mind thinking about his sister. The trail eventually became a road and in the distance Earl could see fields and make out some outbuildings. Sounds of cattle could be heard echoing through the meadow. The river and the forest were left behind. Ahead of him, Earl could just make out a wagon being pulled by a slow walking mule. The driver of the wagon could hardly be seen for the cargo of snow white cotton tied neatly in bales. Gradually Earl overtook them. An elderly black man eyed him suspiciously from sleepy eyelids.

"Afternoon," Earl called.

The man raised a finger to his battered farm hat and mumbled a cautious greeting.

"Where you headed?" Earl asked.

"Gwine to town," the old man drawled. "Gots ta' get dis here load of cotton on d' e'ning train to Memphis. Headed to the cotton gin."

"Mind if I ride along?" Earl asked." I'm headed to Memphis myself."

Yessuh, if'n yous a mind to." the old man replied. "But I spect you can walk a whole lot faster than this here mule be a goin'."

"Well, Sir," Earl replied." I've been walking pretty much all day and it sure would feel good to get off my feet a bit."

"Well then, hop on up heah. Whoa mule." The old man pulled the reigns tight and the mule, appearing almost as old as his driver, stumbled to a halt.

Earl scrambled up beside the driver.

"Go on Mule," The driver ordered. The mule silently stepped forward.

Earl didn't know what to say and the old man didn't seem to have anything to say either. The mule just plodded along and Earl nodded off to sleep to the sound of hooves beating the ground with his bedroll against the small of his back and his head resting against the tall stack of cotton bales. When he woke up, the wagon was stopped behind quite a lot more, all of them looking the same with their white fluffy cargo waiting their turn to be unloaded.

Earl jumped down from the wagon seat thanking the man for the ride. Then he headed to the tiny station house to pay for a train fare from the money loaned to him by Jake.

"Ain't nobody going to Memphis," the station master assured him. "They got the yellow fever there. Everybody trying to leave town." He lowered his head back to the job at hand as though dismissing Earl from further questions.

"I know. There's talk all up and down the river about the fever, but I don't care. I need to get there."

The station master looked back up with annoyance, thinking this boy was purely stupid and asking for it.

"It's two bits", as he pushed Earl's ticket under the window. "Got a trunk?" He asked, all the while stamping papers and appearing impatient.

"No," Earl replied. "Just got my bed roll and a few clothes here. I'll just keep it with me."

The dank interior of the train didn't bother him at all. He found a seat in the nearly deserted passenger car and made himself comfortable. It was his first train ride and ordinarily he would have been curious about everything, but he was just too tired to care. Moving forward with a lurch, the train groaned and the whistle blew. Soon the rhythmic clacking of the wheels was matched with the gentle rocking of the car and Earl relaxed hoping that his journey to his beloved sister was nearly over.

The jolting of the railroad cars jerking to a stop woke Earl. Gathering his thoughts, he picked up his bed roll and his food bucket and made his way to the exit. He approached the depot window and pulled a wrinkled envelope from his pocket.

"Sir, could you tell me how to find this place?" he asked the station master.

"Well, let me see here" the man stroked his face thoughtfully. "You see that yellow column down yonder? Go there and then left you'll need to go down that away, oh about two miles. Just stay on that same street…"

As he continued the directions, Earl listened carefully, having the man repeat one point that was a bit confusing. "But son, I'd be careful about going on into the city…" Before the station master could finish, Earl was off into the night. He couldn't believe he was so close to finding Molly. When this was all over, him and Nathan and Molly would sure have some stories to tell. Feeling a sudden rush of energy, he headed on toward the boarding house. The city was cooling down and the air was crisp. This last stretch of the trip was invigorating.

Approaching the boarding house and walking up the steps, he saw the quarantine sign on the door. He knocked anyway. Molly was sitting in her room working on her sewing and didn't hear the door. When Miss Dorothy called her, she looked up reluctantly from her work. Who was the young man with Miss Dorothy? A sudden recollection filled her heart with joy! Up from the chair she came, dropping her sewing in the floor and reaching for Earl with her arms spread out.

"Earl!" she cried, "Oh Earl, my dear, wonderful brother!"

Earl was pleasantly surprised and embarrassed by his long lost sister's hug. Back at the farm, they rarely had opportunity to show feelings for one another. Every once in a while, they'd show affection the way children do, which was usually by picking at one another. As he took another look at his sister, one thing was for sure. She wasn't a child anymore.

Her changing body was all too obvious to her brother as he shyly returned her hug. Then she stepped back to get a good look at him.

"Oh Earl you've changed so much I didn't even recognize you. You've grown a foot since I seen you. I bet you're taller than Pa."

"I ain't the only one who's changed," Her crimson faced brother said. "Boy it ain't even been a whole year yet and you don't look nothing like you did. If it weren't for those eyes and that smile I might not have recognized you."

"I guess I do look different don't I." As she looked down at her swelling figure and brushed her apron, her emotions turned loose and the tears began to flow . "I'm going to be a mother. Can you believe it?" She touched her stomach again tenderly. I want to go home. I want to have my baby at my own little house with my husband there waiting. Oh, Earl!" And then she was hugging him again. He hadn't been hugged so much since he last saw his Granny, four years ago.

Finally Miss Dorothy rescued him from his sister. "Earl, I bet you're hungry ain't you? Molly, why don't you go into the kitchen and fix your brother a bite. Then ya'll can sit at the table and talk while he eats. Earl, I'm sorry I don't have a spare bed for you but you're welcome to bed down on the couch here."

"Yes Ma'am. That'd be just fine."

Earl followed Molly out to the kitchen and Miss Dorothy went on about her business. She brought down a couple of quilts and a pillow and put them on the couch. She could hear the two of them chattering away in the kitchen. Well, she sure would hate to lose Molly. She was a good worker and a sweet friend. But Dorothy knew how her heart had been aching with homesickness even though she wasn't one to mope around. She also knew that in Molly's condition, she'd be so much better off leaving this city like so many others were doing.

The next morning, Molly brought out her little jar of savings to see if she had enough for a train ticket home. Earl already had his ticket from the money that Jake had given him. It was barely enough. She spent the morning packing her things into the satchel. There was no way everything would go in. The baby things she had made with Miss Dorothy's help would have to be carried in a flour sack.

When the time came to leave, Miss Dorothy opened the boarding house front door to see if anyone was walking by. That quarantine sign was so bright, but she dared not take it down. They'd have the law on her. After seeing that no one was around that early, she motioned for Molly and Earl to come to the door. Molly stood in front of Miss Dorothy trying hard not to cry. Finally she just reached out for the older woman. They embraced and cried as goodbyes were mumbled. Molly tried to pour out how grateful she felt for the generous care she had received when she had no place to turn, and Miss Dorothy couldn't thank her enough for the work she had cheerfully done.

"Now, Molly, you be sure and write me when you get a chance. I'll be wanting to know about the little one."

"I'll write you, I promise."

Finally they could wait no longer. Somebody might come along and catch them trying to leave. Besides, it was good long walk to the station and they didn't want to miss their train.

Chapter 34

Molly was excited about riding a train. First she'd ridden the boat and now a train. If she ever was on a boat again, maybe it would be under happier circumstances. Trains were fascinating to her, but she'd hardly had time to even see one. They could be heard late night and early morning as the steam whistles were pulled sounding the departures.

Earl worried that she shouldn't have to walk so far in her condition, but was assured by her broad smile and quick cadence, that she felt better than ever. He had to admit that she looked better than ever. The good food from the Boarding House plus the exercise of the hard work had done her a world of good. Earl thought she positively glowed. Her health radiated and God had spared her from the fever.

The train was wonderful. Earl, the experienced traveler, had to show Molly everything there was to see. The big black locomotive seemed to have a life of its own. Belching out smoke and steam it seemed frightening to Molly at first. Earl laughed.

"Come on and see where we'll be riding."

There were four long coaches. Painted green with red stripes down the sides, they also had windows that went the length of the coach. The beautiful leather seats were dark brown and supple. At both ends of each coach were two little closets, one for the men and one for the ladies. There was a little stool with a lid for relief and there was a place to wash your hands afterwards. Oh what modern wonders. Molly knew however that it would be embarrassing to have to go to that little closet with everyone else on the train knowing about it. Earl laughed at her again when she mentioned it.

She swung at him and he dodged her with ease.

"You're sure all fired up Mister," She said. "You've only been on a train one more time than I have." People boarding the train smiled indulgently at the young couple who were having such fun.

In no time at all it was time to find their seats. The train let out a mournful whistle or two and Molly's heart began to palpitate as she reached for Earl's hand for comfort. The whistle blew again and the coach shuddered slightly. With a quick jerk it started to roll and they were on their way. Home. Molly was going home. She let go of Earl's hand and grinned at him. Surely Nathan would be waiting. She pictured their wonderful cabin nestled in their beautiful meadow. She wondered about the little kitten she had carried with her under her cloak and remembered how scared and excited she had felt all at the same time. With the rhythmic clicking of the piston rods propelling the train wheels on the tracks and daydreams filling her mind, Molly's head lolled over on Earl's shoulder and she slept.

Chapter 35

Nathan and Charles were working in the barn when Nathan found the words telling this newfound friend that he'd be leaving soon. Fall was in the air and Nathan was restless.

"You and your wife have been great, Charles and I've loved those boys as if they were my own, but I'm ready to move on now."

"I understand, Nate. Why don't you go ahead and stay one more night and try for an early start in the morning. 'Manda can fix you up some food and I have it in mind to let you have that sorrel horse."

"I hate to take your best horse. There's no way I've worked long enough to pay you."

"Well, I say you have. That's the only way I can pay is with the horse. I really needed you this summer and I feel like you earned him fair and square." Slapping Nathan on the shoulder and smiling, he urged them to the house, "Now see here, we'd better get on in for dinner before Amanda starts hollering at us."

Dinner, however, wasn't waiting on the table as usual.

"Amanda," Charles called out anxiously when they didn't find her in the kitchen.

"I'm in here," She answered weakly.

Concerned, both men ran to the parlor where she lay pale faced on the couch.

"Are you sick?" Charles inquired reaching out to touch her forehead ever so gently.

"A little," She smiled as she raised herself slightly from the couch. "It's okay fellas, I'm a little under the weather, 'cause the Turner family is going to have a new addition. Do you think you might be able to help me fix something for dinner before the boys get in from school? I might feel a lot better after I eat."

Charles was too excited about his wife's amazing news to notice Nathan's reaction. A cold sweat had broken out on his face as he heard Frenchie's voice from the past saying, "You know how women get at that time of the month."

"Ain't that great Nathan? The boys are almost teenagers and now we're going to have a baby." Charles was saying as he turned around to face Nathan.

"We're having a baby too," Nathan spoke so softly they could hardly hear him as he rubbed his forehead as though in pain.

"What!?" Charles and Amanda chimed in together.

"Molly, she uh, she's having a baby too."

For a moment neither Amanda nor Charles spoke, then Amanda said hesitantly.

"Who's Molly, Nathan?"

Visible pain was etched on Nathan's face as memories came flooding back He'd wasted the whole summer here in the middle of nowhere when Molly was God knows where suffering who knows what. He started for the door without even speaking to the couple as Charles reached out and grabbed him by the arm.

"Hold on man. Talk to us for a minute."

"My wife…how could I forget…my own wife?" Nathan's voice bespoke the obvious alarm he was now feeling. He was sick and furious with himself.

"Sit down boy. Looks like that blow on your head caused you to have some kind of memory loss. Let's hear the whole story before you take off in a gallop!"

The whole story came pouring out to an astonished Amanda and Charles. Nathan shared the story of his innocent young bride being stolen away by her angry father and his own mission to find her.

"Now I know why I was so far from home. I was searching for Molly." Nathan buried his face in his clenched hands. "I've let that girl down something awful. How on earth could I forget the one I love? Oh God, how could that ever happen?"

Charles squatted on the floor beside him and laid a rough hand on his shoulder. "Well, now son, it wasn't no fault of yours. Every so often bad things happen, even to good folks like you and your Molly. But I always figure if a person can just trust God, well then He can work things out. No problem is too big for Him."

"How can He work out this for me?" Nathan cried out in anguish. "I don't know anything about Him or His ways. Truth be told I'm just a little angry at this whole thing. Someone calls him a loving God, but He let my Molly be stolen from me…"

"That may seem like the truth, but God knows Molly and He knows you. I'm thinking now is as good a time as any to get to know Him, personal like."

Nathan looked up into the face of his friend. "How do I do that?" He asked.

"There's this story in the Bible about a man named Nichodemus. He asked that same question. Jesus told him he had to be born again."

"Born again?"

"Yes, what it actually means is being born in a spiritual way. Learning to let God into your life so's He can guide you and comfort you. It means realizing that we're all hopeless without God and we need to let him into our lives like he intended to be in the first place."

It all seemed so puzzling to Nathan, but because of the circumstances he was willing to listen. As Charles talked, Nathan became more and more receptive. At last he prayed with Charles and relief came flooding into his soul. Real hope filled his heart. Hope that Molly was all right and that he would find her, with God's help.

Although Nathan could hardly sleep that night, anxious for the morning, he had the first peace in as long as he could remember. His anxiety to find Molly and take her back home was tempered by His realization that God cared for him and his Molly. Maybe Charles was right about all things working together for good…

Amanda still felt poorly the next morning so it was Charles and the boys who helped Nathan get ready to leave. Sam and Charlie were fighting back snuffles as Nathan mounted up to leave. He patted them both on the head, "I'll miss you boys a whole lot, but I've got to get back to my own family. Now you fellah's mind your Pa and take care of your Ma." Suddenly mindful of the poor example he might have set in regards to church going, he added, "I want you boys to be sure and go to church. Your Pa knows what's best for you there."

"Sure, Nathan, we'll go." They promised him then turned back toward the house. They were too embarrassed for Nathan to see their tears.

Charles put his hand out to Nathan. "You take care now, you hear? Amanda and me, we'll be praying for you and your Molly. I just feel like everything's going to be alright."

Without another word, Nathan rode off in the direction of Tennessee.

Chapter 36

When Earl and Molly got to the end of their trip and the train was winding down and pulling into the train station, Preacher Brown was waiting for them. Although the times dictated that Molly shouldn't show affection towards a man unrelated to her, she was too happy to comply. To Preacher Brown's delighted surprise Molly ran to him and hugged him.

Pulling her back to get a good look at her, he teased, "What happened to that little girl, I used to know? You've become a young woman."

Molly blushed and laughed. "Preacher Brown, have you heard anything at all from Nathan?" She asked pensively. She was trying hard not to bite her lip but didn't want to bust out crying right here at the station. The happy mood turned somber. "No, child," He answered with regret. "I've heard nothing and neither has Jake. Don't you worry none, though. Me and Sister Prue have been praying every day. I know things are gonna work out."

The threesome gathered Molly's things and went to the waiting wagon. "Now Molly, Sister Prue is expecting me to bring you back to our place to wait until we can find Nathan."

"Thanks for the offer, but I just want to go back to my own little homestead."

Both the preacher and Earl put up a fierce argument.

"You can't stay there by yourself," Earl stated. "With the baby coming on pretty soon not to mention winter, it would be downright foolish to even think such a thing."

"Better listen to your brother, girl. We just can't allow that."

Molly turned on the stubbornness full force. She was having none of it. Her little home was all she wanted. She wanted to get it all ready for Nathan and the new baby. Argue though they might, finally Earl and Preacher backed down.

"Well," Preacher conceded. "I'll just send Prudence out to you as soon as I can. I guess a couple of days by yourself can't do no harm. I know you're a responsible young woman."

"And maybe I can bring Sissy out to stay with you too. Anna is plenty big enough to help Ma with the chores for a little while." Earl added, "If Pa don't pay no never mind. Anyway, I'm old enough now to stand up against him. No more stealing men's wives, even if they are his daughter."

When they finally reached Nathan and Molly's place, night was descending. Molly was so excited she could hardly wait for the wagon to stop. In the dogtrot, a little cat face peeked out at the people descending upon him. Grown now, fat and sleek from a summer of field mice and an occasional slow bird, he shied away from these intruders.

Molly could barely hide her disappointment. "Oh, Boots, have you forgotten me?" He scampered to a safe distance and glared at her.

"Have you been watching out for things while I was gone?"

"Don't worry about that cat. You'll win his trust again," Preacher told her. "Let's get you and your things inside and see how your provisions have fared."

The cabin was clean and the food stored safely in the containers which Molly and Nathan had brought it in. Someone had come in and prepared things for safekeeping. Maybe it had been Frenchie.

Worn out from travelling, the three ate supper and then bedded down for the night. Next morning, Molly made them all a breakfast of cornmeal mush with molasses to sweeten it and poured a strong coffee from the stove to help warm them up for the cold autumn morning. Afterward, Earl and Preacher Brown spent the morning chopping wood to restock the woodpile. There was a lot of wood stacked against the house, but it had dried during the summer and Molly would need some green wood to add with it or else it would burn too fast and be used up in a hurry. During the afternoon, Earl rode out to find Frenchie's place and let him know that Molly was back and would be alone for a day or two. When he came back he had a surprise for Molly.

She heard the bleating of the little nanny goat when she ran out to meet Earl.

"Oh!" She cried scooping the little bundle into her arms. "Where did you get her?"

"Frenchie sent her. Nathan had asked for her before you were taken. Her name is Nellie."

"Oh Nellie," Molly cried hugging her and burying her face in the goat's neck. "I sure am glad to see you. Now we can have milk."

Nellie bleated and nuzzled Molly.

"Come on Molly." Earl said. "Let go of her long enough for me to take her to the shed." Taking her from Molly's grasp, he questioned, "What have you got for supper? Me and Preacher got to get to bed so's we can leave in the morning."

"I've got beans with hot water cornbread. That cornbread sure would have been better if I'd a had some of Nellie's milk in it."

Next morning just as the mist was burning off the grass, the men left out, though it was with great reluctance. They looked back one last time to see Molly waving from the porch.

When they were gone, Molly went to the shed with a bucket to milk Nellie. Boots followed at a safe distance and sat down to watch. Molly playfully squirted milk at the cat and little by little he came closer. By the time Molly was through, he had forgotten to be afraid of her and followed her as she tethered the goat outside the shed and took the milk in. Molly conversed with him continually as she strained the milk and put it in a jar. He answered her with meows but he wasn't quite ready to rub against her legs and he sure wasn't allowing her to pet him when occasionally she'd reach out for a touch. After she had taken the milk to the springhouse and gotten breakfast cleared away, Molly got out the little things she'd been making for the baby. Piece by piece she went through each little gown, diaper and bib. Finally she took them to her chest and put them away. In the chest she found some sewing scraps that Sister Prue had given her. Before long, she had settled in the chair sewing together pieces for a baby quilt, humming to herself. Hours must have passed and she realized that the room was getting colder. "Better put some wood on the fire," she said to the kitty. "It's getting chilly in here." When she went out on the porch to get the wood, she gave a start. The sky was covered by a heavy blanket of dark clouds that could only mean one thing. The first storm of the winter was headed in. She hurried to put Nellie in the shed and then went to milk her for the evening. Thankfully there was hay stored in there for Nathan's horse. If it did come up a blizzard, Nellie would have food. After milking Nellie and closing her up in the shed, Molly hurried to the wood pile. Little by little she transferred as much of it as she could to the porch and into the dog trot. Molly noticed the baby kicking up a storm. "Little darlin, you're kicking a storm up just like the one brewing outside." She patted her tummy and sat back down to rest. If she hadn't had such a restful day to begin with, she could never have taken care of that chore. She felt more than a little tired, she was worn plumb out.

Preacher and Earl had made it to the halfway house, and were watching the sky the cold wind blustered as the shack's thin walls shuddered as though they were in battle. Unsure whether they should head back to Molly or go on to get the women folk, they debated the issue.

Sending up a silent prayer for wisdom, "I'm thinking it's best we push on and get the womenfolk," Preacher Brown finally decided. "Molly will need the women a sight more than us and that's for sure." Earl nodded in agreement and they stepped back out into the cold wind to trudge on to the mercantile.

Chapter 37

In Memphis, the weather was threatening rain, not the snow of the home country, as Nathan rode tiredly into town. He was excited that he could actually be so close to his beloved, but keenly aware that at this late hour, he could do little to find Molly, he sought out a hotel for the night. He paid for his room with the money that Charles generously shared with him. As soon as he wolfed down supper in the dining room he made his way to his room and went to bed. All night his dreams were filled with a frightened Molly begging for his help but always floating away just out of his reach. Morning brought the sloppy rain and the realization that to continue his search, he needed money and that meant finding some work. Nathan went straight to the river front. Maybe he could load and unload cargo. He could earn some money and also to be on the lookout for the boat that Molly had been on. He tried to remember the deck hand's name who'd told him about Molly getting off the paddlewheel in Memphis. He found some quick work that would pay him by the day with no strings attached and that was just what he wanted. He worked the entire day without spying that boat and went back to the hotel feeling a little defeated. Working in the rain had left him with sore muscles and needing a nice hot bath. The hotel manager was willing to put the cost of a bath on the tab since Nathan had worked that day.

Molly woke up the next morning and stoked the fire. She peeked out the door and saw that the ground was covered with snow and it was still coming down. Their first snow was turning out to be a real blizzard. Well,

Nellie had to be milked this morning, she thought. A person can't even see in that swirling stuff. There were even drifts in the dog trot. Then Molly headed for the barn and made sure everything was secure. The little goat didn't give much milk, but that was a good thing. It meant she could go for a while without being milked.

"Now, don't you be eating your rope, Nellie. It's not food. I'll bring you some hay." She made sure there was enough fodder to last, filled the water trough with a bucket of water and then retreated to the cabin. Inside the kitchen, she cleaned out the stove and carried out the ashes and put them in a box. Boots lost no time in using the ashes for a toilet. He wasn't about to go out into the storm. With the storm howling, Molly didn't blame him. Maybe now he'd get over his shyness and come into the cozy kitchen and sit in her lap. That would help keep both of them warm

"See you later, Nellie," she called out before going back into the warm, Boots right on her heels.

Chapter 38

Earl and Preacher Brown were distressed when they woke up to the storm. Both men agonized over their decision not to turn back to Molly and Nathan's cabin. Even so, they had to continue on. They would just have to trust the Lord to take care of Molly until they could get back to her. Earl was trying not to be too worried, but it put an unsettled feeling in the pit of his stomach. He thought Preacher had heard his thoughts as the dear man began to quote Scripture, "Be careful for nothing, but in everything with prayer and supplication, let your petition be made known to God" Looking at Earl he finished, "And the peace of God shall guard your hearts and minds in Christ Jesus". "Yep, Earl, there's no time like the present to trust things to the One who makes us such wonderful promises. Let's get going!"

Both men arrived home looking like veritable snowmen. Sister Prue clucked over preacher and whispered things to him under her breath. Earl was a little curious how a couple their age seemed to be so kind to one another and solicitous. Back home, Pa and Ma rarely talked to one another and certainly not in the little sing song version this couple had. He made a mental note that this was the kind of marriage he wanted, if ever he had the chance.

Preacher had a one man sleigh and Earl started getting it ready to go back. The going would be slow but he was determined to get back to his sister. Prudence Brown brought out all the quilts and blankets she could spare for him to wrap up in and tucked a food basket in under them. Over and over she gave him instructions for birthing a baby, which embarrassed Earl to no end. He'd helped many times with the livestock, but he dreaded the thought that'd he'd have to help his sister. All the same, he assured Sister Prudence that he could take care of it, and at last he was on his way.

Molly sat in her beloved cabin in front of the fire, praying and rocking. She just couldn't believe what a feeling of peace she had now that she was home. It was as though she had been through a war, but now all that was behind her. She knew God had been with her all the time. Boots, no longer shy, had curled up in her lap. The baby Molly carried knotted up in a hard ball, but in Molly's inexperience she didn't recognize that this could be a contraction. The baby wasn't due for about another month, but the stress was beginning to take a toll. After a while, she began to notice a pattern to the knotting up of her stomach. "Oh, Lord," she prayed desperately. "Don't let it be my time, yet. It's too early" She got up and began to pace around the cabin, finding a few little things she could do without too much exertion. Eventually the contractions stopped and her mind eased. Sitting back into her rocker, she began to work through the sewing basket. She straightened the thread and the scraps of material. Morning turned to evening as the day passed and finally it was nightfall. Molly got up and peeked out at Nellie who greeted her with a soft bleat. She was laying in her little pile of straw and seemed quiet content. Feeling that everything was shipshape, Molly snuggled up under the heavy quilt on the little cot in the room. She stretched out, patted her stomach and fell asleep with the cat curled up by her side as though they'd never been apart.

It took the whole day for Earl to get back to the halfway house. From there he could push the weary horse no longer, so he settled in for the night. Although the wind had picked up howling some, he hoped that by morning light the snow would cease.

When Molly awakened the next morning snow was still falling lightly. Boots didn't want to budge from his warm spot when she got up, but when she pulled on the coverlet in an attempt to make the bed, he tumbled to the floor. The cabin was cold and his tail stood straight up.

"I know you weren't so anxious to get up, Boots," Molly soothed as she straightened her bed. "I could have stayed there in the warm myself, but there are chores to do and even if it is still snowing, I gotta get out there to Nellie."

Boots looked up to her and gave a slow meow to answer. Hesitantly he slipped out with her out to the dog trot and took care of his morning business as she gathered fire wood. Even though it was daybreak, the sky was very dark and the snow was beginning to come down hard again. Molly could barely make out the outline of outbuildings. Drifts were rising higher all around. As the wind picked up, small swirls of snow lifted and fell ever so softly. Molly kept up a silly chatter to the cat as she carried in the wood, stoked the fire in the stove, took care of her own morning toilet and then made some breakfast. She dropped three spoons of meal into a cup of boiling water. A little honey for sweetener and some of Nellie's milk to cool it down and her hunger was satisfied for the time being. Finally she was ready to check on her little goat. Dressing herself as warmly as she could, she took a rope from the wall and fastened it to a nail outside the door. Then holding it in her hand, she made her way to the little barn. It was hard walking through the now deep drifts but it wasn't far and soon she was in the barn out of the driving snow. She was greeted by an anxious Nellie as she secured the rope near the door. Now if the blizzard got too bad, at least she could find her way to the barn if she needed to. The warm water she brought with her had lost its heat and Nellie tried to kick out when Molly washed her teats.

"Calm down, girl," Molly soothed her. "I know this is cold, but I'll be through quick as a wink." When she'd finished, she poured the water into Nellie's drinking pail and then pulled down some hay for her. It must have taken only 15 or 20 minutes to finish the chore but to Molly it seemed she'd been out in the cold for hours. At last she closed, fastened the barn door and taking her pail of milk, struggled back into the cabin which by now was toasty warm. Inside, she removed her cloak, scarf and gloves and sank gratefully down into her chair. Feeling more than a bit winded, she noticed that her stomach was once again knotting up as it had the evening before. Molly leaned back rubbing her stomach gently to try and ease the discomfort. "Sleep little one," She coaxed softly. "You shouldn't be born until after Christmas and that is weeks away. We must wait for Papa to come home." She slowly rocked and sang to her unborn child.

Chapter 39

As Jeremy Barnes helped to tie off the boat he stared at the man who was working just a ways down the dock. He sure looked familiar. As if he could feel someone's eyes behind him, Nathan turned. Self-conscious at being caught staring, Jeremy tried to turn away. Nathan had seen him though and suddenly he was standing behind him.

"Excuse me young fellow, but do you remember a woman named Molly Smith who rode on this boat back in the summer?"

The question brought the memory of this man to Jeremy's mind. Of course, this was Molly's husband. He had come to meet the boat in New Orleans. "Yeah, I remember Molly. You her husband ain't you?"

"Yeah and you're the kid who told me she got off in Memphis."

"You mean you ain't found her yet?"

"No kid, I ain't. I need your help."

"Sure, mister. Soon as I'm through here, I'll take you where I last saw her."

Suddenly Nathan had him by the collar. Jeremy began to choke and sputter as the larger man pulled him half off his feet.

"I think it'll be now," Nathan roared, feeling all the rage that he had pent up for months. That feeling of being so close, yet so far away from his Molly was just about the most terrible feeling he'd ever had. Suddenly other crew members spotted the commotion and came running.

"Fight!" Someone shouted. As soon as it was discovered that it was man against boy however, it was three against one as Nathan was grabbed and shoved against the boat. Suddenly he found himself falling into the icy cold water of the Mississippi River. When Jeremy caught his breath, he shoved against his rescuers and raced to grab Nathan and pulled him back.

"Leave him alone!" He shouted to his friends. "He wasn't gonna hurt me! Leave him alone!"

Everyone backed up just staring down at the soaking man who lay panting at Jeremy's feet.

"You alright? Mister, are you alright?" Jeremy asked repeatedly.

"Thanks, kid. I'm sorry I lost my temper. It's just that...."

"It's okay, I'll help you. We'll find her. Waving a hand behind him towards one of his buddies he instructed, "Hey, Jacob, tell Captain, I got some business needs taking care of. I'll work doubles tonight to make up for any lost time."

"Sure kid. I'll tell him."

Jeremy helped Nathan to his feet. "We gotta get you some dry clothes first. Then I'll take you to the person who knows where Molly went."

Back at his room, Nathan quickly changed clothes and then the two men hurried out and headed toward the brothel where Jeremy had last seen Molly. Both men seemed in a hurry and it wasn't long till they were up on the porch at Ruby's place. Jeremy pounded on the door until at last Ruby herself came to the door. Her sour expression changed when she saw Nathan's handsome face.

"Well, hello boys." she crooned. "We're not really open for business yet, but I'm sure I can bend the rules for the likes of you." She reached up to touch Nathan's collar. With obvious annoyance Nathan removed her hand.

"What's the matter, mister? You don't like Old Ruby? Why don't you come on in and let's get acquainted?"

Nathan turned to Jeremy. "You brought Molly *here*?" He asked in disbelief.

Jeremy's face turned cherry red partly out of embarrassment, partly in fear.

"I don't know that many people in Memphis, Mr. Smith. I couldn't just turn her loose in a strange place." To Ruby he said, "Listen, this is real important. You remember that young girl I brought up here last summer? You remember you told me she said she had friends here in Memphis."

Nathan's rebuff had made Ruby feel surly. "Naw, I don't remember nobody. Now if you gents ain't here for business then I suggest you leave." With that she stepped back into the door and attempted to shut it in their faces. Nathan quickly blocked her way. "I think you do remember and you would be wise to remember quickly."

"I don't know where she went. She took one look at this place and took off running."

For a moment anger swelled up in Nathan and he grabbed Ruby's arm. "Hey, let go!" she yelled. "I'm calling the law!"

Coming to his senses, Nathan turned loose. Ruby quickly slammed and locked the door.

"You mean, she really didn't have no friends here in Memphis?" Jeremy stammered.

"I didn't think she had." Nathan answered. "She'd never even been away from home until we were married."

"What'll we do now?"

"I don't know." Nathan felt like whipping something or somebody. "Try to figure out what she would have done, I guess. Let's try this way." Nathan strode off toward the more respectable part of town with Jeremy right at his heels. They walked in desperation for 30 minutes or so and finally stopped at a small park to rest.

"What now? This is a big city. She could be anywhere." The remorse Jeremy felt was overwhelming. He squirmed uncomfortably.

"I won't stop until I find her." Nathan stood to his feet.

"Look," Jeremy responded. "This ain't gonna work, us just running around everywhere. Would she have tried to contact you? You know, write a letter or something?"

"Yeah…maybe."

"Well, then. Just you write a letter and maybe you'll find her."

"Sure," Nathan said resignedly. Together the two men left the park and headed back toward the river. Later that evening Nathan sat down in his room and penned a letter to his friend Jake. Just in case, he enclosed a brief note to Molly.

"Dearest Molly, I'm sorry to have not come to you when you needed me most. I hope you're okay and I hope to be with you soon. Your loving husband, Nathan".

Chapter 40

Earl left the halfway house doggedly determined to get back to his sister, but the driving snowstorm forced him back. It was impossible to follow the trail in the blinding snow and the horse balked every step of the way. Cold and hungry, he settled back into the cabin and sat waiting out the storm and worrying about his sister. "Please God. Don't let anything happen to her."

There was nothing else to do but wait out the storm.

In the quiet of her own cabin Molly fretted. She didn't want to admit that she was uneasy, but alone in the storm, feeling contractions every so often, she really felt distraught. She tried to pass the time alternately rocking and pacing. Every so often she'd stop to replenish the fire. At least there was plenty of wood and enough food to eat. There was Boots for company and Nellie who needed attention. For two more days, while the storm raged on, Molly struggled with her chores and her animals. After having laid down for a little rest, she was unexpectedly awakened from a nap by complete silence. Quickly she got up and looked out to find that the snow had stopped altogether. She hurried out to the dogtrot. The skies had lightened. And, to Molly's delight, a slip of sun was shining and blue sky was peeking out. Everywhere the world was white and beautiful. The little creek gurgled down through the meadow, a ribbon of black down through the white wonderland. The little barn peeked out from the drifts and ice sickles hung from the eaves of the cabin. Across the meadow a rabbit hopped along on the crusty top of the snow. At one point he sunk down in a soft spot and Molly laughed as she watched him struggle out and hop on along. When Boots rubbed against her leg Molly realized she hadn't even grabbed her shawl. It was cold, so she hurried back inside. Her mood lifted, she laughed and sang and went to her little kitchen to prepare some lunch. Thankfully the pains had stopped.

Earl too was glad to see that the storm had stopped. He wasted no time harnessing up the sled and heading out toward Molly's place. The sun was shining, the horse was frisky and the sled fairly flew over the crusted new snow. With the trees now bare and the world so clean and white you could see a long way. Deer darted in the distance. Rabbits were seen scampering everywhere. Earl was ravenous, but there was no time. He just wanted to get to Molly.

Molly shared her meal with Boots and then busily cleaned her little house. Suddenly she felt great; full of energy and pep and happy as a lark. She straightened things that didn't even need straightening. She folded and refolded all her little baby things. Before she knew it the day had passed. She was thinking about refolding a baby blanket when she heard a horse neigh outside. "Nathan!" she cried, running to the door. Instead it was Earl who rode in.

"Earl!" She hugged him shyly. "Where did you get that sleigh?"

"I got it from Pastor Brown," He answered. "You'd better get back in there where it's warm."

"Oh, but it feels warm out here. Look the sun is shining."

"No, the sun is setting. You get on in and let me put this horse in the barn."

"Okay, I'll go in. I'll put us on some supper."

Inside she hurried to warm some beans and get out some bread. It was a good thing she had felt so good today. There was plenty of victuals for Earl's supper.

When they finally sat down to their meal, Earl took her hand and bowed his head. "Thank you Lord for watching out for my sister and thank you for this food we are about to receive."

"And Lord, please watch out for Nathan, wherever he is and bring him home safe." Molly added. After supper, Earl took care of the outside chores and then he and Molly sat in front of the fire and talked way into the night. Morning brought back the sunshine and as the day warmed up the heavy snow began to melt. All day they listened to the drip, drip, drip as the snow melted from the roof. Once they heard a huge thud and it gave them both a start. Earl said it was a slab of snow sliding off the rooftop and he and Molly laughed. By that evening there was hardly any snow left, only mud. The first snow had come and gone and the weather would be warmer for a while. Boots followed Earl outside when he went to milk Nellie and see to Jake's horse. When they came back in, he rubbed his muddy little body up against Molly's legs and skirt.

"Oooh you dirty little rascal! Now, just look at what you've done to my skirt." She scolded. Boots went over and plopped in front of the stove and began to clean up. She and Earl were having such fun together. It was so different than when they were at home. Fun then was only when they were outside away from Pa and his constant foul mood. Now they laughed together as they washed the dishes and replenished the fire. It was wonderful. They were fast becoming friends, able to rely on one another instead of depending on their parents. For the second night in a row, they sat up late just talking. Finally they were off to bed and before long, Earl was snoring away. Molly wasn't sleeping though. The pangs had returned and this time she had a feeling that they might not go away. At some point she slipped out of bed, wrapped one of the lighter blankets around her shoulders and sat in her rocker in front of the fire. Careful not to disturb her brother, she sat and rocked and petted her cat as he lay curled in her lap. When the fire got low, she stirred the embers and wrapped more closely in her blankets. When the morning came, she knew she should be starting Earl's breakfast but the nagging pain was getting more intense. When Earl got up, she was just sitting there quietly, holding her cat and shivering because the fire had burned down low. Alarmed, he got up and hurried to build up the fire again.

"Molly, you okay?"

"Oh, Earl," She answered. "I think the baby's coming and it's early. It shouldn't be for weeks yet."

"Don't worry Molly, I'm here and everything's going to be okay." He tried to soothe her. Inside his gut squirmed. He remembered the preacher's wife talking with him and he'd helped with calving and such. But he didn't know a hill of beans about women and birthing babies. Suddenly he didn't feel like such an adult. He was barely 16 after all and this was his own sister. He mustn't let on to her how scared he was. She needed him to be strong now.

"Do you need to lay down or something?" He asked. "Should I boil some water maybe?"

"No," She answered. "I think this is going to take a while. You go on out and take care of the animals while I take my toilet."

"Okay," He answered reluctantly.

When he left, she stood up. "Oh, Boots. My feet are asleep from sitting so long." But when she looked down, she was surprised at how swollen they were. She hobbled painfully to take care of her personal morning chores and then decided to lay down after all. When Earl came in he found her in the bed.

"You okay?" he asked, feeling her flushed forehead.

"Yeah," She answered. "Go on now and fix you some breakfast. No need to fuss over me all morning."

"You want any breakfast?"

"No. I think I may try to sleep now. I've been awake all night."

Earl could hardly take his eyes off her as she slept. She was restless and moaned sometimes when the pains came, but she did sleep and Earl just sat watching her. He wished someone would come but he didn't dare to leave her alone.

Chapter 41

At the Mercantile, Jake was sorting the mail just brought in. He was thankful that the snow was gone and hoped that Earl had gotten back to Molly okay. He couldn't believe it as he spied a certain envelope in the pile. A letter from Nathan! He let out a whoop and quickly tore it open. His friend was found! The note from Nathan scrawled the information that he was staying at a hotel in Memphis. He was also frantic to find news of Molly. He continued with telling Jake that he could open any letters for him from Molly and wanted to know where in Memphis she was.

Jake wasted no time dashing off a reply and left the store unattended hastening to catch the boat with the letter before it left. Then he hurried off to Preacher Brown's to give them the news. Once he got to the house, he found that Prudence Brown was getting things together to go to be with Molly. Now that the storm was passed she was in a real hurry to get to her young friend. The slushy snow was creating a muddy mess in the yard and the anxious horse kept side stepping as Prudence Brown attempted to place her foot in the stirrup. She was more accustomed to riding in the wagon.

"Now, Old Red, you just hold still for a minute here," She scolded him. At last she was up in the saddle.

"I'll be praying, Prue!" Preacher told her. "You be careful now. I really don't have any business letting you go out there by yourself."

"Don't you worry too much about me," She answered. "Fifty years of living, I've learned I can pretty much take care of what needs doing. With these skies blue as they are now I don't expect any more bad weather for a bit. I'll be to Molly before noon tomorrow." And with that she waved to the two men and took off.

"That gal of mine is a strong woman and stubborn to boot," Preacher commented to Jake as he smiled fondly waving to his wife as he watched her go around the bend in the road and disappear.

"She sure manages to be around when somebody needs her." Jake answered. "I guess she's helped birth every young'un around here for the last twenty years."

"Well, since we didn't have any young'uns of our own, she feels kinda like its her mission to mother everybody else's. I sure have been worried about that little Molly though. I wish I knew what happened to Nathan."

"I was figuring you'd want to know. I got a letter. I sent an answer back down on the boat. Should get to him in three days or so. If he takes the train, he'll be home by the end of the week."

"Thank the Lord!" Preacher was excited. "I been praying about this state of affairs for months, and now looks like I'm seein' an answer to them prayers. Got time to come in for something to eat?"

"Nope, store's been closed all morning. I gotta get back to it. Just wanted to share a little good news.

Earl kept a close watch on Molly all day. His concern was growing. She was feverish now and was so restless that the quilts on the bed kept slipping to the floor. He bathed her face and tried his best to talk real sweet and soft to her but he just didn't know what else to do. Sending out a little prayer to the heavens, he kept watching her. By the end of the day, Molly was very sick and still the baby had not been born. Now, not only her feet, but her whole body seemed swollen. She talked out of her head. When Earl was bending over her trying to cool her face with a cloth, she reached up and patted his face, but her face looked far beyond him.

"Oh, Nathan, I knew you'd come. I'm so glad you're here. Did you see our baby girl? Isn't she just the sweetest thing?"

Tears rolled down Earl's face as he talked softly to his sister. He was thinking maybe this marriage thing was just awful. Who'd want to put a little gal through all this? Still he kept on soothing her best he could.

"Hang in there Molly. Everything's going to be okay."

Throughout the long night and the next morning Earl sat with her, never leaving her side. He dozed occasionally but every little noise from Molly brought him instantly awake. Earl had looked out the window as he made a fresh pot of black scalding coffee and saw that the dawn was beginning to show just on the horizon. No sign of anyone, so he went back to Molly. Next thing he knew, someone was knocking at the door and there was Prudence Brown. Earl was never so glad to see someone.

"Sister Prue! Molly needs help bad. She's been sick for two days and I just didn't know what to do. You gotta help her!"

He took the older woman by the hand and led her to Molly's bed.

"Ma?" Molly called anxiously. "Ma? Is that You?"

"No, Honey, it's me, Sister Prue. Let's see what we got here. Earl, you get me some soap and hot water. I need to wash up and get started. We gotta get this baby born so Molly can get better."

"Yes'm!" Earl was more than glad to let Sister Prue take over Molly's care. He did what Sister Prue asked of him and then he went outside to pace up and down the porch.

After scrubbing her hands vigorously, she wasted no time in breaking the water sac to speed up the birthing process. In about three hours time, a tiny baby girl was born. Prudence quickly washed and dressed the little thing and called out for Earl. He ran right back into the cabin for fear of his sister and was amazed as Sister Prue gave her to Earl so she could get back to Molly.

Earl was in awe of the tiny baby. He'd never seen one quite this small but she was making plenty of noise and waving those little arms around. The clothes Molly had made literally swallowed her up, but they were warm and soft. Earl kept trying to adjust them with his large clumsy hands. Finally Prudence noticed and came over to them.

"Let me show you how to wrap a newborn, Earl." With experienced fingers she took the blanket and wrapped the tiny one up like a sausage with only her face peeking out. "Now you sit down in that chair and rock her a while. I've gotta get this girl's fever down."

Molly didn't even know she'd given birth. Instead, she floated in and out of sleep dreaming of the spring when she and Nathan had fallen in love.

"Molly," she pictured Nathan laughing as she sat in the dirt trying to plant potatoes. "If you're going to sit down every time you put one in the ground, you'll still be planting the potatoes when I'm already digging up the carrots."

"It's easier on my back to sit instead of bending over."

"No, I think it's easier to daydream, when you're sitting instead of bending over." Nathan reached over and plucked her up. Instead of standing up, Molly pulled her feet up forcing Nathan to lift her completely off the ground. He immediately lost his balance and they both tumbled to the ground. Suddenly they were rolling around, squealing and playing as if they hadn't a care in the world.

"So much for the gardening," Nathan said, picking her up and carrying her to a secluded spot just underneath a large oak tree. She remembered him raining kisses upon her laughing face until she stopped laughing and wrapped her trembling arms around his neck. She breathed in the scent of him and relished the strength of his loving arms. He gently touched and caressed her, marveling at her quick response. She remembered him whispering to her,

"Girl, I don't know how I ever lived without you!" The sight of him so close to her made her moan in her fever, and then she watched as he floated just away. She felt herself crying out to him and could hear a soft noise coming from somewhere beyond herself. It was the tiny cry of her newborn that brought Molly back to reality.

"My baby!" She whispered anxiously, trying to raise up on one shoulder, but having no strength to raise up or to talk louder, she fell back onto the cot in a heap.

"Are you awake, Molly?" Sister Prudence came quickly and checked out her young patient. "You've broken a sweat. I declare I believe the fever is gone. Oh Molly, dear, you've been away from us for three whole days. Thank the good Lord, I believe you're gonna be fine!"

"Can I see my baby?" Molly asked again, smiling faintly at Sis Prue. As always this dear woman of God was coming to her rescue. Molly suspected she'd been with her for a while and felt again that pang of wanting her own mother, but thankful for this "motherly" woman.

"Why sure, Honey. Earl bring the little thing over here to see her Mommy."

Feeling a little surge of strength at getting to see her baby, Molly raised her head to see the little bundle Earl brought to her.

"It's a little girl," He said, feeling so proud to show off his little niece.

With shaking fingers Molly pulled back the blanket to see her face. "She's so tiny." She said in awe.

"Well," Prudence said. "Best as I can tell, she's come about a month early I'd say. "Wish I had that scale from the Mercantile. I'm guessing she's 'bout 4 pounds and she's healthy as can be. Thank goodness for Nellie's milk. She's had a little of that for two days, but as soon as you can feel strong enough, I'll let you try and feed her. Let's get Molly propped up a bit, Earl, and we'll see if Molly might like to hold her for a little bit." Clucking over both babe and mother, Sis Prue folded up an extra quilt and replaced the pillows. "Now, here, Earl, hand me that little bundle. I know her ma is ready to love on her. Then I'm gonna get her up and get her bathed and clean her bed real good."

Later, after Molly cleaned up and ate a bite of food, she did feel stronger. Earl and Sis Prue helped her to the rocker. Gently she rocked her daughter, nursing and singing a soft lullaby.

Chapter 42

Nathan stood impatiently at the ticket window waiting for the man to count his change. His hand kept going to his pocket where Jake's wrinkled letter was. The message had been short and to the point. Molly was at home! He couldn't believe his eyes as he went on to read that his first born child would be here soon. A baby! He and Molly had a real family now. God nor man could ever part them ever again, once he arrived at home. Time couldn't move fast enough. With his ticket purchased, Nathan could hardly wait for the train to depart. Sitting still, however, was impossible. He paced restlessly. An older man got his attention long enough to stop the pacing.

"Where might you be headed young man?"

"Home," Nathan answered, beaming. "Home to my family!"

"I'm headed toward Chicago, myself," The man answered. Thus began a little friendly conversing between the two strangers. It sure helped to calm Nathan down and soon he found himself boarding the train and heading on his way, followed by his new found companion. There was no sleeping on this trip. The men discussed everything from hunting ,fishing and trapping, to tanning hides and building cabins. The older man talked of his own youth when he too had forged out a home in the wilderness. Now he chose to live in a big town, having grown weary of the difficult wilderness life. Besides, as the man explained, his family had all grown up and moved away. Once his wife got sick, they figured it was time to get closer to "civilization".

At last the train pulled into the station at Springhill and Nathan shook hands with the man, wished him a safe trip and they parted company. On foot now, with a pack to carry, Nathan struck out on the muddy trail for the ten mile trek to Jake's place. Although he felt he could probably run the entire way, it was wonderful to take in the sights of home. In the blue November sky above him, geese winged their way south. In the trees around him squirrels took advantage of the last warm days to get a few more seeds and nuts stored up for the hard winter to come. Just ahead a deer crossed the trail. Nathan barely noticed as he felt himself push his tired hungry body on another mile and another until at last the Mercantile came into few. Jake bounded out the door as he saw Nathan coming down the street. He was glad to see his old friend. Soup was warming on the stove and ladeled up and eaten quickly. Even though Nathan tried to insist on going on to the homestead, Jake reassured him that Molly was not alone and it would be best that he slept here for the night. With growing weariness taking over knowing that Molly was okay, at last he slept. He was up at first light and could hardly contain himself. Morning brought colder temperatures but no threat of precipitation. Jake put ham and eggs on the table and the whole story came tumbling out. Everything, including the robbers, the Turners and the memory loss of recent events. He questioned all that Jake knew about Molly and was given the packet of letters she had written from Miss Dorothy's. There would be time enough to read them later. He was only a day and a half's journey from her and was anxious to be on his way. He grabbed his friend's hand, put on his hat and, taking Jake's remaining horse, he hit the trail to cover the final distance that separated him from his young bride. It would be the fastest trip he'd ever taken. His Molly was waiting for him!

Molly held the babe close while she ate her dinner. In fact, Molly just didn't want to even put her down, not even for a minute. "Land's sake, girl!", Miss Prue had clucked, "This tiny girl is gonna be some spoiled if you don't let her rest some on her own!" Still and all Prue understood. Although she'd never held her own, she loved on many a small child in their congregation along the years and this little mite was no different.

Since Molly was so worn out, she didn't wake up to the sounds of breakfast cooking. Earl and Miss Prudence let her sleep in at breakfast but now she was stirring. Molly was feeling wonderful and woke up hungry as all get out. They laughed together and both women looked over the little miracle checking again first one hand and then the other, adjusting the sleeping bonnet and the diaper. Earl was amazed at how women were about babies. He wondered if his ma had felt the same way about him. Somehow he found comfort for his own life in this scene before him. Maybe he could find himself a wife and have a passel of kids himself. He smiled as he looked at his sister again. She was even prettier now that she had this baby.

In spite of her early arrival and the face of her tiny existence, the adorable little cherub was thriving. As Molly was admiring their little gift from the Lord, there was a cold rush of wind. Molly adjusted the blanket quickly and looked for the culprit of the cold air. The door had been flung open and even though Molly was still weak she was on her feet rushing to the arms of the handsome man who stood there. Her beloved husband had found his way back to her. Then his arms were holding both her and the baby tight against him. Tears of joy flowed down her face as she looked up into his eyes once again. Earl quickly closed the door behind them to shut out the cold. Finally, Nathan released his hold on her just a little, though, as he'd promised himself and God Almighty, he never intended to let go of her completely again. They went to sit on the cot together and Molly began to gently pull the blanket back from a tiny fuzzy haired infant.

"Nathan, this is our daughter. I hope you don't mind, but I called her Faith. It just seemed right somehow, that she be given a name that went with our life. Throughout the summer, I kept faith in my heart that we would find each other again and be a family."

Nathan took his little daughter and held her gently in his big strong hands.

"Faith." He smiled and turned to gaze at Molly's face. He couldn't keep his eyes off of either one of his beautiful girls. "I see how your faith in God has only gotten stronger. As for mine, well, I can say, I couldn't have made it without Him being with me, with you, with us. I'm here for you now and with God's help I will be here for you always."

Molly knew in her heart that what he said was true. Silently she thanked God that her little Faith would have a father that was strong and yet not rough. Gentle and yet not weak. Nathan was going to be the kind of father to their children that she'd always dreamt about. A father who could love his little daughter. And, she would have a daughter who would never be afraid. She realized all of a sudden that God does indeed answer prayers, even ones that were whispered in secret when she was just a little girl. With that she began to hum a little lullaby.

Chapter 43

In some woods not far from the river, men were cutting trees. It was cold and snowy but they worked just the same. The hard work kept the blood flowing and provided warmth to the body. With the sap not flowing, the trees were lighter and easier to cut. Nearby, the mules waited patiently for the next log to pull. They liked the winter too; no pesky flies to bite and sting. From the nostrils of both man and beast, foggy white breath was exhaled. A loud cracking noise signaled a tall tree coming down. It didn't make it to the ground, however. The top caught against another tree and it leaned precariously. For a split second there was silence, then voices began to swear and complain.

"Sam!" One man hollered out agitated at the situation, "I do believe it's your turn to do the dirty work."

"I ain't doing it. I'll be a son of a gun if it ain't Johnson's turn. He'd better do it."

Johnson responded. "You'll do what you're told, Meyers, or you ain't workin for me."

With his usual menacing scowl, Meyers cursed under his breath, "I'll get it down alright. You watch me, I'll get it down."

He strode over in a huff to the tree that was keeping the other timber from falling to the forest floor. Angrily he began to chop, one two, one two.

"Hold it! Hold it!" Meyers, thought he heard someone shout but kept right on chopping.

With a mighty groan the suspended tree began to sway and Meyers realized that he had in fact heard a warning. The mules scurried in fright as their tack jangled in the frosty air. As Sam Meyers turned to run, his boot got entangled with the mule's reigns. He realized too late that his angry response was gonna cost him this time. As the tree began to fall, time seemed suspended. Limbs brushed his back and he was propelled to the ground. For a moment he was stunned. While he strangely felt no pain, he knew the big tree was pinning him down. It was eerily quiet for just a moment as the earth seemed to acknowledge the situation. Suddenly, men were scurrying forward with axes and saws. Mules were hastily unharnessed and brought around to the tree. Chains were tied to it as well. As if the sounds were coming from far away, Sam could hear the commands given to the mules.

"Gee, boy. Pull, pull, pull."

As the tree was pulled from his mangled body, the pain came like a flood. Meyers screamed in agony and then blessed blackness covered him. When he came to himself, he realized that someone was trying to clean his face. He had thrown up his lunch.

"We've got to get this man to some help." His boss stood over him while others looked on.

"Where will we take him? We're miles from any house." Most of the men really didn't care much what happened to Meyers. Although they were all a pretty seedy lot, even they thought Meyers was a hard and mean fella. He never helped anyone and often took advantage of the younger men.

Once he had mentioned a family and Ol' Grub hollered and guffawed, "You married? God Almighty man, she must be some woman to be puttin up with the likes a you!"

Johnson thought for a moment. "Didn't he talk about knowin' that trapper in the big meadow over towards the hills?'

"Yeah", another man responded. "He did for a fact."

"His cabin is not that far. We'll take him there. Maybe they'll take him off our hands." He started to laugh, but felt better of it. Don't kick a man when he's down, he thought, not even a no good fella like Meyers.

They took two poles and fashioned an Indian sled out of them with some rope. After they made sure it would hold, they carefully lifted the injured man and laid him on it. Again, Meyers hollered out in agony.

Great sweat drops formed on his forehead and his upper lip. Blankets that smelled of sweaty unwashed bodies were wrapped around him to keep him warm. The sled was harnessed to a mule. Then the boss motioned for a couple of men to go along with him and they led the homemade gurney down the snowy path toward the cabin of a man they all thought to be Samuel Meyers friend.

Nathan was in the yard splitting wood for the fire, his jacket laying on the woodpile, having been abandoned with the heat of the work. He needed to stock up before any more winter weather same through. He wanted to make sure his tiny new born daughter would be kept safe and warm. He turned when he heard the shouts of the men bringing Sam Meyers to his door. At first he was unaware who the injured man was.

"Hey!" one of the men was yelling. "We got an injured man here. We need some help."

Nathan hurried to see. One look at the man being packed in by mule and Nathan's face turned to stone.

"You'll not leave him here. Take him somewhere else. Better yet, leave him right here. He can rot for all I care. I'd take better care of a bobcat than I would him. He ain't welcome here, by God and all His creation!"

The men from the wood hawk camp were astonished.

"Why, it's the dead of winter," one of the hawks called out, as the others nodded their heads in agreement, "he won't survive if we try to take him further."

"I said you won't leave him here!" Nathan held up his axe for a moment, thinking he could end this all right now. This group of hard hearted men were aghast at the response. Nathan struck the axe in a piece of wood and turned toward his cabin and opened the door. "Best get him outta here before I decide to take matters into my own hands!"

Molly heard her husband's unusually harsh voice outside and was compelled to see what the commotion was all about. Spying the men and the mule packing someone, she ran into the yard without bothering to get a wrap. Nathan tried to grab her by the arm, "Molly, don't look! It's just a piece of trash." When she saw the injured man her face blanched and her hand flew to her mouth.

"Bring him in." she said.

"I won't *have* him in my house!" Nathan bellowed.

"Nathan, I wouldn't turn away a sick dog. I can't turn away my own Pa."

Ignoring Nathan's flaming stare, Molly brushed past him and opened the door wide so that the men could carry Sam into the cabin. She instructed them to lay him on the bed. Nathan did nothing to help. Sam groaned in pain. Molly pulled away the stinking blankets and handed them back to the men. They stood in silence not knowing what to do. Nathan glared at them and reluctantly they all filed out of the cabin. For a minute, the boss stood at the door, trying to figure out something to say. As Nathan walked towards the door, he turned quickly and left with the others. Nathan watched them leave, thinking his wife had lost her mind.

Molly set to work, assessing the situation and began trying to remove Sam's tattered clothing but she wasn't strong enough to lift him. Childbirth had left her weak and she didn't sleep much because of the baby's feeding schedule, up every 3 hours, feeding for at least 30 minutes each time was wearying but worth it. Nathan saw his wife struggling. Finally, he could stand it no longer and went over to help. He didn't say a word as he lifted the injured man like a sack of flour and helped to remove the shirt and trousers. Molly went for a basin of water and began to bathe her father. He screamed in pain at every touch. While there was very little blood, except for a cut here and there, his injuries didn't seem apparent but she could tell something was very wrong. As she tried to get him to help a little, she saw that he wasn't able to move his legs. They just hung there as though they were inanimate objects not even attached to Meyers. After some cleaning up and giving him a drink of milk and a bowl of bean juice, the story of what happened began to unfold. He did manage to tell them that a tree had fallen on him. Finally he was resting a little.

"Someone should go for Ma." Molly said as wiped her brow and sat in a heap in her rocker. She was exhausted and Nathan knew it.

"I'm not leaving you and Faith alone, especially not with him here." Nathan said. He wanted to snarl again, but Molly had begged him not to.

"Nathan, we got to do right no matter what he's done, so that God will look down favorably on us. We got to forgive"

He replied, "The weather could get bad and you can't tend this man without my help. Meyers was going in and out of a restless sleep. Faith began to cry and Molly went to her. Wearily she sat down in the rocker and began to nurse her infant. Nathan glanced at their bed. He and Molly would need a place to sleep. Taking an empty mattress tick from a drawer, he headed for the barn to fill it with fresh hay. They would have to sleep on the floor. That just about made him curse.

With Faith fed and changed, Molly walked to the kitchen to start supper. No sooner than she started to peel a potato, her father cried out. She hurried to his side. He wanted to go to the outhouse.

"You can't go." She told him. "You'll have to wait for Nathan to help you."

When Nathan came in it was too late. Once more she cleaned him. Later she tried to feed him potato soup but he was too sick to eat. The night was hard. Between her father and her infant, she hardly slept at all. Reluctantly Nathan cared for Samuel the next day, allowing Molly to get a little rest. Two days passed by in monotony of caring for the one man neither of them thought they'd ever have to see again.

They woke up the third morning and saw that Earl was riding up into the yard. The wood hawks had gotten word to them and he had come to help. Molly rushed to him and wrapped her arms around his neck. She was so glad to see him. He had rescued her once and here he was again. Nathan was glad for the first time since the wood hawks had brought Samuel to their door. Earl could lift his father and bathe him. Nathan could get back to his trapping and not worry about Molly and the baby. Earl looked at Faith with pride.

"I told Ma about her." Molly smiled and a tear crept from the corner of her eye. Ma, my how she wanted to see her Ma.

"She's changing and growing like a little weed!" he exclaimed. He picked up the bundle. Tiny fists waved in the air and bright little eyes looked into his face. She worked her little mouth until she forced out a sound.

"She's talking to me." Earl laughed with absolute joy! From across the hall Earl heard the all too familiar voice of his father.

"Earl? That you boy?" Earl looked at Molly as he tenderly laid the baby down and answered his father, thinking how weak the man's voice was. He went to see him in the other room.

"Yeah, Pa. It's me."

"Did you bring me some tabacky?" Pa bellowed, even though they were in the same room.

"No, Pa." Earl answered. "Sorry." The old feeling knotting up in his stomach. Thinking to himself that he was a man now, but that Pa still held that old feeling over him.

"You sorry all right. You always was." Meyers' head fell back on the pillow forlornly.

Earl's face burned beet red. He looked at his Father lying there feeble and vulnerable. He had come to help and already his Pa was criticizing. How he ached to hear some kind of praise or a good word. All Earl's life, he'd just wanted the one thing it seemed his Pa could never give. He could see that wasn't ever going to happen. He turned his attention back to his sister and his niece.

"Earl," his Father whined, "Can you come back here? I need some help."

Reluctantly, Earl walked to the bed and looked down into Pa's face. Sam's face held a gray pallor and there were shadows under his eyes where deep circles had taken hold. Up until this moment, Earl hadn't dared to look his Pa in the eye. The comprehension of the frailty of the man lying there shocked him. This was not a man to fear. This was a shell of a man, still trying to roar like a lion but unable to turn himself over. Overcome with the severity of his pa's circumstances, pity filled Earl's heart. Letting out a sigh, he bent to help the man who had always been so incredibly cruel to him and his siblings. It just didn't matter any longer that Earl's father couldn't understand his own hard heartedness. Earl half prayed half cursed to himself and made a silent pledge to try to forgive the man on his own. It seemed to lighten Earl's own feelings as he made his decision.

Molly for one was relieved to have Earl there. She was finally able to get some much needed rest. It was great for Nathan too as it gave him someone to talk to and help with the daily chores. Since Thanksgiving was approaching, the couple was determined to make this week extra special. Nathan went to the woods to get a deer. Molly was hoping he would be successful. Maybe he could even find a persimmon tree with some fruit still hanging, for a tart sweet pie. When he returned a few hours later, he was grinning from ear to ear. "That buck I been spying finally let up on his wariness. I got a shot off before he could turn and run." Nathan proudly displayed the huge set of antlers still on the prize. Earl went out to help him with the meat. Nathan had field dressed it out in the woods, being careful to make every piece of meat count, before bringing it in. Now he and Earl cleaned the carcass with fresh straw. They suspended the deer from a tree upside down by the hooves. With expert precision the hide was cut away. It was obvious that Nathan has learned how to dress an animal as a young boy. As the men worked to prepare the meat, Molly was alone with Pa and the baby. Butchering took a long time. Molly made potato soup and sat down to feed Pa. He refused to feed himself, so she spooned it to his mouth. He was perfectly capable of lifting the spoon and she felt resentment well up inside each time she lifted a bite to his mouth. Inside she was seething, but on the outside she was the perfect patient dutiful daughter. She tried to repress her feelings but silent tears began to flow down her cheeks. At last she wiped his mouth and took the empty bowl away. Not so much as a thank from the man who could do nothing for himself. Well, at least not much. Maybe he could do a little more than he let on. Molly was feeling lots of emotions at the thought of once again being used by the man who was so abusive to them all.

She walked through the cold dogtrot to the kitchen only to realize that Faith had been crying. She picked up her infant and sat down in the rocker to nurse her. She was unexpectedly overcome with a rush of emotions and she began to sob. Startled, the baby also cried. When Nathan and Earl walked in, they found Molly pacing the floor with her screaming infant in arms. From across the dogtrot, Meyers was yelling. Earl went to see about his pa and Nathan led Molly back to the rocker, petting her shoulder and helping with Faith.

"I'm a bad daughter!" Molly cried out in anguish. "I don't want him here. I don't love my own Pa. I don't want to take care of him. I just can't take care of him anymore. When I left home to be with you, I thought I was away from him for good. But now I know, he's never leaving. He's always going to be in my life. I just can't take this!" Heavy sobs racked her body as she slumped in the rocker. All the feelings that she had held back for her entire life, including the terrible thing her pa did by stealing her, yes, stealing her away from Nathan, came streaming out.

Nathan squatted down beside the chair and with a gentle hand, lifted Molly's swollen wet face and pushed back a straggle of hair. "You could never be a bad daughter, Molly. You have done the best you could for an ungrateful man. It's going to be alright. We are going to work this out. You don't have anything to worry about. You'll never have anything to worry about ever again." Then he stood up and walked across the dogtrot. He picked up the mattress from the floor and carried it across to the kitchen. Earl had returned to the room and upon hearing their conversation was worried that Nathan might be ready to put Meyers out. He followed Nathan anxiously.

"For a while," Nathan told him, "Molly and I and the baby are going to live on this side of the cabin and you and your Pa will live on the other. It's just too much for Molly. So much trouble and hurt from his hand. I should never have let the wood hawks leave him here."

"He had to stay somewhere," Earl answered, "Or else he would have died. I wish there'd been something else they coulda done. Sometimes I wish Pa coulda just…" As Earl's voice trailed off, too afraid to speak what was really on his heart, deep inside, he ached for his sister. He knew the torment she was feeling. Pa had always dished out more mistreatment to her, probably because she was the oldest. There was some relief in Earl's mind that never again could the old man draw a hand back to him. He knew that one day this day would come and he could walk out on the old man. Already he felt that he was becoming more of a man, more ready to handle his own responsibility. Pa's demands and harsh words were becoming less and less effective to him. More and more, he saw this shell of a man before him. A shell of a man who was old, worn out and hurt. Only for Molly the pain continued. He figured she was feeling every ill treatment their pa ever dished out over and over again, each time she had to wait on him. The insolence of the sickly old man just made Earl a little sicker.

Silently Earl prayed for his Sister. Prayed that she'd find the faith and the strength to overcome the past. Prayed that somehow she'd be able to forgive. Not so much for Pa's sake, but for her own, so that she could deal with it, so that she could be happy and lighthearted again. All Earl wanted was to see Molly happy and he had seen that before their pa was brought here. He'd do whatever he could to keep the load of caring for Pa off of Molly's fragile shoulders.

Molly was comforted that she didn't have to see her Pa. The remorse she felt about her feelings, however, gnawed at her. She went about her tasks acting as if she was cheerful, but deep inside, her heart ached so much. Partly for the loss of a father's love she saw mirrored in her own Nathan as he dealt with little Faith and partly for her own inability to just forgive and forget. She thought of the words in the Bible: 'Honor thy father and thy mother that thy days may be long upon the land which the Lord thy God giveth thee.' How do you honor someone who has never given a reason to be honored?

At last it was Thanksgiving day and Molly prepared a fresh venison roast . There were only turnip greens for vegetables as that was the only crop that still grew unattended in the garden. Molly tried to be thankful when she Earl and Nathan bowed their heads for prayer, but she felt deceitful. Her heart was full of resentment, not thanksgiving. Resentment hung on her shoulders like toe sacks full of rocks. It was weighing her down no matter what she tried to do to shake it off. This should be a joyous day. It was her first Thanksgiving with her husband and her newborn daughter. After months of anxious separation the two of them were together and had much to make up for lost time. Try as she might to shake the image of the horrors she'd been through, Molly just could not set aside her feelings against the man who had caused all her childhood pain to top it off with the separation from her new husband.

Earl quietly got up and made a plate of food and carried it across to his father. He stoically fed him and cleaned him and made him as comfortable as possible.

"Earl," Sam pleaded like he did every day, "Take me home to your Ma."

"Can't do that right now, Pa." Earl shook his head, "It's winter and you're not well enough to travel."

"You take me anyway," Sam demanded, wielding his weak fist through the air. "I'm your Pa and you do what I say!"

Earl just looked at the man then turned and walked back across the dogtrot.

Molly and Nate were sitting at the table. The baby slept snuggly and contentedly in the little crate they'd fashioned into a bed.

"He wants to go home." Earl stated matter of factly.

Molly quickly stood to her feet. "Take him! If that's what he wants, take him."

Earl stared at his sister. He could see the emotions displayed across her face. He knew the grief that she had suffered from the actions of their Father but his thoughts were far more practical.

"Can't move him just yet, Mol," He answered. "I know his mouth is full of bitterness but he's just not strong enough."

Molly's face became rigid. She knew that. She just didn't care. Feeling that she was trapped in a situation that once again she could not get out of, she started stacking the dishes from the meal. Slinging them was more like it. After nearly breaking a plate, she realized how she was behaving and deliberately forced herself to slow down and get a hold of herself. The men got up from the meal and went outside where they made their way to the wood pile and began to work. One was splitting, the other tossing, the split wood into a pile.

"She's been through too much," Nathan began to speak aloud what both men were thinking while they were busy. He finally conceded, "I don't think she can take the pressure much longer."

"Yeah, I know," Earl replied. "I can deal with it. I'm not afraid of Pa anymore. But with Molly it runs too deep. I don't remember ever seeing her so angry and resentful." He paused for a moment. "Nate, would you have a problem with me building a little lean to out back? Me and Pa could stay out there 'til I could get him home to Ma."

"No problem with it. It's too much work for one man though, Earl. I'll go fetch Frenchie. The three of us can put up a little cabin pretty quick."

Earl felt relief. "Maybe I can get the wood hawks to help. I'll head out for their camp tomorrow."

Having felt they made a decision that solved at least some of the problem, the men smiled for the first time in a while and went back to their work with renewed energy.

When they came in for supper, they shared their plan with Molly.

"Molly," Earl pleaded. "If you can manage Pa's care for just a week more, shouldn't be any more than that, then I'll have him out of here."

Realizing that this would be an answer to prayer, one that Molly felt a little sorrowful about , Molly agreed.

Early the next morning, the men left, one headed for Frenchie's place and one headed for the wood hawk camp.

Molly washed some dried beans to put on to boil. Thank goodness for some stored up things she on hand. Nathan's hunting was providing plenty of meat and the beans and things stored away were providing extra sustenance. Ever patient on the outside, Molly tended to her father. Between Pa and the baby, she was too busy for her resentful and angry feelings to surface.

By late afternoon she was surprised by an influx of helpers. The wood hawks brought men, mules and equipment. Frenchie brought his wife and baby.

Delighted with the thought of woman talk, Molly came to the door with her arms outstretched to Clara. On Clara's back, held tightly in place with a shawl, a baby peeked around at this woman he didn't know hugging his mother.

"I am so glad to finally meet you!" Molly cried sincerely. "Come on into the house out of the cold."

Inside, Clara untied the shawl and laid it on the floor, sitting her little boy on it. Dark eyes stared at Molly from a little chubby face with red cheeks. Two tiny teeth showed from a little bowed mouth. With a tiny finger he pointed to Molly's face and chirped a baby sound to her.

"And what is your name?" Molly asked him as if she fully expected him to be able to tell her.

"We named him Robert," Clara said, "But Robbie is what we call him."

"Hi, Robbie," Molly cooed to him. He looked to his mother for approval and then bounced happily to Molly trying to put his finger in her mouth as she stooped over him. She took his tiny hand in hers and kissed their softness. Then she rubbed both hands to warm them. He was cold after his trip to Molly's. Clara was busily inspecting the newborn in her box.

"Oh, she's so tiny." She exclaimed.

"Tiny, but mighty," Molly laughed. "Just wait until she tunes up for dinner."

Clara's presence had lifted Molly's mood wonderfully. Here was someone to talk to. Someone who could advise her about babies. First, though, they needed to address the needs of several hungry men. Clara picked up the lid on the bean pot. Thankfully, Molly had cooked a lot.

Clara then went to the door and yelled out to Frenchie. He brought six squirrels to her already cleaned and ready to be cooked. Molly brought out the seasonings and flour. Clara heated a pan and Molly started on biscuits. You would think that the two women had been friends working together forever the way they coordinated in the tiny kitchen. One thing Molly was grateful for was Miss Dorothy's instructions on preparing large meals. While they worked, they both kept a watchful eye on Robbie, crawling about underfoot.

By the time the meal was ready to dish out the men had worked out a plan. They would put up a small cabin a short distance from the main house and they would enclose the dogtrot while they were at it. Molly was surprised and pleased. It would add another room which was much needed space.

The men lined up to the stove filling the plates that they were given. Earl filled a plate and took it across the hall to his Pa. The rest of the men just made themselves comfortable in the open dogtrot. Some stood while others leaned on the wall or sat along the floor. The winter day had turned out quite mild, just right for all the outside work that was planned. The men's voices were loud and boisterous and Molly closed the door so that she, Clara and the babies had a semblance of quiet as they continued their work.

After the men had eaten, they set to work on their plan. As soon as some large trees were cut and trimmed they were dragged to the site prepared by two of the men for the little cabin. Everyone worked steadily until the daylight began to turn to dusk. Then a campfire was made in the yard and the men ate the evening meal. As the night came on it became colder and soon folks were spreading out the blankets and bedrolls in the relative protection of the dogtrot. The women and babies made themselves comfortable in the kitchen while Nathan, Frenchie and Earl bunked in with Meyers.

When Molly was awakened in the early morning hours to feed Faith, she couldn't help but laugh at the snores and grunts of the men sleeping in and around the dogtrot. It sounded like a cave full of bears. After Faith was put back into her little box near the stove Molly began to gather things to start breakfast. Clara heard her moving around and she too got up and helped get things started. By the time the men started rising, a big breakfast was ready. Having Clara there with her eased Molly's conscience where her Pa was concerned. Earl was still doing most of the bathing and caring for the man, but the instant Earl left the cabin, their pa would start bellowing for Molly. Molly and Clara had begun to clean the kitchen from breakfast when the loud voice began his demands again.

"Girl! I need some water."

"Coming Pa," Molly answered as she rinsed a cloth in the dish pan. She turned to finish wiping the table.

"Mol," He hollered again, "Can't you hear me? I said I'm needing me some *water*."

"I'm coming," She retorted. Hurriedly she scooped the dipper into the water bucket and poured it into a cup. Noting Molly's grim demeanor and how her face paled every time he called gave Clara insight to feelings that seethed there. Clara saw too, the rugged strength of this girl woman as she watched the day unfold . It was pretty obvious that regardless of how she felt inside, Molly would do what she thought was right. Even so, it was apparent that the old man was pushing her beyond her limits. Clara watched her cross the hall to the other room and entreated a quick prayer.

"Lord, you promised in your word that you would take care of your children. I ask that you would help Molly and give her strength in this that you have set before her." When her new friend came back into the room, Clara couldn't help but notice that Molly's hands were shaking, so she gently guided her to the rocking chair.

"You sit right down here for a minute. I can finish up this chore. Then we'll just sit and enjoy ourselves for a bit before its time to start dinner."

Suddenly Molly was crying.

"I just can't do it any more, Clara. I don't think that my Pa ever loved anyone in this world but himself. In fact, I can't see as how he loves himself. After all, who'd want to be so cold hearted and hateful? I just can't tell you what I've been through having him for a pa. Me, my Ma and my brothers and sisters all went through. I've always thought I should be an obedient daughter and I've tried, Lord I've tried. The only time I rebelled against him was when I married Nathan, but I will never, ever be sorry about that. One of the few good things that's ever happened to me; Nathan and Faith there." Molly motioned towards the babe and for a moment her mood lightened.

"No, of course not!" Clara answered. "God sent Nathan to you to deliver you from that bondage. You are a child of God, not a child of rebellion. The same God who sent Nathan to you is the same One who will help you through this. God can change anyone and you have to keep reminding yourself. Do you have a Bible? Get it out and look up Scriptures. They're not just for the preacher you know. They are life and liberty for all of us who call on Him!

We will pray together and you and I will pray when we're apart, ok? We will pray hard for your Pa. Nothing like praying for someone to ease our own burdens about them. And, starting right now, you're going to quit feeling guilty about things that you haven't caused. Why Nathan's face around you is proof that what you and him did is good and right. Shucks, girl…" Clara waved into the air as though she was batting against an imaginary candle fly.

"I just can't see it, Clara." Molly began to sob again, "I've lost my faith. I've lost my hope and my joy."

Clara reached out for Molly and pulled the girl's face up even with her own. She wiped that tear streamed face with the dish towel she held and pushed back the damp strands of hair from her face. She prayed tenderly to the Lord and into Molly's ear and soothed her until she began to calm.

"Lord, remind Molly that she is not the sum of her childhood, that she is more than a conqueror, that she is more than just Nathan's bride. She's the bride of Christ! Amen!" She gave Molly one more good hug and said, "Let's get back to work and have some joy around here!" Just at the moment little Faith let out her first belly laugh and both women burst into laughter too. It was as though God Himself were speaking to them all.

Out back just a ways from Nathan and Molly's own cabin, Earl measured off a spot in the cold earth. He dug the hard soil and placed the large stones he'd already collected where the corners would be. He was winded, but pleased with his own work, although it was barely ready when the wood hawks' mule team dragged up the first huge logs. Two of the men joined in with Earl to begin much smaller version of the bigger cabin. The men were experts at this kind of work and chinkless notching was used so that no gaps between the logs would let in the cold. Although this method took a little longer because each log had to be grooved and filled as it was laid in place, this would be better in the long run as no clay would have to be used over and over to chink the logs.

The men worked together so well that it made for quick work anyway. Because it was winter, the logs were low on sap making them a little lighter and thus easier to handle and cut. Logging was always easier in the winter. For one thing, no snakes in the woods and the men, though they would get sweaty, didn't have the problems of heat stroke like in the muggy summer weather. No nails were needed. This log cabin would be sturdy, rainproof, and inexpensive, just like the bigger one. Well practiced axes and hatches cut out the notches. They were none too deep as this would weaken the logs, but with many hands working, it seemed as if the little log room just rose out of the ground. Openings were left for a window and a door. For the time being, a soft deer skin would cover the window. The door was fashioned from three large split logs battened together. Leather hinges were created and a latch was created to fasten the door. The men all nodded that this cabin was gonna hold good and tight, picking up a tool here and there, they began to realize it was getting late. Once again the day had passed and the hungry men lined up in Molly's kitchen to eat.

As the men were assembling to eat the sky was darkening. Low clouds began to gather and you could feel a blast of fresh cold coming through. As night fell, the clouds opened up and cold rain began to fall. The men left the cold dog trot and crowded on the floor in the two bedrooms. Molly, Clara and the infants stayed in the warm kitchen. The little log house was filled to the brim with people but everyone was warm. Sounds of sleeping men came through the door from every direction, but somehow it was a big comfort to Molly. In the wee hours of early morning, as Molly fed Faith, she heard the rain change to the pinging of sleet. Winter was truly here. By morning, the world was covered with white. Ice and snow made a wonderland of the surrounding forest and completely covered the little cabin that was being built in the back. There would be very little work done outside and the cabin was mighty close quarters for all the people inside. Nathan, Frenchie and Earl got up and prepared to go hunting. Food was needed for this bunch. At least Molly didn't have to worry about taking care of her Pa, there were many hands to attend to his every need. In fact, from the noise and laughter, Molly knew that they were keeping his spirits up with lots of entertainment. She guessed that someone had produced a deck of cards as the hardy noise indicated they had a game going in there. She and Clara had made biscuits and gravy enough to feed an army, but it disappeared so fast, she couldn't even save some for the hunters. Clara noticed that Molly's mood was lightened. Not having to tend to her Pa probably had a lot to do with it, but Clara knew that God was answering prayer. The men kept the fires going all day long, not letting Molly or Clara carry one stick themselves. They were having a grand time resting up and fellowshipping because of the weather. Molly had poked her head through the door on their side of the cabin once to ask for more firewood and the stench almost knocked her over. It made her eyes water. It was too cold for all those men to go to the creek for a bath. Well, for all they were doing for her family she wasn't going to complain about that.

In a couple of hours, the three hunting men were back. They had a nice mess of squirrels and a couple of rabbits. They cleaned them at the barn, checking on the needs of the horses and mules while they were there. Soon they were stomping snow off their boots as they walked in to present Clara and Molly with their gifts.

The women were thankful for the meat. With all these mouths to feed, food was running short, and now with the weather being bad, no one could make the long trip to town for supplies. It was also getting close to time for Christmas. The men would want to be going home. Molly began studying how she didn't think that the cabin would be finished by then. As she worked preparing the food, grim lines began to form on her furrowed brow. Anxiety gnawed its way back into her heart. Clara noted the change in Molly but watched in silence as she sat nursing her own baby, Robbie. Her heart ached for this new friend she had. Molly was such a young woman with so much to look forward to, yet she was carrying the weight of the world on her thin shoulders. Clara wanted to relieve that burden. She knew that the Word of God offered peace from a troubled heart. A merry heart was better than medicine. There was no way she could quit praying for Molly and she was going to ask God to do something miraculous for her friend.

After eating, someone noticed that a warm sun had crept out from the clouds. The sun was causing the whole world to glisten and then everything began to melt. The men were glad to get out of the cramped quarters and back to work. It sure was creating lots of mud as they traipsed around the place. Soon the little cabin was finished. Fresh straw was spread on the dirt floor to hold down the mud. The small window was covered with hides to help keep out the cold but could be held open with a stick to provide a little light. A tiny pot bellied stove was recovered from the barn. It had been Nathan's to use in the lean to before he carved out his place. One by one, the men began gathering up their tools to leave. They were itching to get back to their own homes to celebrate Christmas. Being around a young family reminded them of their own youthful homes. Some of the men were older and many had led hard lives, but the love that was obvious between Nathan and Molly was like a tonic to them all.

Next morning when the little cabin had a chance to warm up from the fire that had been set in the stove, Earl, Nathan and Frenchie carried out the straw tick bedding. Ropes were stretched tight across the wooden frame they made for the bed. This would hold the mattress off the ground. Then the three men carried Samuel out to the cabin. At last Molly could have her space. Earl would be in charge of the care for their father.

Once Earl had Pa settled, he, Frenchie and Nathan began to tackle the debris left from the cabin raising. Decent logs were put aside to help enclose the dogtrot. Limbs were stripped and chopped for kindling and firewood. Too green to burn at present, it was stacked near the barn.

"Look at this," Earl exclaimed. From under the debris he pulled a perfect tree top. "I've found a Christmas Tree!"

"Molly's gonna like it and it's just the right size." Nathan responded. "I'll carry it in to the womenfolk." He grabbed two squared up pieces of split wood to make a stand and carried it in.

"Oh!" Clara cried out delightedly. "A tree! Robbie and Faith will have their first tree."

Robbie chortled when he heard his name.

"What can we use for decorations?" Molly asked as she began thinking of ways to dress up the diminutive green tree top.

"Oh, we'll find something." Clara answered. "This little tree will make it feel more like Christmas."

Molly became silent. She had no decorations, no presents, not even a Christmas goose. She thought of her younger siblings and her Ma and that this must be a meager Christmas for them. Until they got word from the wood hawks, they wouldn't even know that Pa had been hurt. Ma probably expected him to show up with a little money to buy winter supplies. Molly kept her composure until Nathan went back out and the silent tears began to flow.

"Do you have any popcorn?" Clara asked. "That will make some decorations." She turned to Molly with a smile. Then she saw the stricken face and the flowing tears. Quickly she guided her friend to the rocker. Molly not only felt a heavy sorrow, she also felt embarrassed.

"Oh, Clara, I'm sorry," She sobbed. "I should be happy. I'm back with my Nathan in my own little home. I have this beautiful baby daughter and all I feel is sadness and grief."

"Molly," Clara soothed, as she looked Molly square in the face. "You've been through a whole lot in your short life, but there's more to this melancholy I think. I suspect you've got a case of the baby blues."

"Baby blues?" Molly asked.

"Yes," Clara answered. "It happens sometimes. Not only is the little one keeping you from getting sleep, you haven't been able to get rest because of your Pa. And then we all crowded in here making more work than you should need to handle. Why don't you just go rest and I'll work on these things for a while. Frenchie and I don't have to be home just yet. Old Mr. Toliver who lives near us is taking care of our animals. We don't have any worries causing us to need to hurry home."

"I…I just can't let you do all the work," Molly protested, holding her head in your hands.

"Yes, you can" Clara insisted. "You need to be strong to take care of Faith. She's so tiny and winter has just begun"

Reluctantly Molly agreed that that maybe she did need a little rest. She climbed into the bed. Softly Clara breathed a prayer for Molly's exhausted body and the sad emotions that overwhelmed her. "Lord, watch over my new friend. Keep her safe and let her rest, Amen." The soft words lingered in Molly's mind as sleep descended and much needed rest came. When the men came in to eat, Clara met them at the door and let them know that Molly was resting and they should be quiet. Nathan was at once concerned and wanted to go to her.

"You can go to her later." Clara said. She put Robbie in Frenchie's arms and instructed him to feed their baby some mashed beans and let him sip some of Nellie's milk from a cup. Then she picked up Faith and put the tiny baby to her own breast. Many times, she had seen her own Mother nurse some one else's infant when needed and she was thankful that Robbie wasn't totally weaned. After the men had eaten, Earl prepared a plate for his Pa and the men silently filed outside to resume their work. The weather had turned almost balmy, at least for early winter, and the snow and ice was almost totally gone leaving the yard swimming in mud. Nathan just couldn't get into the frame of mind to work. He and Molly were given so little time to be together and now she was exhausted to the point of being ill. What could he do to help her? He noticed how Frenchie helped out with Robbie, but he had no idea how to help with Faith. When he picked her up, she was so small and fragile he was afraid she would break. Because of the cold, Molly kept her wrapped like a little cocoon. All a person could really see was the tiny red face with two little fists occasionally escaping from the blankets. Nathan remembered his friends in Mississippi, Charles and Amanda and how he'd stayed and worked the summer with them after the incident with the robbers. They were the ones who taught him about trusting in God. Nathan wished now that he could pray for his family the way that Charles did. He just didn't know how. When dusk came, he went alone to the barn to feed the horses and milk the little goat. He sat on the milking stool and pressed his forehead against Nellie's soft side. She turned her head to look at him and bleated softly. From the depths of his heart, a silent petition rose before God. His soul struggled for the thoughts to send to the Heavenly Father for the young wife who had been through so much and the tiny baby born early. He'd never known love before and especially like the love he felt for those two. He'd do everything he could to protect his family. They were given to him by God, Nathan knew this in his heart. He thought back to the moment he first saw his young wife there in the mercantile. She was so young and small yet she had proved how very strong she was. Suddenly he knew. Her strength, her faith would get her through this. God was here. He finished his work and went to the house. His friends were here. Molly had awakened. Gratefully she ate, then sat and rocked the baby while the others tied ribbons made from little fabric scraps on to the branches of the Christmas tree. Clara popped some corn to string. While Clara strung the popcorn, Frenchie and Nathan went out, rifles in hand, to try their luck for a goose.

Robbie was fascinated by the tree. He pulled at the ribbons and begged his mother for kernels of pop corn. Clara laughed with her child and did her best to pull Molly into the joy of decorating the tree. Molly sat quietly, gently rocking, rocking, rocking. Her tiny baby slept, then roused for nursing. Soon Clara fed Robbie, and then nursed him to sleep. She laid him down and turned to her friend.

"Molly, you know that the Lord cares for you. He knows the secret most thoughts. You don't have to share with me if you don't want to, but it might help."

"Oh Clara," Molly sobbed, "If he knows my secret thoughts, then he knows just how bad I really am!"

Clara stood to her feet and reached for Faith.

"Oh, Molly. You have got to quit tormenting yourself. You're one of the sweetest, kindest people I've ever met. You're generous to a fault. Why look at how you worked to take care of everyone so your pa could have himself a cabin."

Molly seemed to dismiss her friend's kindnesses and replace them with the grim facts.

"I hate my Pa. I have tried to help care for him, I have tried to forgive him but I can't. I just can't. Here it is Christmas and I don't even have a present for anybody. Not even my tiny baby girl. What if she gets sick? What if God takes her from me because I can't forgive my Pa?"

Gently Clara laid Faith down beside Robbie. Then she sat on the floor by Molly's chair.

"Oh, my dear sweet friend, you need relief and we're gonna ask God to do it for you." She took Molly's hands in hers and began to pray, " Lord look down on this Christmas Eve and touch Molly. Give her peace in her heart. Heal the hurt that is there. Give her assurance in her heart for her little child. Help her to understand that Christmas is about You, dear Savior and the only gift we need is your love." As Clara prayed, Molly actually felt her heavy load start to lift. She sighed and a smile broke out just a little across her tear streaked face. Somehow the "prayer of faith" had actually helped Molly. What a friend! In no time at all, she felt lighter and was ready to help Clara with cooking for their Christmas meal. Soon the men were back with not one, but two plump geese.

"Molly, remember your were wishing for a goose? Now look, God brought us two geese! He doubled your request and our men were used by God to answer your prayer for you, for us all!" Clara, laughed and Molly chuckled, realizing just how good a God they had watching over the whole bunch. Outside the cabin their laughter and talk could be heard as they cleaned the geese and made them ready for roasting. They would have a good Christmas dinner. Finally, everyone had finished their many chores and began to settle down. The cleaned fowl were placed in a roasting pan and set in the oven. The stoked fire would roast them slowly over the night. Out in the little cabin built for Earl and Samuel, a lamp flickered. In the dim light, Earl sat whittling from a scrap of wood. Before long, the shape of a tiny wooden horse began to appear. It would be placed by Robbie's plate at breakfast. Earl couldn't wait to see the child's face light up. In the house Molly and Nathan were finally able to retire in their own comfortable bedroom, with the glow of the banked fireplace giving off just enough light for Molly to see the infant curled safely in the curve of her arm. In the darkness, Nathan silently gave thanks for the smile that had returned to Molly's face. Back in the kitchen Clara put in the finishing stitches on a soft blanket. In one corner was Faith's name and birth date. Finally she too lay down by her family, hugged her Frenchie tightly and began to drift off to sleep. As she dozed off she could hear her own pa reciting the Christmas story from Luke chapter 2, as he had all of Clara's childhood, "And she brought forth her first born son and wrapped him in swaddling clothes and laid him in a manger for there was no room for them in the inn, And there were in the same country shepherds abiding in the field keeping watch over their flock by night. And, lo, the angel of the Lord came upon them, and the glory of the Lord shone round about them; and they were sore afraid. And the angel said unto them Fear not; for, behold, I bring you good tidings of great joy, which shall be to all people. For unto you is born this day in the city of David a Savior, which is Christ the Lord." Such comforting memories rocked Clara fast asleep.

Christmas morning dawned with a beautiful sunrise. Temperatures promised to be pleasant and Molly fairly bounded out of the bed as she was the first one up. Faith was awake and demanding to be fed. On the other side of the dogtrot, Frenchie got up and stoked the fire. Before long Clara was up too. Her husband turned from the fire to give her a smile and she went to him and hugged him, laughing sweetly at her man.

"Merry Christmas, Mon Cher!" she spoke in his native tongue. She was glad he had taught her a few phrases, such as this one which meant my darling. She looked him in the eye and as he returned a quick wink, she laughed again! Dancing around a little, she put a pot of water on the stove to boil for oatmeal and then hurried to the outhouse. From the tiny cabin out back, Earl heard the animals stirring and got up. The little homestead was coming to life for the day.

Frenchie went out to get the secret presents for the ladies that he and Nathan had made yesterday. They were so pleased with themselves that they could do something for their wonderful wives. Frenchie kept insisting that his Clara was the best. To which Nathan responded, No my Molly is! They laughed and Frenchie gave his friend a good whop on the back!

After Faith was fed and changed, Molly searched in her sewing basket and withdrew new clean hemmed handkerchiefs, stitched back in the summer when she was at Miss Dorothy's boarding house. It was impossible for everyone to set out their gifts in secrecy, but they tried. Everyone was smiling. Earl and Frenchie brought Pa into the big cabin for the Christmas breakfast. His face was pale and he was in need of a bath, but even his sorrowful countenance couldn't repress the joy of this Christmas morning. Every plate had a present beside it. For each of the men, a new handkerchief waited. For Clara and Molly, long clean goose feathers secured to a handle by stout string, made for a lovely duster. Baby Faith received the soft blanket that Clara had worked on into the night. Robbie had two gifts. He crowed excitedly over the little wooden horse from Earl. Also by his plate, was a dried gourd, found hanging in the barn. It made a wonderful rattling sound. Molly was overjoyed at realizing she couldn't remember a better Christmas and her spirit fairly soared. After breakfast, the geese that had been simmering in the oven of the stove in a big pot all night were brought out. The meat was so tender and juicy that it fell off the bones. Molly stirred flour to make dumplings. In the corner, Robbie played happily with his little horse. After all of the morning activity, Faith slept peacefully in her little box. Across the hall, the three men filled the wash tub with warm water and there in front of the fireplace, they carefully shaved and bathed Samuel and dressed him in clean clothes. Then his dirty garments were washed in the bath water and taken to the line outside to dry. Meyers certainly felt better, even if he was embarrassed at having grown men help him.

Earl pondered in his mind the poor condition of his Pa's body. He doubted his Pa would live to see the spring and he wanted to take him home to Ma. He would approach the subject with the other men later, after the festivities were over.

"I wish we had something to make a pie, or eggs to bake a cake." Clara said.

"It would be nice to have cake or pie," Molly answered remembering her ma's sugar cake and that persimmon pie. But I'm so glad for the goose and dumplings."

"We are blessed." Clara told her friend, "And I am so glad to see a smile on your face today."

"I think God is truly forgiving me." Molly answered. "It's still hard to look at my Pa, but I think with God's help, I can forgive. I know that I have to be strong for Nathan and Faith. I love them both so much. And Faith is growing stronger every day."

"Yes, she is," Clara replied. "And she's as pretty as her Ma!"

Molly blushed at the compliment. It was so wonderful to have Clara. The older woman was so uplifting, a good example and a true friend.

Across the hall, resting comfortably in Molly and Nathan's soft bed after his bath, Sam Meyers felt better than he had since his accident.

"Molly!" He called.

Across the dogtrot, Molly heard his voice, freezing at the sound of the old patronizing tone, and her spirit cringed. She did what Clara had taught her to do and recalled a memory verse about kindness and remembered too that she had asked for forgiveness toward her Father. She walked across the open hall and went into the room where he was.

"Fetch me something to drink, Molly girl, and I need some tabacky."

Pleased at least that he was feeling better, she went to do his bidding. She brought him coffee and the little bit of tobacco that was left.

"Is that all the tabacky?" He asked irritably.

"Yes, Pa, I'm afraid so." She answered.

"Humph," he grunted. "Then somebody better go get some more."

A bubble of impatience surged up in Molly. "Pa, we aren't close enough to the Mercantile to just run out and get some more. It will have to wait."

Samuel stared up at his daughter's face. "Are you getting huffy with me girl? I'm still your Pa, you know."

Before Molly could stop herself she responded in anger.

"Well you may be my Pa, but I'm not a girl anymore. I'm a woman. I have a husband and a child and I will not take your surliness any more, is that clear?" Before he could respond, she turned and went back to the kitchen.

She flounced to the stove and began to sling the leftovers together and slam the dishes into the dish pan. Clara looked up in surprise.

"What happened over there?"

"I want him back out in his own place!" She stormed. "Where's Nathan? The men need to take him back out. Christmas is done and he doesn't need to stay in here, hollering at me and ordering me around like he does."

"They're outside, Molly. I'll get them." Clara hurried to the door, pausing to get her cloak and calling to the men as she went out the door. When they came in, they went straight to Samuel and begin to gather the blankets into a sling to help carry the man.

"Hey! What cha doing?" Samuel protested. "I like it just fine right here. I'm not ready to go."

"We're just taking you back to your own room, Pa." Earl soothed.

When they got him settled back in his own bed, Earl sat down beside him to calm him while Nathan and Frenchie headed back into house. In the kitchen, Nathan found Molly by herself angrily sloshing the dishes around in the dish pan. Clara had taken the babies into the other room.

"Molly," Nathan addressed his young wife. "We need to talk."

"I want him out of here! There's nothing to talk about." She stormed. "This is my home. I came here to get away from him and now here he is, ordering me around just like before." Suddenly she became weak in the knees as her anger dissolved into tears and she crumpled into Nathan's arms. Silently he held her tight. His anguish to see her in such pain tore at him. His mind went back over the past months. So much had happened since last spring. He had watched her blossom from an innocent young girl into a beautiful woman only to have her snatched from him by the very man who was grieving her so at this moment. She had carried their child in a strange city not knowing where he was and unable to reach him. She had offered to take in the injured man and care for him even though he had put her through so much. After all, he was still her Father and she felt responsible to him. Well, no more. He would make sure that that man was out of her life for good.

"Don't you worry over this another minute." He told her. We'll take him back to his home now." He gently kissed the top of head and then headed out to the little cabin that had been hastily built just days earlier. He pushed open the door and addressed his brother-in-law who was sitting next to the bed. "We're taking him home. I should have never allowed him to stay here in the first place."

Earl stood to his feet, not sure whether he was feeling pain for Molly or his pa. "But we built this room so that he could have a space outta sight to get better. I don't think he's well enough to travel yet."

"I won't have him bullying Molly one more day. You're taking him home."

"Today?" Earl inquired, suddenly becoming uncomfortable about the whole thing. "Shouldn't we wait till morning?"

"We're not waiting." Nathan said forcefully. "You gather up what we need to wrap him up. I'm hitching up the wagon." Nathan strode out up the cabin and headed to the barn.

For a moment Earl just stared after him. He had a great deal of respect for Nathan. He also knew his Father's caustic personality. With a sigh, he turned and looked towards his Pa.

"Well, Pa, looks like your Christmas present is to get to go home."

Frenchie followed Nathan to the barn. "Wouldn't it be better to wait until morning?"

"Nope," Nathan responded flatly. "The sooner he's on his way the better. I'm done with him and Molly's past done with him. We did the best we could and he's remained ungrateful and hateful to her no matter what. That man has not got one good bone in his whole body. I'll be dad burned if I'll let her keep weeping and having all these feelings when he could just be gone!"

Frenchie didn't argue as he silently followed his friend to the barn. He knew the pain Nathan was in as he and Clara had talked at night when they were alone. But he also knew that traveling on a winter day, even with the mild weather would make this trip very difficult for a man in Meyers' condition. It was bad all the way around.

The horses looked up from the hay where they were feeding and greeted the two men with soft whinnies. Nathan strode to his horse and rubbed him affectionately behind his ears. "Come on boy, let's get you some water." He led him out to where the spring trickled from the spring house to a little pool dug out and lined with rocks. The horse was more interested in his master's attention than drinking. "Come on," Nathan coaxed. "Drink some water." He pulled his head down and the horse took a step forward and began to drink noisily.

Inside the barn, Frenchie was gathering the harness, blanket and feeding bucket that would be needed. He filled a large bucket with oats for the trip. When Nathan brought the horse back to hitch him up to the wagon, Frenchie headed to the house to have Clara prepare some food for the trip. After the wagon was readied for the trip, Nathan led the horse to the tiny cabin where Earl and his Father were. Between the two of them they managed to load the straw tick mattress into the wagon and lift Meyers up and settle him on it. Earl surrounded his Father with blankets and propped him in as comfortable a position as he could. Though Earl and Nathan hardly spoke as they worked, the old man chattered non-stop.

"It's what I wanted in the first place! Just wanted to go home. Told 'em not to bring me here. No, none of them would listen. 'Bout time somebody done what I wanted. It's bout time…"

Frenchie came out with a pack of food Clara had prepared. He hesitated a moment and then spoke quietly to Nathan.

"Clara and me need to go back home."

Nathan turned and looked at his friend. He reached out and shook his hand. "Thanks for all your help."

Again Frenchie hesitated, "Are you sure Molly be alright alone?"

"She'll do fine. I'll talk to her before we leave. She'll be fine." Nathan seemed to be reassuring himself more than his friend. He left Earl to finish up the loading and walked back to the house where Molly was. Her face was pale but stoic. "Can you manage being alone again, girl? I know I promised but…" Nathan asked her.

"Oh, we can stay a bit longer," Clara interjected.

"No," Nathan answered. "You and Frenchie have done more than enough. Molly and I have got to get back to normal and the sooner the better."

"I'll be alright," Molly said. "Just as long as Pa is gone, I'll make it just fine." Nathan kissed her cheek and went out.

Clara reached out to hug her but Molly turned away. "I'll be alright." she stated again, partly to prove it to herself, partly to keep from crying for Clara. The moment was gone and Clara went back to putting the food away. She had packed most of the Christmas leftovers for the men to carry. She was concerned about Molly being well enough to take care of herself and the baby for what could be more than a week, but her own husband's uncompromising face told her that they did indeed need to return home. While she was glad to be seeing her cabin again, in her heart she was aching over the situation but she knew that it was out of her hands. Silently she gathered her things and Robbie's things. She no longer knew what to say to her friend. She knew the blues that Molly was suffering could affect her health but she also knew that God was in control. God had been with Molly before and he would be again. Outside she heard the sounds of Nathan and Earl leaving. Within the hour, her own little family would be on the way back home to their own farm. Molly would be left alone to deal with her tiny baby for several days. Outside, Frenchie was saddling up his horse. Before he left the barn, he put out hay for the little nanny goat and milked her. He carried in the milk and set the pail on the table.

"Molly," He said. "Nellie is settled in for the night. I left her plenty of straw and water. She won't need anything more until morning…"

"Thank you Frenchie," Molly responded, "you've done more than any friends I've known and I want you to know that I appreciate it beyond words." She walked over and picked up the little pail of milk. She stretched a clean cloth over a clean pitcher and carefully strained it. Then she rinsed, soaped and rinsed again the cloth and hung it on a nail near the stove to dry. It was time for Frenchie and Clara to leave. Clara stood in front of Molly holding her little boy in her arms. He was protesting the tightly wrapped blankets and trying to free his little hands. Clara patted his back to soothe him and reached over and kissed Molly on the cheek. "Now, Molly, I don't care if you can take care of everything yourself. I'm sending Frenchie back in a couple of days to check on you and that's that." She said.

"No need," Molly answered. "The two of you have been a real help, more than I deserve. You've been more like family than friends." As she walked Clara to the door, she finished, "I'll be fine."

With their last words hanging in the air, Clara turned and went out the door and walked the length of the dog trot to where Nathan waited with the horse. She handed Robbie up to her husband and then allowed him to pull her up behind him. As the horse turned to take them home, she silently prayed in earnest for Molly that God would protect her and heal her wounded heart. "Lord, You've just got to take care of her, body soul *and* spirit".

Alone now, Molly turned to the little box near the stove where her baby slept. She would be waking soon wanting to be fed. Molly gazed at the tiny beautiful face. Instead of joy, Molly felt an overwhelming sadness. Being alone in the cabin didn't give her the assurance she had hoped for. Rather it just increased the deep sadness that wanted to swallow her up. She reached over and scooped up the little bundle. Startled awake, Faith waved her little fists in the air and blinked little blue eyes. The warm smell of her mother caused her to turn her tiny face and search for nourishment. Molly sat down in the rocker and began to nurse, rocking the baby slowly. Silent tears began to spill onto her face. Where was her joy? Where was her love? Had her heart just totally turned itself off?

Chapter 44

As the wagon rumbled down the trail, Meyers realized that going home in his condition might not have been a good idea. Every jolt and bump caused him to wince in pain. The usual complaining and whining began. Nathan turned and silenced him.

"I'll not have it, Meyers. You said you wanted to go home. You have gotten what you wanted. Best not complain about it."

Earl looked back at his pa and frowned. Meyers realized he'd better keep quiet and knew not to give Nathan any grief. He suffered in silence. On the wagon seat beside Nathan, Earl mulled things over in his mind and tried to figure out where God was in all of this. He understood his sister's pain. He understood Nathan's standpoint, but the suffering man in the back of the wagon was his pa. Somewhere during the past year, Earl had come to know that his Father's life was ruled by something the preacher had talked about years ago. That old sin nature. He knew enough about people to know that his father could have died from the devastating injury he had received. He knew also that a two day trip in a wagon, especially in the dead of winter, could be the death of him. He wished that he could talk to his pa like father and son, and could share about God so as to lead him to the Lord. Everybody needed peace and his pa surely had none. But he just wasn't sure how to go about it. Until the accident he had always been subservient to Pa and considerably afraid of him. Now that he was growing into manhood himself, he could see what a pathetic individual his Pa was. He blustered his way through an unproductive life taking out his anger and frustration on his wife and children. Now he was in a bad way what with the injuries. Earl knew all his father knew was how to sling out hurtful words. The fear Earl had felt all those years as a boy was gone. The truth was, Earl now realized that it was up to him to be the head of this family. He was a man. He could take care of his Pa and his Ma and his younger siblings. He knew that Nathan would take care of Molly and Faith. Earl had spent a lot of time worrying over his sister. From her disappearance and then through the premature birth of her baby, he had done everything he could to help. He loved Molly and was thankful he had a good sister like her. But now he also knew she could be released from his responsibility. He knew that Nathan was a good man and that he loved Molly and Faith with his whole heart. Earl felt a real burden released from his shoulders as he realized the new one he was facing. No matter, he loved his family and he'd do whatever he felt led to do, no matter what.

As the wagon plodded along, the three men rode in silence. The only sounds that could be heard were the clip clop of the horses hooves as they moved, along with the occasional jangle of the tack as one of the horses would shake his mane. Every once in a while a squirrel could be heard chattering at them from the tree tops as the wagon passed beneath their fortresses. For the most part the squirrels and birds had made their preparations for the cold weather to come but although it was nearly January, the weather continued to be mild. At least the weather was one good thing. Had it been colder or wet, this trip would have been much more difficult. Darkness fell and still they plodded on. The injured man slept fitfully, moaning every now and then. And although Nathan and Earl were both hungry, they were holding out until they reached the halfway house. There they would settle in and they would eat from the pack of food Clara had made for them.

Chapter 45

Back home, Molly noticed the darkness settle in, both in the house and in her heart. She was alone after days and days of noise and people. First those who loved and cared for her after the birth of little Faith, then the woodsmen who had brought her injured Pa. Those same men had come back to the farm and toiled with her husband and brother to build the injured man his own space.   After Faith was done nursing, she cooed and smiled at her Mother's face. Molly smiled at the beautiful little face as she laid the little bundle on the bed. She poured some warm water from the tank at the back of the stove into the wash basin and went back to the bed to get her little baby. Carefully, she undressed Faith near the warmth of the fire and began to bathe the tiny pink body. Little Faith let loose a good strong cry at this intrusion and Molly began talking and soothing her child. Little by little peace began to steal its way back into Molly's well being. It was impossible to let the joy of tending to this child keep her from feeling the pleasure of her newborn baby.

Unbeknownst to Molly, the prayers of Clara and Earl were being answered. Molly dried little Faith and dressed her in clean clothes. The workout left Faith sleepy and as soon as Molly laid her down she washed out the baby clothes and the diapers in the bath water. They too joined the nail with the dish cloth to dry near the stove. Molly fed herself with slices of Christmas goose and warm milk from Nellie. Then she rocked slowly with only the light of the stove flickering lowly. She began sorting out her thoughts one by one. She hadn't prayed much in recent days. It was so easy to talk to God when you were pliable, just searching and needing answers. It wasn't so easy to talk to God when you were feeling resentful and angry, trying to hold onto worldly feelings. Alone in the quiet, a loving God tugged at Molly's heart. She faced her resentments and angry feelings. One by one, verses memorized from Prudence Brown's classes came to her mind, along with ones Clara had shared recently. 'Honor thy Mother and Father that thy days may be long upon the earth.' 'Love those who despitefully use you…' and 'How can you love God whom you can't see if you cannot love your fellow man whom you can see' That one gave Molly a pang in her heart.

With that pang, she knew she had to take responsibility for causing her parents, especially her ma, unjust fears and anxieties with her actions. She asked Him to forgive her for not letting Him help her with her difficult relationship with her Pa. In her heart she knew that God had taken the situation and turned it for good. He had given her the love of Nathan. He had kept her safe when her Pa had carried out his evil intentions. God, in His mercy and grace, had given her a healthy baby even though she came into the world a little earlier than she should have. All these things rolled through her mind. When the tears came this time, they were tears of repentance and of her grateful heart towards God who loved her so much. At last her mind lit on the one most difficult thing she'd ever faced. Could she truly forgive her pa who had caused her so much pain? She wasn't sure. One thing she did know, God was telling her she had to try. With God's help, she would work on it.

At last she got up and prepared for bed, pulling the straw tick mattresses over near the stove. It was too cold on the other side of the cabin as the fire in the fireplace had gone out, but all was cozy in the kitchen that Nathan had built and that Molly now called home. She snuggled her tiny baby close. As she fell into the deepest and most restful sleep she'd had in a long while, she dreamed of last spring when she fell in love with a handsome young man who had swept her away to a brand new life. Although the scene was from before Pa came and stole her away, strangely enough Faith was with them and she played in the garden they had planted. In this dream, she was a happy and beautiful toddler and Molly woke the next morning with more peace in her heart than she had felt in a long time.

Chapter 46

As the wagon approached the halfway house, Meyers woke up. Even though the temperature had fallen in the dusk, sweat trickled from his brow. The jostling wagon had caused him much pain and he moaned out loud. Earl turned to look back at him.

"Are you alright Pa?" he asked.

The older man mumbled incoherently.

"Just a few more minutes, Pa, and we can get you in out of the cold."

Samuel grunted. He wasn't feeling cold, he was hot. He attempted to throw back the covers that were tucked in around him. The wagon came to a halt and he moaned again. Nathan and Earl jumped down and opened the door to the cabin. Nathan took the shovel that stood in the corner and scooped ashes from the fireplace. Earl gathered sticks and a few pieces of wood. Soon a fire was burning and the glow lit up the tiny space. The two men went back to the wagon and worked to lift the sick man out. "Hold on a second." Earl cautioned, "Pa, you gonna be sick?" With that Meyers made a guttural sound and laid back.

"Best to get him in and settled as quick as we can." Nathan responded.

"Okay," Earl answered, and they hustled him into the cabin and laid him on the bunk.

"Oh, my god, oh my god!" Samuel muttered loudly. "Somebody git that tree off my legs."

"It's alright, Pa." Earl couldn't help but soothe the injured man. He left him for a moment to wet a handkerchief with water. He returned and gingerly wiped his face.

"Where's your Ma at?" Samuel looked at Earl quizzically. "Tell her to git in here and bring me my supper right now!"

"Ma's not here. Remember we're on our way home. We've stopped for the night at the halfway house for rest." Earl responded. He was worried at this new turn of events. Pa was clearly befuddled and his face was hot and flushed.

Nathan turned and left the cabin to tend to the horse. He realized that the man had taken a turn for the worse. If her pa should die before they got him home, Molly would carry the guilt of turning him out forever. He thought of his friends Charles and Amanda. Their example of praying and trusting God came to mind. Mentally he cried out to God. He prayed for his sweet wife Molly who had gone through so much. He prayed for Earl as he ministered to his father. Then he asked God to help him to deal with his own feelings toward Samuel Meyers. God knew he was justified in feeling anger for what this man had done, but maybe at some point, with God's help, his feelings might change just a little toward him. Shaking his head, he picked up the food pack that Clara had prepared for them and carried it into the cabin.

He walked in as Earl was raising his father's head and attempting to pour water into his mouth. Most of it just trickled down his chin.

"Pa, you need to try and drink a little water. Come on now and try to swallow a little bit."

Samuel tried and then laid back his head and closed his eyes. "Too tired." He said. "Try again later." He breathed heavily and appeared to be sleeping. Earl looked helplessly on.

Nathan touched his back. "Let him rest if he can. Nothing else we can do right now." He held out their food bag. "Let's eat and get some rest. We got a lot of road ahead of us tomorrow."

Earl took the bag and pulled out a biscuit sandwiched with goose meat. He took a bite but it just felt dry in his mouth. Silently he chewed the dry biscuit as he watched Nathan devour his own biscuit. After Nathan had eaten his supper, he unrolled his blankets on the floor of the tiny cabin and stretched out to sleep. Earl simply sat where he was, watching his Pa's labored breathing by the light of the moon shine coming in the window. His thoughts were many as he watched. So many times, the man who lay there had caused such suffering for his family. But now he was just a shell of a person as he looked so small and helpless. How could this man have caused so much grief and suffering to his family? Earl couldn't help but wonder if his Pa had ever prayed. Did he know anything about God or getting saved so he could go to heaven? Earl doubted that he did. He could be kind. It always seemed to be the hard drink that caused him to get abusive. Or maybe it was something else. Earl wasn't sure. There in the darkness Earl talked to God. He didn't pray aloud, just sincerely from his heart. He, like his sister, prayed for the courage to forgive his earthly father. Hadn't he learned from Preacher Brown that children were to obey and honor their parents? That was a difficult thing to do when you were hungry and your pa hadn't been home in a month. It was hard to do when you'd been yelled at and embarrassed in front of folks. It was hard to do when your hide had been tanned harder than normal and you didn't understand what you were supposed to have done wrong. Tears began to slide down Earl's face. Angrily he brushed at them and rubbed his eyes. In spite of everything he loved his Pa just like every child loves a parent no matter what the circumstances, that's how Earl loved him. God was trying to speak to his heart, he knew as the hard memories in his mind were replaced with memories of the Pa who had taken him fishing. The Pa who helped him learn to bait his hook. The Pa who taught him how to use a gun and to hunt a squirrel or a deer. He recalled his pa's tales of the wood hawks working and hauling wood to the steam boats for fuel. Some of his stories were quite comical and made them all laugh. There was good in there with the bad. He reached over and laid his hand on top of his Pa's hand. It startled the man and opened his eyes.

"Winnie?" he called. "Is that you?"

"No, Pa. It's me, Earl." He hesitated then asked, "Pa? Pa I got a question for you. Would you care if I asked God to help you?"

"Huh?" Samuel queried, turning his face toward Earl.

"Pa? Can I *pray* with you?" Earl asked a second time.

Samuel stared in the darkness for a moment, and it seemed an all too quiet eternity. Just as Earl was about to get up and get into his own bedroll, his father answered. "Yeah."

Softly Earl began to pray and from his bedroll on the floor Nathan was listening.

"Lord, this here's my Pa and he's mighty sick. I pray that you'll just touch him Lord. Help him to know you're here and you're looking out for him and be with him in his time of need."

Suddenly Samuel's body trembled. It took a few seconds for Earl to realize that his Pa was crying. He'd never in his life seen his Pa cry.

"Pa!" Earl cried out, "Pa, are you okay?"

"Don't know how," the older man muttered. "Ain't no God in no heaven wanta listen to a mean old codger like me. Don't know how."

"God listens to anybody that asks." Earl said.

In the background, Nathan got to his feet and stoked the fire to give a little more light and then he came and stood behind Earl.

"God listens to anybody who asks." Earl said again. "All you gotta do is ask."

For a moment there was just silence. Then with a heaving sob, Samuel said the words. "Oh, God! Forgive me if you can. I'm nothing, just a mean old man." Meyers grabbed Earl's hands, "Son I don't know how you could, but if you can, please forgive me. I been all wrong." Samuel clutched Earl's hand in the night. "Earl, boy, couldja tell your Ma, tell your sisters. I'm sorry. Nathan?" Meyers called out. "Nathan?"

"I'm here." Nathan answered.

"You tell her. You tell Molly now, you hear. Tell her I am real sorry. She deserved better."

"I'll tell her." Nathan answered, thinking to himself how hard that would be. He, more than anybody, knew the suffering this man had put his Molly through.

All that effort had tired Samuel out. He closed his eyes. His loud labored breathing filled the room. Earl and Nathan just sat in silence. At the moment there was nothing that they could do. They were waiting for the dawn. At some point they both fell into an exhausted sleep. At first light, the whinnying of the horse woke them. It took a moment for them to realize that the room was quiet. Too quiet. Earl staggered to his feet and looked at the figure of his Pa laying so still.

"Pa?" He called out. "Pa?" He turned to Nathan panic stricken. "What'll I tell Ma?" he asked. "What'll I tell Ma?"

Nathan said nothing. He put his hand on Earl's shoulder. His own feelings were mixed. He didn't feel like grieving for a man who had caused him so much trouble. But he cared about Earl. They'd come to know and respect one another while working on the cabin. He had much to thank Earl for. He'd watched this boy become a man, practically overnight. He'd found his sister. He took care of her when her baby daughter had been born three weeks early on a cold winter day. He'd taken over the care for his Pa when it was too heavy a burden for her. Now he stood grieving for a man who had placed that entire burden on his young shoulders. Nathan turned and walked out of the cabin, leaving Earl with his Pa. He tended the horse and made ready to hitch him to the wagon. In spite of it being the beginning of January, which was normally the coldest month of the year, the day was strangely warm.

Earl looked at his Pa's face. It seemed amazingly youthful. The eyes were closed as if he were sleeping. The weathered face looked peaceful. His hands lay outside the blanket. Earl touched them and they felt cold. He lifted them and put them under the quilt. He stood there a moment longer, breathed a little prayer, and then went out to help Nathan get the wagon ready. It was time to take his pa home.

Chapter 47

When Molly went out to tend to the little Nanny goat, she stopped and looked toward the sky. The weather was promising to be nice. Her spirit was almost joyful. She felt a peace inside. She thanked the Lord for her blessings as she looked again toward the beautiful heavens. Something for sure had been lifted from her heart. She hurried to tend her chores so she could get back to Faith who had already waked up and was looking quietly around, cooing and making little shrieking noises to entertain herself. Molly scooped her up and watched with wonder as the little face looked into her own. She was so beautiful, this tiny little gift. A toothless gummy smile lit up the room and Molly swirled around in a little dance. For the first time, she was here with her baby daughter and no one else was around. Granted, she was grateful for all the help, Frenchie and Clara, Earl and the men from the wood hawks, but she no longer needed them. She was here in her own home with her precious child and all they needed now was for Nathan to come home to them. He would. He would be back before they knew it. Back before the ice and snow would come, to make sure they were taken care of in the cold Kentucky winter. He would be home very soon she told Faith. Then she lay her baby down and cleaned her and dressed her all fresh. She put the soiled things in a pail to soak and then she made herself some breakfast. Later in the morning, she wrapped Faith securely to keep her warm and together they went out to tether the little goat outside to nibble at the dry winter grass. Molly couldn't remember the last time she felt so free and happy. It was as if she were just now feeling the great joy that the birth of a child can bring. When the sun was beginning to set in the sky to the west and the little goat was safe back in the barn, Molly sat and rocked her baby and sang the songs that her own Ma had sung to her.

Chapter 48

At the house of Molly's childhood, that same sun was low in the sky. The old hound dog came out from under the house and began to bay at the approaching wagon as it rattled in. Winifred came to the door and watched. She shielded her eyes for a better look and saw that it was her own boy riding there on the buckboard with the man who was married to Molly. She went down the steps and began to walk toward them as they came. She could tell something was wrong as Earl looked away from her gaze. She saw something in the back of the wagon and her intuition told her it wasn't good. Word had already come to her about the accident her Samuel had been injured in. She knew the damage had been significant and had wanted to go to him. But she couldn't leave her children alone at the farm. Now she knew without having to hear it that her husband was dead. Sissy had also heard the dog barking and the wagon coming and followed her Ma out the door.

"Whoa!" Nathan called out to the horse and brought him to a halt. Winifred simply walked to the bed of the wagon without saying a word to Nathan or Earl and looked in. It was just a bundle of quilts, wrapped tight. Earl jumped down from the wagon seat and walked to his Ma. He put his arm around her and they stood together staring at the bundle, neither speaking a word. Sissy stood hesitantly back. She too knew without being told. Finally she turned and went back into the house. As she closed the door almost to, she shooed the two younger children back in where they anxiously peeked out. One of the cats darted out between their feet but no one paid him any mind. Then Ma was coming in the door. At first she didn't seem to know what to do, then she ushered the children to the bed in the corner that served as a divan, to sit. They obeyed quickly, staring at their Ma with wide eyes, waiting to hear what she had to say.

Finally she spoke.

"You all know about your Pa getting hurt in the timber woods." She said. The little ones nodded gravely. "Well, the good Lord went ahead and took him on to heaven." she said.

Finally Seth asked in a quivering voice, "Is he in the back of that wagon?"

"Yes," she answered. Then she turned and went to the kitchen where she had been preparing supper. Sissy followed her. Winifred took the pot from the stove and attempted to set it on the table. Her hands trembled and the pot tilted on the edge. Quickly Sissy grabbed a dish rag and caught it and set it right. Although heat from the boiling pot came through the rag, she didn't mind. It only smarted a little and she could run her hand through cold water if needs be. Right now all she could think of was to help Ma. Winifred slumped down in the chair, lowered her head and raised her apron to her eyes. Tears began to flow and sobs began to rock her body. All three children came and gathered around her, unsure exactly what they were supposed to do. The pa they had feared and who had spent more time away from them than with them was gone. He had missed their Christmas morning and now he wouldn't be there ever again. Each one began trying to recall to themselves if there had ever been anything really to miss. By the time darkness had set in, the preacher and Miss Prue had come. Nathan had gone to get them while Earl had laid Samuel in the back room. Miss Prue had scurried around finishing up the supper but no one felt like eating. Finally she put the little ones to bed and asked them to say their prayers, which she really did for them. Each one stayed quiet as a mouse.

Outside in the barn, Earl and Nathan set to building a coffin. Inside, Miss Prue tried her best to comfort Winifred. It was hard though. Everyone knew that Meyers had been a hard man, hard on his children and hard on his wife. Giving another quick prayer thanking God for her own kind husband, she and Sissy worked in the kitchen. Miss Prue started in making some pie crusts and rolling them out to bake some pies for the bereaved family. She helped Winifred to a more comfortable chair and gave her a drink of strong tea that she had made.

"A cup of this will help settle your stomach, Winifred." Patting the grieving widow and placing a shawl on her shoulders, she went back to work. It would be a long night that was for sure. Finally, Sissy could take it no longer and she asked to be excused. "Child, you rest now. You're ma's gonna need you a lot in the days to come." Miss Prue sent her out of the kitchen and went back to work.

At first light, a tired Nathan bid everyone goodbye. He told them he wasn't staying for the burial, that he wanted to get back to Molly and baby Faith as soon as he could. Winifred insisted that he take some of the baked goods Sister Prue had stayed up all night to make. She also told him she understood and to give Molly and the baby her love. She thanked him for taking good care of her Molly and gave him a quick hug. As he got into the wagon, she stopped him.

"Tell Molly I love her. I wished I could have been with her when the baby was born. Also, Nathan, please tell her I can't wait to see that baby girl." She looked down and walked back to the porch.

"I'll tell her Mrs. Meyers. I will." As the wagon rattled away, she contemplated her life. It was so strange; the husband that had caused so much grief was the man she had loved, at first anyway. She'd tried to make a good home. She'd tried to help him with his temper, his drinking and his other vices. She'd kept her problems to herself and not even asked for so much as a prayer from the preacher. That thought caught her heart a little. What if she'd shared some of what they were going through? She realized she'd carried that load all by herself. By not asking the preacher to pray, she'd really not even been counting on God for answers.

Then, this past year had been so hard. And the stress of it all showed strongly in her face. Although she had been the one who took care of the children while Samuel was frequently gone off and living the way he liked, she was painfully aware that what little money he had brought in from working with the wood hawks would now be no income at all. How would she ever manage? She hated herself for feeling relief and yet worried more about her children now more than ever. While one problem seemed to be alleviated more problems were probably coming. Winifred had lost hope in her own future and that of her children a long time ago. Molly had been her shining example as the escape brought some mixed joy to her own life. If God hears, then maybe, just maybe, things would work out. She went back into the house and set to work making potato stew. She made a mental and spiritual recommitment right there to count on God more and to look into His Book more to see how He felt about His people. Maybe she could get her own feelings back in order and be able to share this with her children. Maybe it wasn't too late to teach them about God's love and care. With the newfound hope, she stirred the pot.

After exchanging good-byes with Nathan and sending a kind word to Molly, Earl had a feeling of renewed strength and vitality. He could take his responsibility as the man of the house seriously and he liked what God was doing in his life. Again, he silently vowed to God that he would do a better job than Pa had done, God rest his soul. He was grateful for the opportunity to live for God before he got old and injured. He also said a silent prayer for what future wife might come his way. "Lord, if you'll help me, I'll serve you the rest of my days."

He had a talk with Preacher when they went out to the barn to finish making the coffin. He had shared with the man of God about the death bed confession of his Pa and believed with all his heart that Pa had truly been saved. Now he intended to step up and take care of his Ma and his younger siblings. Preacher had tried to tell him he was too young to take on such a load, but he knew the young boy was more than able. The one thing that Samuel Meyers had left behind was a heritage of good children. Preacher felt sure that none of them would follow their Pa's footsteps down that reckless path that had caused so much difficulty for their young lives. At least they had been taught God's love from an early age and young as they all were, they knew what hard work was right down to the littlest of them who gathered the eggs every days and could fetch in a pail of water even if it wasn't filled all the way to the top.

In the house, Winifred went through the motions of the morning. She knew that folks expected her to grieve, but her mind just felt blank. She returned her thoughts to the early morning thinking again about the time, early on in their marriage, when she had felt such overflowing love for Samuel. Back then he was a real talker and quite handsome and healthy. She also recalled her own mother insisting that marriage was the best thing for her. Although Samuel was quite a bit older than her, Winifred felt no option was open to her. She had felt pangs of concern, with the way he would occasionally drink too much, or talk offhandedly with her, still her mother had felt marriage was always the best decision. Besides there was the whole thing about her own pa dying so young and leaving her own Ma in such bad shape.

She couldn't say marrying him had been a mistake, because without that she wouldn't have had her children and they were her greatest blessing. A blessing she'd have never had if she hadn't married Samuel. For that at least, she could give thanks to the Lord. And be grateful to the man who had ultimately brought her so much grief. God would make a way for her.

Samuel's body had been prepared and now he lay, a corpse in the front room as was the custom of the day. Although there were funeral directors in the bigger cities, there was nothing like that where they lived. Winifred knew that no one would likely visit the home before they buried her husband. He had never been one to make friends, not really among the wood hawks even, though occasionally he would talk of one fellow or the other.

Earl had shared with her how those men had stepped up to help at Nathan and Molly's farm. It made her feel a little better knowing someone had cared. As she and Earl talked and made plans for the burial, he told her about how her Samuel had made his deathbed confession. She had heard him one time singing a hymn in the barn out back and she had asked him where on earth he'd ever heard it. He got all mad and red in the face and told her to get back in the house. But she remembered the song just then and knew it would be good to sing at the burial. She also remembered the little worn out Bible her mother-in-law had pressed into her hands as she and Samuel left that day so long ago. They had just stood in Samuel's mother's living room with some preacher only the mother had known who pronounced in a single flat monotone about marrying forever. She remembered too how she'd found some marked places in the Bible and a note inside the flap where Samuel's mother had written "Favorite Bible Verse - 1 Chronicles 16:34 O give thanks unto the LORD; for he is good; for his mercy endureth for ever." She told Earl that would be a good verse to share. She didn't know if Samuel had ever known about any Bible verses or that his mother had given her the only Bible the poor soul had ever owned. But it would have to do. Again she found herself grateful to think that someone in her husband's life had known God.

Unexpectedly, she was overcome with it all and found herself weak at the knees. She stumbled over to the bed that doubled for a divan and sat down. Pictures rolled through her thoughts. Molly, her sweet Molly, and the day she ran away with Nathan and had gotten married. He was a stranger and Winifred had been so afraid for her. Her naive young daughter, feeling that life would be better with someone totally unfamiliar to her than to stay in the only home she had ever known. Tears flowed down Winifred's face as she remembered her anguish on that day and how she'd prayed so hard that God would take care of her sweet child. She found herself thanking God yet again, for the couple who had gone directly to the preacher's to make things right before they left the community Molly had been raised in. Now she was a mother to a precious new baby whom Winifred had not yet seen. Winifred hoped that she had taught Molly a few things about caring for babies, but she hadn't gotten round to telling her about birthing them. Earl didn't tell his mother the whole story, but he had told her enough to put Winifred at ease. At least her oldest daughter had not been all alone when the time came. Winifred was so glad that she had met the stranger who was her son-in-law. She knew right away that Nathan was a good man, even if his jaw was set as he rode into her yard that day. She figured it was because of Samuel's ill temper that Nathan had decided to get him on home. It didn't take long for her to see he had been a huge part of God's plan for Molly all along.

As Winifred grieved it was not so much for the loss of her husband, but for the guilt she held in her heart because she hadn't been able to protect her children from their Pa's mean spirited ways. She grieved for the times they were punished unjustly while she stood by helplessly. One by one the children, upon hearing their mother crying, came to her side. Sissy, who had been her mother's greatest support after Molly left, put her arms around her mother's shoulders and stroked her hair as she cried. Winifred could not tell them what was really causing her grief. Someday she might tell them, but not today. One of these days she'd try to get the courage to tell them how sorry she felt for being so weak. She truly wished she could have stood up for them more. Wiping back her tears, for now she'd simply told them how much she loved them and gave each one a tight hug. They were marveling at how their mother, crying about all the things happening, had actually seemed stronger.

Chapter 49

Nathan had done everything he could for Molly's mother and Earl. Although he was sad to part ways with Earl, they had become good friends, he was itching to get on back to Molly. With his horse fed and rested, he was now headed home. All he wanted to do, and it was indeed his greatest desire, was to just leave here, put the past behind him and start fresh with his Molly and their precious tiny baby.

He found himself talking to God as the wagon lumbered along, empty now of its burden. His thoughts were of a dead man he'd hated. He'd hated Meyers because of the way the man had been so mean and despicable. His vile ways and his hateful actions towards Molly were unforgiveable. He'd hated him so much he felt he could have killed him, yet for Molly's sake he'd allowed them to bring him into their home only to watch her fall apart from the stress of it all. And after getting to know Molly's ma just a little, he realized that he felt a fresh surge of anger for how the whole family had been under his curse of sorts. An old sermon he'd heard came to mind about the sins of the father. Somehow it helped to think that Meyers might be a victim himself.

As he rode along, his thoughts changed. He didn't realize but he wasn't so clench fisted anymore as he thought it was funny how such a strong feeling as hate could dissolve when you just turned it over to God. After all was said and done, he'd come to understand what a weak man Molly's pa had been. He'd bullied his family because of that weakness. All the way home, Nathan meditated on God. Slowly, as Nathan dealt with one issue and another, a real cleansing came, and the resentment eased. Nathan found that instead of feeling a heavier burden, it was so much lighter. Forgiving folks sure can make a man thankful.

There were only brief stops to rest and quickly grab a little meal from the sack of things Molly's ma had packed for him. It wasn't much as her stores were quite meager, but he knew Earl would take good care of them. This trip continued without stopping at the halfway house on the return home. The horse set his own rhythm and didn't seem to be too tired. As night fall, the sounds of the woods were somehow comforting in the cool night air.

As dawn broke and the sun was gently pushing up into the sky with purples and golds streaking along the horizon, the cabin came into view. His cabin, their cabin. What an awesome feeling. Nathan could make out a flicker of light coming from a window. Molly was probably up feeding Faith. He wanted to rush into the cabin and take her in his arms, but he had to drive to the barn and unhitch his tired horse. He rubbed him down with clean straw and gave him water and food. He made a mental note that as soon as he had greeted Molly, he would come back out and milk the little goat. As he walked toward the cabin, Boots, the same cat that had been hidden away with Molly the first of their life together, now came up and curled around his feet nearly causing him to trip. "Watch it Boots!" He smiled as he reached down and picked up the little cat in his arms and petted him. Boots started purring contentedly.

Molly was surprised to find herself more rested than she'd felt in a long time. As she went out to take care of the little nanny goat, she almost felt like skipping. Quickly getting the goat milked, she went back in to find little Faith laughing at a speck of sunlight dancing across the wall. "You little darlin' you are so happy aren't you?" Molly strained the milk and set the cream into the churn. She'd get back to that in a while. She dipped down to scoop up Faith and changed her diaper.

She was glad she had made a pot of stew last night. It was still simmering on the stove top for her Nathan. He would surely be home today. Not once had she felt fearful. She guessed it was because her pa was laid up in the wagon. No way he could get to her anymore. His hurt and pain he inflicted on everyone was part of her past. She couldn't help but be thankful that he was gone. She did worry about her ma, but it was best.

Getting Faith settled back in her little bed, Molly began to straighten up the cot and poured herself a cup of coffee. Sitting down, she found herself humming a tune from childhood. It just felt good to be in her own home, with her own baby, waiting for her own husband.

He walked up to the door and tapped gently so as not to startle Molly, his beloved. In an instant the door was flung open and she stood there for just a moment, with the firelight and the lamplight making a silhouette behind her. Then in an instant she was in his arms. He walked in fairly carrying her, and for a long moment they simply held one another without speaking. Then he spoke softly into her ear. First he told her how much he loved her, how much he appreciated her strength, her integrity and her love for him. As they sat together at the table, he shared her ma's message. Molly smiled as she thought of her ma and her siblings. It was good to know that they were okay.

Nathan held her hands in his and began…

"He didn't make it. Your Pa didn't make it home Molly dear". She stiffened just a little at her pa's name, feeling a strange sadness, but complete peace. Then she looked up into his face, the face of her beloved husband, who would never leave her or forsake her.

"Oh yes," she answered. "Yes, he did make it home. God showed me. All is forgiven."

CPSIA information can be obtained at www.ICGtesting.com
Printed in the USA
LVOW080408140412

277567LV00003B/4/P